ACKNOWLEDGMENTS

Most folks know of Shoeless Joe Jackson the baseball player, but no one ever told Katie's story. Her thoughts and emotions remained largely unspoken. Those who knew and loved Katie Wynn Jackson gave the spark of life to this fictional account, and I am indebted to them for sharing their memories.

The boys from Bolt's Drug Store – Gene Estes, Ned Clay and Rex Carter – spoke both of the businesswoman who could keep books with the accuracy of a trained accountant, and of the loving wife forever by her husband's side. Attorney Leo Hill talked of Miss Katie with such gentleness that it was obvious how profound an influence she had. John Burgess delivered newspapers to the Jackson household, and offered glimpses of two people completely devoted to one another.

Ethel Copeland spoke of her Uncle Joe and Aunt Katie with unabashed devotion. Gilbert and Elinor Rogers wrote a wonderful letter about being neighbors to the quiet folks who lived next door. No one talked with more passion about Joe and Katie Jackson than Joe and Katie Anders, a young couple welcomed into the lives of the older folks.

Special thanks to those whose expertise added deeper colors to this love story. Joe Thompson's memories of Shoeless Joe, and Carrie White's help in gathering information on the Jackson's days in Delaware during World War I, proved invaluable.

My deepest gratitude to those who wouldn't let me give up. Mac Kirkpatrick, researcher extraordinaire, was available to chase down those elusive questions whose answers gave exquisite flavor to Katie's moods. Lisa Senn, my friend, gave advice and encouragement in exact doses.

Thanks also for the newspaper columns of Scoop Latimer and to Mike Nola, a fellow Joe Jackson aficionado.

Most of all, to my wife Donna and daughter Meghan, thank you for your love and patience. You were always there.

And the Lord God said,
"It is not good that man should be alone.
I will make a helpmate for him."
...
And Adam said,
"This is now bone of my bone,
and flesh of my flesh"

Genesis 2: 18;23

Just Joe:
Baseball's Natural,
as told by his wife

Thomas K. Perry

Pocol Press
Clifton, VA

POCOL PRESS

Published in the United States of America
by Pocol Press.

6023 Pocol Drive
Clifton, VA 20124
http://www.pocolpress.com

Publisher's Cataloguing-in-Publication

Perry, Thomas K. 1952-

    Just Joe : baseball's natural, as told by his wife/
    Thomas K. Perry. – 1st ed. – Clifton, VA :
    Pocol Press, 2007.

        p. ; cm.

        ISBN-13: 978-1-929763-30-6
        ISBN-10: 1-929763-30-1

        1. Jackson, Joe, 1888-1951–Fiction.
    2. Baseball players–United States–Fiction.
    3. Chicago White Sox (Baseball team)–Fiction.
    4. Jackson, Katie–Fiction. 5. Baseball stories.
    I. Title.

    PS3616.E779 J87 2007
    813.6–dc22   0704

Cover photo restoration by Mike Nola, Official Historian, Shoeless Joe
Jackson's Virtual Hall of Fame (http://www.blackbetsy.com).

FOREWORD

This is a love story. It is the life of Shoeless Joe Jackson, an extraordinary baseball player in the early part of the twentieth century, told from the perspective of his wife, Katie Wynn Jackson. At least, it might have been from her perspective, had anyone talked with her at length and listened as she gave the details of a most interesting life.

Many of the events are real, others the product of one writer's imagination. The timeline, where Katie and Joe were at any given period in their lives, is precisely followed. In those periods, their thoughts, conversations with one another, and interactions with other people are best described as congenial lies. Did they happen just that way? No one can ever know. Are they possible, given what we know of their love story? Absolutely.

During the research and writing of this historical fiction, I got to know Katie Jackson. Conversing with her friends and family added a depth to this lady who took on all the slings and arrows of outrageous fortune, and at the end of the fight stood tall and proud. There were times when the writing flowed so smoothly that it seemed the dear lady was dictating. There were other times, certainly more numerous, when she raced ahead and tossed a backward glance that could only mean "come and see".

Joe Jackson's story, especially his involvement in the 1919 World Series as a member of the Chicago "Black" Sox, has been told many times. Guilty or innocent? Consummate manipulator or ultimate scapegoat? Those who have heard it form strong opinions, and no arguing is going to sway them. But this is Katie s story, as it might have been. She is quite a remarkable lady, and Shoeless Joe Jackson the most fortunate of men. I hope you enjoy sharing their journey.

Chapter 1

Understanding Mr. and Mrs. Joe Jackson isn't easy, but if you're going to try, start in 1939. Joe always said his greatest sorrow was not that he was thrown out of baseball, but that we did not have any kids. Mine, too, because it accounts for a lot of this silence around the house just now. All swept, dusted and tidied up, and open windows let in the breeze of an early spring morning. But it's empty except for the footsteps of an old woman echoing off hardwood floors.

McDavid Jackson was Joe's favorite nephew, and years before there had been talk among the family about us adopting the boy as our own. I felt barren. And selfish, wanting my man for myself even when I knew this would make him happy. "He won't be ours by blood, but he can be the son I couldn't give you, Joe."

"You're always first in my heart, Missy," I heard him say, and was even more ashamed of myself. I remember looking up at him and smiling through my tears.

"I know, I know," was all I managed, and pressed tight against him. Thinking all the while, 'But he's what I couldn't give to you, and I hate myself for it!' My sobs were lost in the white cotton shirt he wore.

Can't remember what stopped it all, but it never happened. He was a good boy, stayed close to his Uncle Joe, and the two of them were a sight together, walking the downtown streets on a Saturday evening, sharing a bag of lemon drops and quiet conversation.

Anyway, McDavid finds him a nice girl in Miss Lila Hunt, and the two of them were married in '39. Like I said, you have to understand all this if you're going to understand my man Joe. October of next year, they're expecting a baby, and Uncle Joe is running around town buying this and that for the child's nursery.

Seeing Lila grow big with that child, and McDavid with a smile brighter than a harvest moon, made me think again, and bitterly, of what Joe and I never got to feel. Wasn't very becoming at all, especially when my man was so genuinely happy for them. But sometimes we get lucky enough to realize how wrong we've been, and have a chance to set things right.

Joe was at their house one day, putting a coat of primer on the nursery wall. His favorite stop was Breazeale Hardware, couple of doors down from our store in West Greenville, where he and Mr. B. had already mixed up two cans of paint, one light blue and the other of course light pink. He bought stencils of lambs he was planning to color in white after he painted the walls. At lunch, I picked up two BLT's and vanilla shakes and drove over to share a meal with that hardworking loveable man. Not long after I drove up, here comes the happy couple.

1

"Uncle Joe! Aunt Katie!" McDavid yelled, spun me around and hugged me, then grabbed Joe in a bear hug. Lila stood smiling at us, walked over, held my hands and kissed me on the cheek. She was always so sweet that way. Like I said, it was me that needed changing, not that lovely little girl whose face was framed by rings of black hair. The men had gone back to the kitchen for something, and Lila spoke to me.

"Katie, would you like to feel the baby? He's moving and kicking to beat it all, raring to go!" I wanted to offer a short 'no, thank you', but couldn't do it, couldn't turn away from her dark eyes filled with so much kindness.

"Yes, yes I would," and was more than shocked at my willingness. Still, I drew back when my fingers were only an inch or two from her belly.

Afraid of what?

Of touching what I could never offer my own husband?

No, more than that. Of having to knock down the wall, open up and share their joy. Give up my self-pity and really mean it when I said how happy I was for the both of them. Not faked, like so many times before.

"It's okay, Aunt Katie," and she smiled when I looked up at her. First time she ever called me that.

"Won't hurt him a bit." She took my hand and laid it on her belly. Think my heart about beat out of my chest when I felt the child kick hard. Lila gasped and bent over a little, those bright eyes closing a bit as she winced.

"No doubt he's a boy," she laughed. "Little girls couldn't kick that hard."

I reached up, put my arms around her neck and kissed her on the cheek. "Your son is awfully lucky," I whispered, all I could manage at the time.

"To have you and Uncle Joe watching after him, yes, yes he is." Don't ever let anyone tell you angels don't walk the earth, because I had one of God's inner circle standing in front of me to prove it.

The men didn't have a clue how much things had changed when they walked back in. It was a love I wasn't afraid of anymore, and it felt wonderful.

But toward the end of the month, whatever measure of joy we had was swamped by wave after wave of sadness, and you just wanted to give in to the undertow and die. Joe's old soft cotton handkerchiefs are still handy for wiping away the tears even a dozen years removed from the horror of that day. Lila went into labor but something was so very wrong. The doctor kept running in and out of the front bedroom in

2

their little bungalow, now a half finished nursery, getting more hot water and clean rags and shutting the door behind himself.

"What's going on, Uncle Joe? It ain't supposed to be happening like this, is it? It's supposed to be joyful, waiting to hear a baby cry, dreaming of all the things you're going to do with him or her. Ain't that right?" He was holding tight to my man's arms, knuckles turning white. The boy looked for some kind of hope in Joe's eyes, but saw only fear and resignation.

Lila screamed, and there was a long silence before she began to cry softly. The young man did, too. Not long after, more silence, and when Dr. Clatworthy came to the door and closed it behind him without looking up, I think we all knew what happened. Joe reached his arms up around McDavid's shoulders and mine and pulled us close. Lila, and the baby boy she tried so hard to bring into the world, had died.

"Boy, I am so sorry," my man said. Doc walked over and muttered much the same. I think he still didn't believe what happened, and laid his hand on young Jackson's arm. He mouthed words, but could give no voice to them, the grief was so overwhelming. I know, because I did the same.

"You did all that was in your power, sir, and you're a good man to have tried so hard for Lila and McDavid," Joe said through his tears, putting out his hand to shake the doctor's. "You have the thanks of the Jackson family." The worst thing of all was that it hurt so badly and you couldn't change it for those you love.

A late October sun came through the living room windows, and bathed us in a soft glow. But it only accented the quiet and the soft sobs of McDavid. Joe walked over and held me tight, and I could feel his tears falling on my neck.

"Oh God...Oh God...Oh God" was all he said.

It was warm the day we buried Lila and her little boy, the sky that deep autumn blue, oaks and maples turning to reds and yellows, even flowers still blooming. Two things I remember most: the white caskets covered with red carnations, and a preacher who didn't know how or when to keep his mouth shut.

When I touched the tiny white box I remembered the baby kicking just a few days ago, and maybe I came as close to understanding motherhood as I was ever going to. I wept silently, holding onto Joe's hand but never lifting my eyes. It was a personal grief, and I had to be alone with it.

"Jesus, help us," Lila's mama sobbed.

"It ain't right, God. Ain't right." Her father's big hands covered his face, and tears rushed through thick fingers, disappearing under the soiled cuffs of his white shirt.

3

"Boy, hold on, hold to me." Joe had his arm around McDavid, and I think without my man his legs would have given way.

"God's here, boy, helping...and I am, too." Despite his tears, Joe's voice was deep and strong. Everybody around him took comfort in his ways, family and strangers alike.

The short meditation and Scripture, Jesus' words about not letting your heart be troubled, were comforting to the crowd gathered around the funeral home tents. Then the damn fool preacher goes and tries to create a revival altar, complete with hellfire and brimstone, at the expense of our grief. He was louder than Poe Mill fans when they used to shout at us Brandon folks when we played them at Little Egypt.

"If you ain't saved, come to the Lord now." I loosened my hand from Joe's, my jaw beginning to tighten.

"Don't be late. Join these two in heaven." That was the last I heard, turning and walking away from the crowd, though no one besides my man even noticed. Maybe some were listening to his raving, maybe some shut him out, I don't know. I believed we were here to honor the dead, and that's where I was going to leave it.

I stepped back in after it was over, took McDavid's other hand, and with Joe walked him back to the car, followed by David and Helen. The Jackson men got in the back of the Packard, the women in front, and I drove, guiding the line of mourners back to Brandon. The young man cried, the only sound on the ride back home.

Time went by slowly, but it did go by, and Joe tried to get the boy back out into the world.

"Every time I took off for the vacant lot to play ball with the kids, I'd run over and pick up McDavid. Sometimes, Missy, he'd come along and sit on the little stone fence behind home plate. 'Let's play ball', I'd yell and run to the mound, motion for him to follow me on out with Burgess and Thompson and some of the Negro children from down at Meadow Bottom and Hellman Street. He kind of sat and stared, maybe walk out on the field a minute or two, not try to catch nothing and pretty soon wander off by himself.

"'What's wrong with him, Mr. Joe?' one of the kids would ask. And I'd tell them he was fighting being alone after his wife and little boy died. They'd shake their heads yes, but I don't think they really understood. But then, don't guess I do either."

My man did try. With the war keeping everybody occupied - blackouts, candles in the window, gas rationing and such - Joe would spend as much time as he could with McDavid. Get him over to Bolt's Drug Store for a milkshake and sandwich, for a game at Brandon between the Braves and maybe arch rival Mills Mill or Poe. Sometimes they'd just walk like before, up and down the streets of Greenville in the evening, covering most of West Greenville and Pendleton Street and Augusta too, and it seemed to do them both good. After a bit, McDavid started to go out with friends and even played ball with Joe and the kids. Toward the end of '44 he came into the store one day and told us he'd met a nice girl and was going out with her. It was the first sign of beating that deep depression that had kept him chained and miserable.

"She's a fine girl, Aunt Katie and Uncle Joe, and Cindy's...well, she's full of life and laughs and makes me feel alive again. We met downtown last night and saw a movie, and I walked her home, holding hands, and I felt even Lila understood. That's what made it okay for me. It is okay, don't you think?"

"'Course we do, boy. Don't we, Katie?" And he reached out one of those big hands that swallowed mine, and pulled me close. Looking into McDavid's brown eyes, you could see light breaking through all the sadness he'd bottled up for six years.

"Of course we do," I echoed my smiling overgrown kid and hugged them both there in the store. Probably would have hugged them harder and longer if the bell over the door hadn't interrupted when two customers walked in.

The courtship between McDavid and Cindy went along fine, and they got engaged on Valentine's Day, 1945. You wouldn't ever see two happier people, and throw Joe in the mix and you've got a joyous Saturday night flaming fiddle square dance going full blast. It was good to see the Jackson family getting their lives back in order. Thank the Good Lord the darkness was finally slipping away, replaced by a measure of happiness we'd all been denied so long.

The wedding took place in January of '46, and with the "I do's" the McDavid Jacksons settled in at 14 Lowell Street on the Brandon mill village, which suited Joe just fine. Come spring, he'd grab me, lock up the store, grab them, and head down to the ballpark to watch one of the textile league games. We must have been a sight entering that grandstand, too. Young couple all happy, waving at well wishers, Cindy's light brown hair blowing about, McDavid's a little darker and tousled by the early April breeze. Me, the old lady in a plain brown cotton dress, with flats, and Joe, his belly straining against a white shirt half in and half out of his blue pants, a white Panama covering that bald head. Everybody started speaking at once, to each other and all the folks sitting and waiting for the game to start. My man's eyes glistened and his laugh was full and downright catching. I hauled off and kissed him full on the mouth right there in front of fans and teams and mill officials and who the hell else cared to look. Oh, I loved that man. Folks cheered as loud, I believe, as for one of Mr. Jackson's Saturday Specials in that same park some forty years before.

5

"Missy, come here, there's somebody I want you to meet!" He'd run off to answer the knock at the door, setting Skippy off his lap, which would last only until Joe found his seat again.

"This is Joe Tinker, shortstop of the old Cubs and..."

"Tinker-to-Evers-to-Chance fame," I finished for him, smiling.

"Hustling ballplayer and great competitor."

"My pleasure, Mr. Tinker. Visits from former ballplayers seem to be few and far between these days, but are always welcomed." And why wouldn't they be, the way Joe's eyes lit up when these hard-boiled men, fierce rivals all, came to talk about the old days. About glory. About the game that decided it had no need of my man.

"Pleasure's mine, Mrs. Jackson", he said, still clasping Joe's right hand. Was it just me that noticed, or did all players of that era have huge hands? He let go, took my much smaller ladies' model and held it with surprising gentleness. His voice was softer than I expected too. "I've wanted to come and talk with your husband for a long time now, and only got around to doing it now. We bumped into each other a few times in Chicago, maybe drank a beer together once. And I just got the urge to talk with the old southern boy again. Years are getting away pretty fast now, and it's nice to talk old times with folks who shared them."

"If you'll excuse me, gentlemen, I'll leave you to your glorious war stories. I'm glad you came, Mr.Tinker," and I extended my hand again, which he took with that soft touch like he cradled many a ground ball before starting a double play, I'd expect, "and I know Joe is, too."

"Ma'am," he said. My man gave me a wink as I turned to leave the room. Then he and Joe stayed up most of the night, and they tried to be quiet, but you understand how a laugh came out a bit louder than intended when a certain memory got the better of them.

Last I heard was the clock striking 3 AM as I turned over in bed. Yes, maybe better times were coming for me and Joe and all of the family, and I said a little prayer for that as I drifted off to sleep.

By Christmas time in '47, we were finally going to celebrate again in style. We were thankful for the war being over, for the happiness that McDavid had found with Cindy, which looked like it would last, and for the general well being of the extended family. Joe and I went all out, decorating our Wilburn Street home to the nines, and we either made or bought every kind of cookie and candy and cake you could imagine.

"Here's the holiday punch, Missy," my man said, setting down the cut glass bowl on the oak dining room table. "And over here's the real special batch," he gave that deep laugh of his and splashed in some rum. Reaching out and taking my hand, he pulled me under the mistletoe and kissed me real sweet.

"Thank you for being there through all the pain and the hard times, Katie Wynn. I think you got your own special place in heaven just because of the way you are." It was one of those times I wished it was just him and me, but that would have to wait an hour or two. The knock at the front door announced the first of the Jackson family beginning to arrive for the Christmas Eve celebration. The cold night stopped at the door, because inside was love and family and the joy of that special season. Coats and sweaters got piled in the guest bedroom.

McDavid was absent, probably running a little late, and I could picture him and Cindy having a quiet time together before setting out for this Jackson hoopla. There was another knock at the door, more forceful than the others, and Joe covered that distance as quick as his first steps out of the batter's box on a grounder to second. I was right behind him.

"Officer Cabiness, Mr. Jackson. Mrs. Jackson," he tipped his hat and we remembered seeing him walking the West Greenville beat. Joe closed the door behind us as we stepped onto the porch, and the younger man seemed stuck for words.

"Something's wrong, ain't there?" Joe put his hand on the policeman's shoulder. "What's wrong with the boy?" My man's voice began to break. Of a sudden I couldn't...no, didn't want to make sense of what was happening, and that cold dark held away by the Christmas lights shining through the window suddenly became powerful and swallowed us all up. It wasn't the cold that made me shiver so violently.

I remember snatches of words and phrases - "accident" and "suicide", and "not sure which, too hard to tell right now," and "maybe we'll never know."

"I'm sorry, folks," and Officer Cabiness' voice shook as he fought back tears of his own. "We all thought he'd made it back, and now he's slipped away from us for good. I know you loved him, Mr. Jackson, showed in all you did for McDavid. Not just the last few years, but since he was a chap taking after you to the ballpark." He steadied Joe when a sob pried its way out of a broken heart, grief and sadness made more alive by the wind kicking up.

"I'll go on over with the officer, Missy. Throw me my coat, and tell 'em there's been a terrible accident and McDavid's gone." Nobody noticed too much when I slipped in and out quickly with Joe's hat and overcoat. Watched them drive off in the black-and-white, watched Joe's eyes set hard, preparing for what he would find. Set my own jaw hard, turned and walked back into the house, and like a witch transformed a season of birth into a night of death. Never knew I could feel so helpless, so empty.

There were lots of tears and hugs as the clan filed out. Quick as possible, candles got blown out, presents still left were stuffed back under the tree, and lights were turned off. I cranked the Packard and headed back down to the house on the village, thinking 'you don't ever get away from this plot of land that has a choke hold on you from the time you come into the world until you leave, and only God calling the sinner home is enough to break the bonds.' Up the eight front steps, trudging like a condemned prisoner up a scaffold, nothing to look at but a drop into blackness.

It was a season suddenly horrible. Joe's brother David and his wife crying for the loss of their son, Cindy in shock, the doctor holding her hand, policemen showing Joe as best they could how things must have happened. And my man walking down those steps behind the draped body of his nephew, so close to being a son. Nobody else with even the courage to look, including me.

Graceland Cemetery was a monument to civic forethought. A few uptown ladies decided the lintheads needed a burying ground all their own, conveniently distant from our betters, and it was there, out beyond the Brandon Mill village, where we laid McDavid to rest. A strong wind cut in and out of the rows of gravestones, etching odd designs in the light snow that fell overnight. The Jackson men, dressed in black, were protective of their women, offering an arm to make sure we didn't wind up on our backsides. Overcoat collars were pulled up against the stiff breeze, and we cried. All but Joe. Whatever crying he figured was necessary, he had done, and now he was strong for the family. But I knew my man, knew his heart was breaking, could tell by the way he took my hand and held it like he was afraid I'd be gone if he didn't. I squeezed back, hard, for the same reason.

"Missy…"

"Here, Joe. Always right here."

Words only the two of us heard, and that was as it should be. The wind swallowed up my whisper.

There were other words meant for the family.

"The boy was of a gentle nature," the preacher said. "There was a deep hurt in his life he never overcame," and I pictured an autumn day when Lila and the baby boy were buried, white caskets and red carnations and a crowd of folks who came to mourn. "But God loved young McDavid, does so even now, in a place where no hurt nor tears are allowed, and He welcomes him home now." His words were gentle and comforting for all of us.

8

"Take the Packard on, and get 'em all comfortable at the house," Joe spoke softly to me, his lips close to my ear. "Something I've got to do before I can leave."

"Say your good-byes to the boy," and I kissed him on the cheek, still not ready to let go of his hand, still afraid the darkness would swallow him up and take him from me.

I was last in line, as the cars pulled out onto Highway 123, waved on by Officer Cabiness, who had stopped traffic and saluted as we went by. I glanced back. Removing his overcoat, Joe was there in his fedora and black suit, rhythmically digging a shovel into the hard mound of earth, working in perfect time with the two black gravediggers to finish the job at hand. No doubt they knew him, probably expected him to grab the shovel and join in.

"It was something I had to do, finish it so the boy could go home," Joe told me, sipping coffee in the small trophy room, two chairs cramping the four-by-ten space. I had cut one of the two cakes the neighbors brought in, coconut if my memory serves me, and used the blue china saucers and cups to serve everyone. His brother David came and stood in the doorway.

"It was a good service, Jefferson Walker," using the nickname he had given his brother so many years ago when we were all kids. If any of the Jacksons were ever allowed to be kids. "There was no way I could have…done that." The words came in a soft monotone, all his emotions drained away. Joe squeezed past me, shook his brother's hand, then hugged him as they both broke down in tears. I always marveled at how my man cried, biting down on his lower lip to make sure the sobs didn't escape, letting the tears fall silently, tasting the blood when he swallowed.

"Lord," I prayed softly, "let him remember the preacher's words about peace and healing. Don't let this tear at Joe, eat him up. Let him live, Lord, and stay with me for years to come." It was selfish, but when you can hear the wind echo in your own emptiness, I think maybe you can be forgiven for a prayer or two of desperation.

After the funeral, folks went back to their own lives, leaving each other alone to deal with a death no one understood, and with a grief no one wanted to face. Joe didn't say much. Took charge of paying for everything, got Cindy moved back in with her folks, and though grateful, she never really kept in touch. We saw her very seldom, maybe passing each other uptown when she was shopping or going to a show at the Bijou.

Maybe more than any of us, my man was different. I knew he was looking for answers, trying to understand McDavid's death, but he kept so much inside that no one could fathom the depths of his pain. His

9

walk was slower, his shoulders slumped with the burden of a life he wasn't able to save. The skin on his face drew tighter as he started skipping meals or at best barely picking at what was on his plate. Except for the kids who came down to the store to talk baseball during the winter months when spring was still a lifetime away - "over to Bolt's, boys, for milkshakes. Know you can't come in the store, and it's way too cold to stand on the sidewalk" - he spoke little with anyone, and saved his smiles for them alone. They may not have understood his pain any better than the rest of us, but they loved him, accepted his warmth and the smiles and praise he offered, and demanded nothing of him.

"They are his salvation," I remember telling my sister Mattie one day. "Keep him going when I think maybe even he doesn't want to."

"He'll be fine when baseball gets here, Mrs. Jackson, you'll see. He's going to smile again," one or another of those sandlot dreamers would say. And I hoped maybe they were right, that it could all be put back in order. I hoped, until Joe had his first heart attack, missing Opening Day with the boys and girls for the first time in years, that big heart broken in two by a tragedy not of his making.

We'd face this together, too, him and me, like so many times before. Somehow we'd find a way to slide safe at home, dust off the bad memories and keep on going, waiting for the next turn at bat.

Chapter 2

Never seemed like there was ever a time I didn't know Joe Jackson. Papa owned a gristmill up toward Paris Mountain for awhile, then took a job laying curbs for the city, and that's when we moved into town. Our house, and some land we bought, wasn't far from Brandon Mill village, and somehow Joe's mama and mine came to know each other.

When the weather was good, Miss Martha Ann would walk out most mornings to the little open area the mill gave to each family for raising a pig or keeping a cow or having a row or two of vegetables. She'd be in a plain cotton dress, a color washed out and faded though it could have been blue at one time. Old brogans were half a size too big as she shuffled along the path. And my mama, Alice Phillips Wynn, she'd walk out and hang clothes on the line to dry, and it wasn't long before she made her way down to where Miss Martha Ann worked her plot, wet grass sticking to Mama's bare feet, smoothing her brown dress and dark hair, introducing herself. That was her way, never meeting a stranger.

A head shorter than Mrs. Jackson, she would cock her head and squint in the morning sun when the two of them would sit on the back steps snapping green beans and drinking a glass of water from our well. She'd listen to the older woman, whose age you could not guess, and you'd be way too high if you tried, tell the story about coming to Greenville from way up in Pickens County. And sometimes I'd stop my running and playing with my brothers and sisters, crawl up next to Mama, and listen.

"That journey we made by wagon," she said, slipping her feet out of the shoes and digging first her heels and then toes into the grass that ran under the first step, "and it seemed awful long. George Elmore drove, keeping the mule going at a steady pace, and me and Joe, my oldest and at that time only child, sat on the seat next to him. Wasn't nothing much to do, and since my man didn't do a lot of talking, me and the boy hummed whatever tune come to mind and watched the land flatten out.

"Farming up there was a hard life and it was a fight every day to scrape out a living. So when we heard about these cotton mills being built and needing workers, we took out toward Greenville. First village I ever laid my eyes on was Pelzer, and there right by the Saluda River that big old mill sat just humming and eating bales of cotton at one end and spitting out cloth at the other. George Elmore stopped the wagon at the company store and a Mr. Jordan, kind of short plump fellow with a brown apron draped over coveralls, directed us to the plant super's

11

office." Miss Martha Ann patted down a strand or two of brown hair too soon going gray.

She took a sip of cold water and wiggled her toes. "But settling into that mill life, we gave up a measure of freedom we'd come to know back in the mountains. Hard as it was up in Pickens, our clock was the sun and wasn't nothing but the open land outside our house. At Pelzer, we had a life controlled by the mill whistle blowing to get the hands up in the morning dark at half past four, at quarter of six to set 'em walking, and again at six to start the shift. Blowed again at noontime to send 'em home for dinner and at one to get 'em back. Blowed one last time a six that evening to chase 'em home for the evening."

Sitting out here in the sun it was hard to see giving up the light and air and green grass and pretty flowers for a life directed by a whistle. Miss Martha Ann put her rough hands on my shoulder and smiled. "Got to remember, child, we about starved trying to farm, so regular work and pay, and a house provided by Captain Smythe's mill company seemed a good trade." Mama and I agreed she was a good lady as we listened to her stories on that spring morning. The older woman got up and started toward her little farming plot, then on back to the mill village just beyond the tall oaks.

"Bring your boys next time," Mama called after her. "They can play with my young 'uns while we talk."

Miss Martha Ann didn't make it back over until nearly mid-summer, but one morning I saw her walking slowly up to our house, followed by her two boys. Mama reminded me the older was Joe and the younger David, and she was now expecting a third, probably a boy, too, by what Sunie Jones the midwife down on the mill hill figured with her sticks and tea leaves. Mama explained to me about Miss Martha Ann losing three sets of twins at birth between Joe and David. How do old people take so much sadness and keep on living? I didn't have any kind of answer, and there wasn't time for asking Mama before our visitors arrived.

It was sort of strange to see Joe toting his little brother on his hip. "Other boys down on the village make fun of him, but he goes about his duty, doing what he can to help me," Miss Martha Ann said, putting her hand on the boy's head. "Joe, this is Mrs. Wynn, and her daughter Katie."

Joe looked shyly at Mama and only said, "Ma'am". He only said "Hey" to me before turning away to watch David picking up rocks and dropping them in a tin can he'd found in the yard. The overalls Joe wore hardly came to his ankles, he was barefoot and shirtless, the straps crossing tightly over his thin shoulders. A lock of brown hair fell across his forehead and hung nearly in his eyes.

12

"Katie, go talk with him, make him feel at home." Mama pushed me a little toward him.

"But he don't hardly talk," and I begged not to be sent after him. He took off chasing his little brother, staying just close enough to guard against anything bad happening to David. There was to be no arguing when Mama gave me that look, so I slipped around the puddle and followed along behind Joe Jackson.

"Don't see you out much," were my first words to him.

"Work in the mill mostly. Been there since I was six, started sweeping floors and now I'm learning to doff in the Spinning Room. I like that, using my hands and stuff and..."

I screamed to high heaven, my toes bumping up against a slithering monster making its way through the tall grass in the field. That set the women folk running our way, not knowing what had happened. When they got there, Joe already grabbed the green snake and was carrying it off a ways, letting it loose down close to the creek. I held to Mama tight.

"My little one don't like snakes and such," Mama smiled, stroking my hair and calming me down. "Thank you, young man, I'm obliged for what you did. And I know Katie would say the same thing, soon as she stops shaking."

I could only nod and try to blink away the tears. Did manage a quick "uh huh" between the waterworks and sniffles. Joe had David back in his arms and was walking off with Miss Martha Ann.

"Come back, and we're obliged for your help, young Joe." Mama waved, and I watched the three blurry forms disappear through the trees.

When the steam whistle at Brandon sounded early the next morning, I knew Joe and his pa would be heading for the cotton mill, to be swallowed up by the noise and lint until it was nearly dark. Daddy told me before about the hard work the lintheads did, and he didn't say the word hatefully like folks uptown did when they'd see one of the mill workers coming toward them.

"Sweeping floors with brooms bigger than he is," I said, crawling up in Daddy's lap. He curled strands of my hair around his finger, let them fall and started again. "Don't he have to go to school like me? Why does he have to work in the mill when plenty of kids I know don't help earn money for their family?" Lots of questions from a female, but I guess he was used to it by now. Mama had taught me well.

"Mills hire men with big families, Katie, figuring they can get cheap labor that way. When the kids come of age, six or seven years old, they start walking with their folks into that big old building, working sixty, maybe seventy hours a week."

13

"So boys like Joe can't ever be a kid, can't run and play and read and stuff. They get all of that snatched away from them, and go and start work, stuff they are going to do 'til they die."

"Your friend is a little man, yes," he reached for his pipe, already packed carefully with Prince Albert, and lit it. I liked to smell the smoke, but Mama scowled at him like she did every time the aroma sifted through the house.

"Get to school, young lady, and you to work, old man," Mama said, pretending to be mad but not doing a real good job of it. "Maybe Saturday afternoon we can go and visit Miss Martha Ann and her family," then she smiled at me and touched my face. There was a faraway look in her eyes when she told me I was growing up too fast to suit her.

We started out for 312 Mason Street after cleaning up the kitchen from Saturday dinner, just me and Mama since none of my other brothers and sisters seemed to care much about going. Down along the path by Miss Martha Ann's garden, I looked down to make sure I didn't step on anything slithery, while Mama stopped to get a few tomatoes and squash to carry to her new friend.

"Glad to have company," Joe's ma said, opening the front door as we climbed the last of the eight porch steps. The front room where we sat had three chairs fashioned from rough pine, a worn brown oval throw rug on the floor in the center, and an outdated Chero Cola calendar hanging by a nail on the wall. Light streaked through dirty thick glass windows, framed by dyed cloth curtains.

"Fabric is seconds from the mill. George Elmore brought some home they wasn't gonna use and I colored 'em up a little." Then they started talking and I looked around, swinging my feet, which didn't quite reach the hardwood floor from that lofty perch.

"Boys are out back with their pa, if you want to be outside," Miss Martha Ann smiled and pointed toward the kitchen and the back door. I didn't need a second invitation. "Careful, 'cause a board or two on them back steps is loose," she called after me.

Joe and David were throwing a ball back and forth out near the clothesline, at least when Joe wasn't running over to pick up baby Jerry every minute or two. Their pa was sharpening some knives and an axe with a file over near where his woodpile was, probably I should say where the wood was still laying since it was cut awhile ago and hadn't been stacked. He drew that metal file back and forth and the sound set my teeth on edge, but didn't seem to bother the old hound dog lying at his feet. Mr. Jackson looked up and nodded, but didn't say anything, which Joe told me later wasn't unusual at all.

14

"Come on and throw with us, Katie," Joe called, waving me over. It was a ball made of tightly wound yarn around a knot of cloth, the only toy I saw anywhere. Joe was tossing underhand to David, who'd rare back and throw it almost straight down in the dirt, then race his big brother for it. The two of them would tangle up and fall to the ground laughing.

"Do 'gin, Joe," was the little one's favorite words. Pretty soon it was the three of us tossing and chasing and falling all over each other.

Joe's ma came to the door and called for David to come in for his nap. Joe picked up Jerry and carried him up the steps, handing the baby to Miss Martha Ann.

"Ma, can me and Katie go down to the game?" her eldest raised his eyes and stared at her through his too-long hair. She looked at Mama, and the two women smiled and agreed it was okay.

"Brandon Braves is playing the Ravens from over at Poe Mill, and it'll be a good game," he said, so excited he could hardly talk without gasping for breath.

"Fool game" was the only comment Mr. Jackson gave as we hurried out of the yard, our feet slapping the hard ground and kicking up dust.

Figuring he wasn't going to say anything to break the silence after we slowed to a walk, I asked Joe how he'd been doing.

"Learning that doffing job real good, Katie," and he showed me the method for taking the full quills off the spinning frame and putting empty ones back on. "Best thing is making my rest, then heading outside to play baseball with the other fellows. Just got to make sure I'm back in by the start of the next doff cycle. Second hand can't come and drag me back in now like he used to when I snuck out from my sweeping. 'Course, I was only six back then, just a kid, but now I got a real job with that doffing, and in another year or two I can play baseball on the men's ball club, and get out of work for practice."

When we got to the field, he jumped right in to being a part of the game.

"Come on Charlie! Hit it hard!" He offered encouragement to the batter as we came up on the first base side.

"How'd you get so hot about baseball, Joe?" and I watched those brown eyes of his sparkle when he talked about this game he loved so much.

"When we lived at Pelzer," he said as we sat down on the grass past where the Brandon bench was, "the big game was always with Piedmont Mill up the road five miles or so. Them boys would go at it with spikes flying, and spitting tobacco juice at runners when they'd round the bag or even when they chased a foul near the bench. Pelzer

15

had fine players like Mac Bannister and Ben Lark, but they was three on that Piedmont team I watched real close 'cause they was so good. That was Rome Chambers, Davy Crockett, and Champ Osteen."

I'd gotten caught up in his excitement and didn't realize it when Joe lunged past me and caught a hard hopping foul ball moving straight for the back of my head, then flipped it to the first baseman. But I did notice the man said "Nice catch, kid" and there was some clapping from the grandstand up behind us.

"That's twice you already protected me, Joe, first from the snake and now a ball." He just smiled, and I did the same back. "Maybe I can watch you play when you're on the Brandon team in a few years," and I gave a laugh when he blushed. Folks around us got a kick out of the two of us, I think.

It wasn't like Joe Jackson dropped full grown in a baseball uniform down into Greenville and started turning heads with his wonderful talent. He really was a little boy who laughed and cried, worked in the mill pushing brooms as big as him, took care of his younger brothers and sisters, misbehaved and got whipped for it, trusted and was betrayed, loved and was loved in return.

Some of those mill workers who saw us at the park that day, they remembered him sneaking out of the mill and playing ball on his breaks. One of them, a loom fixer I think he said, gave those boys a picker stick he took out of one of the machines, a solid and smooth and flat piece of wood about an inch wide at the bottom and three or so at the top, and about three feet long. It was a passable bat. And with some electrician's tape and some yarn, they fashioned a ball.

"We'd watch 'em from one of the windows in the weave room, and your boy here was good, little miss," and how that Joe could blush when he was fed a compliment. "Some of the hands, they'd talk about them lazy kids sneaking away, laying out of work to play, but hell they was only six and seven year olds. Let 'em have fun, I'd say. One thing sure, not one of us denied the boy had a talent for the game."

Big fellow stuck his hands in the pockets of his greasy overalls, spit tobacco juice off under the grandstands where it wouldn't bother any one, and smiled. "You got a keeper there, Missy." Guess he thought we were going together. I did look a little older than eight, and Joe, though he just turned twelve, looked more like fifteen.

Champ Osteen, to Joe's delight, came to Brandon to take over the team, and that first year young Jackson was batboy. At practice, he'd copy every move his hero made, fielding, batting, sliding. This was school, his sums, reading, writing and spelling all rolled into one. Some of the big men pushed him around, called him "little boy" and such, but the next year, after a winter spent out on that field with Champ, it was

16

different. When it was too cold for anything but sitting by the fire, the two of them would be out there, going over and over throws from the outfield and firing it to the inside of the base where the runner had to come. Extra time on his homework made for straight A's in Champ's class.

All that work with Champ during the winter, throw after throw from deepest center to the base of that tree out behind the backstop, and running down fly balls, it would figure he'd be the catcher that first week of practice. Being the youngest, that's where the veterans stuck him, and that lasted about as long as it took for his first baseball injury.

"They started on a Monday, and he came home that very day with blood running down his face," Miss Martha Ann told me one evening later that spring when we were all sitting on the porch steps. "One of them pitchers cut loose with a fast ball that Joe didn't have enough strength to stop. Drove the glove back into his home-made mask, and the mask into his forehead, and left a deep cut." She laughed and brushed his hair back to show me the scar, and said he was more upset that the catcher's mask didn't hold up. "He took off to practice again soon as I was done doctoring on him."

Joe said, "Katie, I was so scared the first day I walked out on the field with them men I couldn't see straight. They was old hands in the mill, fixers and doffers and mechanics, tough fellows who could run their jobs all day long and still have energy for baseball when shift change rolled around. Me, I was a skinny thirteen year old they stuck behind the plate 'cause they wasn't sure what else to do with him.

"So I gathered me up some scrap wire from around the mill on my break, and at home fashioned me that mask. Gave me a measure of comfort 'til one day Josh Tenton's fastball ripped the webbing out of that flimsy mitt and kept on coming, hammering square into the metal. That was what I called my 'mistake behind the plate'.

"Champ smiled and waved me to the outfield when I got back, and I used his glove to catch some fly balls. This made a sight more sense to me than getting my brains beat out all the time." Joe laughed just like his mama, and he reached out to give her hand a squeeze.

"Walking out of that mill in the middle of the afternoon, to play ball, nobody coming to drag me back in to push brooms or run a doff box, oh Lord Katie you'd think it was just about heaven." To watch him, you'd know he was right. When he was there on the field, I think he felt God's pleasure.

As you might expect, he spent most of the year as batboy and late inning rest for the regulars. Joe's biggest thrill, I think was being part of the team picture, and how he went on and on about it.

17

"The day the manager passed out them uniforms, oh dear Lord-a-mighty how proud I was. Dark blue they was, with that big fancy 'B' embroidered on the jersey and that gosh awful high collar clinging tight to your throat. Even the stirrup socks, alternating wide dark blue and white stripes running sideways, made you feel special.

"It was the first time I ever got paid for playing baseball, and I ain't going to tell you I didn't enjoy that extra two whole dollars a week on top of my regular pay at the mill - five whole bucks a week when you add 'em together. It was a feeling I can't describe when I could help Ma buy groceries and clothes for the young 'uns, and Pa he even looked a little like he was proud of me holding my own with them men. Though I don't think he ever understood somebody being paid to play a silly game. No, for him the outdoors was only for hunting and fishing.

"It was more than money, and in fact money didn't mean all that much. But baseball, it got me out of the mill, free to roam and yell and breathe fresh air and enjoy the sunshine. I could finally be a kid, something took away when I was six and walked with Pa every day except Sunday to work in the spinning room. For those blessed hours practicing and playing this wonderful game, there was a freedom like nobody could imagine, and how I loved that feeling.

"One day they lined us all up single file and took a picture of the team. I still laugh at the short brimmed caps we had, like little boys wear now, but wasn't no one laughing then. Me and all the fellows had a serious look while we was staring at the camera, like it was all business 'cause if we showed we was having fun they might not think it right and put us back in the mill that very minute! Hell, they couldn't of done that neither, not without risking a riot of some sort from that bunch of angry lintheads who come out regular to watch our games.

"Me standing there propped on a bat, big old left hand covering the knob and swallowing up the first four or five inches of the handle. Always did have hands way too big for the rest of me, like when I'd scoop a grounder I'd come up throwing ball and rocks and dirt and whatever else happened to be in the area of the ball. Second baseman or shortstop who had to make the cut-off had a time picking the ball up out of all that debris flying at him.

"Katie, how I loved the game, it was so simple and pure! Playing and feeling the joy just in legging out a double and sliding hard into second, didn't matter the rocks on that rough infield created some nasty strawberries stretching from the back of my knee near to my hip. You remember those, and how I'd hit the ceiling when Ma slapped alcohol on 'em. Neighbors two blocks away said they could hear me yell!"

18

It's hard not to remember him that way, like the little boy, I mean. Couldn't anyone but a little boy really understand the way he felt when he played baseball.

The season went on pretty much normal, the team nothing spectacular but a solid bunch. The park rocked like a Saturday night tent meeting in the hot summer when us linthead fanatics cheered the Braves and hissed the Poe Ravens or Judson Redcoats or whoever the enemy was that day. I'd sit there, soaking it all up, watching carefully the little part Joe played in the game, and I'd be the first standing and clapping when he'd head to right field, or maybe go behind the plate in the eighth or ninth inning. There was a moment, though, a single play in a meaningless late August game, that maybe showed me how special Joe Jackson's talent really was.

The Braves were getting hammered by Poe, something in the neighborhood of 15-1 when Joe came up in the top of the ninth. He'd already been kicked around behind the plate, slid into three or four times, and had a good deal of Little Egypt red dirt on him. Sweating like he was, that stuff streaked all over his face until he looked like an Indian brave, at least the one I'd seen in a book at school. Fans were yelling at him, "little boy, go home, your mama's waiting" and such, but Joe never flinched, just settled deep in the batter's box. It was quiet solitude for him, a discipline he understood and took comfort in. Me, I was a nervous wreck.

He took the first pitch for a strike. "Outside! Outside!" I yelled, and got a round of applause from the Brandon folks and a raspberry or two from the Poe faithful. There was a ball and another strike, and then one came in low and a bit off the plate. The bat whipped off his shoulder, and next was the sound of hissing of horsehide torn apart by timber and screaming past the second baseman before he moved. Next man, Childress, flied out to end the game.

"That infielder, Hub Fleming, he come up and just looked real hard at me. Stuck out his hand and said, 'Boy, that ball would of killed me 'cause I couldn't never got this glove up in time. Hardest damn thing I ever saw hit, like a bullet out of a rifle. Keep going, young man.' Then he walked off, glanced over his shoulder one more time, and I guess I just about floated off that field. Ain't that something, Katie?" He popped me playful like on the shoulder as we rode in the wagon bed back toward home with some of the players and their families. Since Papa knew Mr. Johnson, owner and driver of the rig, I got to come, and was just about the proudest girl in the whole park. Just sat there with my legs pulled up, chin resting on my knees, my brown faded dress near covering my toes, and watched the sun set as we made our way back across town. And didn't even mind it when I heard them familiar words,

19

"think you got a keeper there, Missy." I sneaked a glance at Joe, and the handsome fellow smiled and didn't even blush.

If there was a game, this girl was there watching it, unless Mama said I was needed at home. Then I'd sulk through afternoon chores or school lessons or watching the young 'uns for her. Joe had his own problems, too, after his pa got in some disagreement with the plant super and decided he'd go into business for himself as a butcher. Mr. Jackson had a few customers among the mill hands and he'd make Joe deliver the orders. That boy ran a bunch of laps for Mr. Hatch, the new manager, when he was late to practice. Champ, you might remember, left for the American League and the New York Highlanders after last season.

Folks said Joe was getting better, and started talking about him. Even Mama and Miss Martha Ann came to a game now and then with me, and learned to cheer at the right times. The line drives were now "blue darters", and infielders swore they sizzled as they went by. The home runs, some of them slammed way over the center field fence at Brandon and into the trash dump, became "Saturday Specials" in honor of the one afternoon mill hands got off work to enjoy.

Oh, it used to embarrass Miss Martha Ann when her little David and Jerry passed the hat after one of those long hits, going through the stands where a penny or nickel got tossed in. Sometimes maybe five whole dollars came from the crowd at a big game, and one time I heard her whisper "Thank you, Jesus." Papa said Mr. Jackson didn't do too good with his butcher business, and I knew better than to think Joe's mama would take charity, so I reckon it was the money she was grateful for. She leaned over and patted my knee and smiled. "But I still wish they wouldn't do it," she said.

Joe became "The Pride of Brandon" and "The Candy Kid" because his playing was so sweet. Running down a tough chance in the outfield, he'd take long elegant strides, then just reach up and pluck the ball out of the air. And if it was the last out of the game, why he'd run on to the deepest part of the outfield, then turn and throw the ball back toward home, clear over the backstop on a dead line. "Show out! Show out!" that crowd would yell, and I'd stand up and wave and yell the loudest of all.

Things started happening fast for Joe, and everybody wanted to know about this Jackson kid. By the time he was fifteen, he was picking up $2.50 a game and even his pa thought the money was good, but had changed his outlook only by one word: "damn fool game". The people who watched him, though, saw something special. Look out that window there you can see the smokestacks of six, maybe seven cotton mills, and where Joe came from is where Greenville came from. It was the folks from Mills Mill, Poe, Monaghan, Dunean, Brandon and a host of other mill villages who loved him, respected him for his fierce will to win, and for his refusal to do it at all costs. They looked and examined everything he did, and liked what they saw.

They still poked fun at him, though, especially his teammates. One story said he was playing barefoot in a sandlot game where the field was more rock and broken glass than dirt and grass, and after a few innings Joe came in from the outfield and said he was done for the day. Asked if the glass and rocks were bothering him, he answered, "it ain't that, but they cut up the ball so bad I can't throw it." Don't think it was to make him feel bad, but to Joe it pointed to all the things he didn't have, and that fierce pride that sat right next to his will to win kicked in with a vengeance.

So he started looking for ways to make more money, provide for his ma and brothers almost like the head of the family, and get out of being seen as poor and ignorant. It was baseball that gave him his chance. In those days the mills regularly tried to lure the best players into their fold, and Victor Mill up in Greer succeeded in doing just that to young Mr. Jackson.

"He's a taking off up yonder to play ball, Missy," Miss Martha Ann told us out in her vegetable garden, and I could feel a lump in my throat. I brushed the hair, and a stray tear, out of my eyes. Don't know if Mama noticed, but her friend did, and she gave me a quick wink, like telling me everything was going to be all right. "It's a better offer, and he'll make more money, and Lord knows that will help. And he gets room and board up there, too."

I didn't like the sound of that, and when I was told that he'd pretty much be living up there during baseball season, that was too much. Like a bat out of Hades, I bolted down the path, not even mindful of anything slithery, and on up the road to the Jackson house. If the rocks and clumps of dirt hurt my feet, I didn't know it. Joe was sitting on the front porch keeping an eye on David and Jerry, the two younger boys tossing that rag ball back and forth. He started toward me when he saw I was out of breath.

"It ain't like I'm going to be far away, Katie." Here I was twelve years old and crying like a baby in the middle of the street. Maybe it was the first time I admitted to myself I loved him, and when he took my hands in his, these little ones disappearing into his big rough mill worker-ballplayer hands, maybe I knew it was the first time he was admitting the same thing.

"But you won't be here, and I'm not going to have anybody to sit and talk with, or go to the ballpark and watch. Greer might as well be in China or Chicago or somewhere!" I managed that much between the

21

tears, but Joe stood there patiently until I quieted down a bit. We walked back and sat on the steps, and thankfully the boys hadn't skipped a beat in their game of catch.

"I'll be home every Wednesday. There's a truck from the mill that runs burlap bagging back to the cotton gin down in Fork Shoals, and picks up cotton bales, and I've been promised a ride home. I'll catch the train back up on Thursdays in time for practice. It won't be long, you'll see," and we sat there and watched the dark settle in over the village. The noise of the looms carried through the open windows at the mill, easier to hear as folks started settling in for the evening. Joe walked me back up the path, his brothers tagging along, and helped his ma with her load of beans, squash and tomatoes.

"'Night, Katie," he said soft and gentle.

"Thank you, Joe," and I ran on past his ma.

"Missy, it'll be fine, you'll see," Miss Martha Ann said.

"Yes, I believe things will be fine, for him and you," Mama put her arms around me. She didn't scold me when I started crying, and only offered "I'll tell you in a bit" when Papa asked what was wrong. Sitting here now, I realize how much I miss the comfort of her touch that was so real that night.

I was missing him, but the folks around Brandon were madder than hornets in July at losing their best player to Victor.

"He was a great natural hitter, not a finished ballplayer by any means, and guess I never imagined he'd make enough of a reputation to get clear of Greenville," one of Papa's friends said when he stopped by. Bit my tongue because dear Mr. Wynn would have popped his daughter's behind if she'd raised a fuss.

Another time at the ballpark, when Papa had walked with me, one of the second hands spoke as we went by. "He's the best example of what a man can accomplish in this world totally without brains." I pulled up, ready to speak my mind on that one, Papa or no Papa around, and nearly wound up on my face for it because he grabbed my hand and didn't stop.

"Ain't no need, Katie," he whispered even as a few people were laughing at the supervisor's comment. "Never let somebody control you by making you mad." Maybe it was my first look at ridicule and spite, and it wasn't by any means going to be my last.

Joe was right, though, about not being away long. Late in the summer he was on a tear and Victor was stringing wins together over anyone who cared to take the field with them. One of their contests was against the semi-pro Greenville Near Leaguers, and Joe did pretty well. After the game ended, the Leaguers offered $75 a month, plus meal money, and got young Mr. Jackson out of the cotton mills and back

22

home. I was waiting at the steps with Miss Martha Ann when he walked in from the train station, then he took off running over that last hundred yards, bounded up the steps and grabbed us both in a big old hug. I swear he was better looking and twice as strong as when he left, and oh I was so content to have his arms around me.

The Near Leaguers didn't really keep hold of him long either, but it was time enough to saddle him with his nickname for the rest of his life, and how my man despised it. Probably was the only thing he didn't forgive Scoop Latimer for, and yet it was something bound to outlive us all. Funny, isn't it, how significant moments just slip right on by and leave us wondering how we were so stupid not to see them.

Scoop was covering the game for the Greenville *News* that afternoon in August of '07, and the Leaguers were in a tight game over in Anderson with the local Electricians. First time I think in Joe's life he got caught breaking in a new pair of spikes in a regular game, but mind you I'd been warning him for weeks his old ones were about to come apart, and they did even before the road trip was over. Those blisters, though, were just part of history waiting to happen. Since he couldn't talk his manager into taking him out - and who in his right mind would bench Joe Jackson? - he hustled out to play centerfield in his stocking feet in the last of the seventh.

Scoop always laughed when he'd tell it all again. "Not one of those Anderson fans noticed our boy in his socks until he slammed a long triple to drive in the winning run. He was welcomed by a leather lung diehard when he pulled up at the bag. 'Oh you shoeless son-of-a-bitch!' Sorry, Katie," he'd say, knowing full well I enjoyed the repeat performance as much as he craved giving it. "You know the good Baptists would have hung me if that got in my sports column, so we squeezed out 'Shoeless Joe' instead. Little bit nicer sound, don't you think?"

The chubby little guy started giggling again, and if Joe was close by he'd say, "Yeah, thanks Scoop. Not only did they think I was stupid, but now my very fashion sense was called into question!" But he loved the old guy, and he poked him in the ribs, knowing good and well Scoop did him a great favor.

All through his life Joe was a quiet and humble man, uncomplicated, sweet natured. He had a child's heart and his love for this game was just contagious. Even in his first professional tryout with the Greenville Spinners, there wasn't a whole lot of scared in him. He wasn't being arrogant either, but when he stepped between those chalk lines he was the knight in shining armor, the magician who could do just about what he wanted.

Tommy Stouch was the manager, and he arranged for Joe to come over to Meminger Park to show his stuff. I hopped a trolley over there without Joe knowing it, assuring Mama I was all of fourteen and nearly a grown woman. Told the conductor, Captain Martin, what I was about and asked him to hurry as much as he could. I missed Anderson when my man was given his one-of-a-kind nickname, and wasn't about to do the same again. As soon as that car slowed approaching the park, I jumped off and hit the ground running, gray cotton dress flapping in the wind, and made my way through the oak trees that stood just up from third base.

Billy Laval was warming up. A good pitcher, I'd heard folks say, and Papa used to tell me teams would hire him for when it was a tough game and they needed a win. I swallowed hard hearing the sound of the ball popping loud into the catcher's mitt. Lordy he was fast.

There was the expected round of insults when my man got set in the box, from "busher" to "barefoot boy", with a few unmentionables and even a "linthead" floating in from the outfield. Joe and I laughed about the same time on that last one. I mean, how stupid can you get? Here's a team, the Spinners, named after one of the most skilled jobs in the cotton mill, and some crafty old veteran comes out with that bunch of nonsense.

He lifted a high foul back behind first and then took three balls that I thought looked pretty good. The chorus of taunts got louder, topped off with, "What's wrong, mama's boy? Froze in place 'cause you scared?" The next three balls hit the fence in right-center on a dead line, just about before either fielder could move. A little squeal of laughter got out of my mouth before I could stop it, and by then Laval had stretched and thrown again.

He was keeping the ball low, and Joe pulled two down the right field line. The last one was between the first baseman and the bag. That big kid didn't even have time to turn his head, much less move. Stouch was taking every move in, signalling for his pitcher to change location or go to a breaking ball. Laval turned his back to Joe and loaded up his spitter - it worked up to the plate slow and got out of the park fast. The next two came back through the box, the last one about taking the bill of the pitcher's cap with it.

Joe launched a half dozen more stinging drives to all parts of that outfield, then another one straight back through the middle.

"Where the hell you going, Laval?" Stouch yelled to his friend, who by now was taking his wind-up three steps behind the mound.

"He's a getting my slow spitter and then I'm running for centerfield. Big son-of-a-bitch is hitting 'em too close to my head, and I ain't got no desire to be the first Greenville pitcher killed in the line of

24

duty. Half inch outside he don't swing, smidgen inside he can let it go, then throw one a foot off the plate and he nigh kills you with it!" Another shot kicked up dust behind second.

"You come throw the damn ball if you want to see him hit any more!" Laval threw his glove toward where Mr. Stouch was standing near the third base dugout and proceeded to leave the field.

Oh how I loved watching my man set these professionals on their ears. And I had wings on my feet catching up with the trolley, and a motor on my mouth relating every minute of the tryout to Captain Martin. He was probably glad when we got back over to Brandon.

"Mr. Stouch walked over to me after it was all over and told me to be ready in the spring," Joe told me that evening when he walked over to our house. It stayed my secret that I watched my man pass his test. And Papa's, since he gave me permission to go. And Mama's, since she didn't disagree and make me stay at home.

"He told he $100 a month and I just swallowed hard and said 'Yes sir'. Great Lord-a-mighty, Missy, bankers don't make that much! Do they, Mr. Wynn?"

Papa shook his hand, and Mama hugged him, telling him they were real proud of him getting a good job away from the mill. "It's what you love, boy, and that's what makes all the difference. Do it with all the talent God put into you," Papa said, puffing that pipe and Mama shooing him to the back steps before you couldn't see in the house.

We walked down to the Jackson house holding hands, him talking about telling his folks the news. We stopped near his mama's vegetable garden, and Joe put his arms around me, bent down and gave me a slow, sweet kiss. I knew now why that unbelievable sum of money was so important to him. For the first time, or at least the first I was brave enough to admit it, Joe Jackson was going to ask me to marry him. Got to say I returned his kiss with a lot of feeling. The fresh smell of turned earth was all around us, and it was almost quiet, though you could hear the looms over at the mill.

"Missy, I'm just wanting you to be more than my girl, if...if you'd just consider being my wife. Now I know we're young, 'specially you, but I don't think I could ever love nobody more."

"Joe Jackson, I'm nigh fourteen. A woman, I'm telling you, holding a job clerking after school at George Conduras' candy store up on Main Street. And yes," I reached up on tiptoe and kissed him again, then said real soft, "I'll marry you."

We decided then and there to wait until next spring, making sure the Spinners' job worked out before we'd ask our folks for their permission. Getting their blessings wouldn't be a problem. I mean, we had been closer than a brother and sister for going on how many years?

25

Miss Martha Ann was happy as could be about the baseball job, knowing her eldest would be helping to provide for the family and filling a need his pa never really would. She gave him a big hug, and me too. Even Mr. George Elmore got up and shook his hand, though all he said was "Damn fool game", but he gave his son a smile this time when he said it. That was as close as I ever saw him come to praising his boy.

"Ya'll got to see this," and Joe pulled his copy of the contract from his hip pocket and unfolded it. I took it and read out loud, "Contract of Greenville Spinners Base Ball Club". On the bottom, over the word "signature" he had crudely marked "X". I was the only one standing in that room who could read what was in the document.

Just after Christmas we told our folks about the plans we had made, and like I said it wasn't a real shock for either side of the family. There were a few hugs shared, questions answered about when it would be - summer, most likely -, and what took you so long - ask Joe -, and that was about it. We decided it would be best to use the empty bedroom at the Jackson house to start with, and then we'd find us a bigger place after baseball season was over.

That winter Joe did some work with the village crew at the mill, fixing up the houses, setting poles to run wire for electricity, delivering coal and wood to the families. He had talked with Champ Osteen, took a trip to Piedmont to do so, about helping him with his workouts for the coming season. The two of them started getting together almost every afternoon for two or three hour drill sessions, unless it was raining or snowing, and sometimes that didn't slow them down much at all.

"He knows so much, Katie," my man said, all excited, soaked with sweat and rain finding its way drip by drip to the kitchen floor. The shoeless one did remember to dump the muddy cleats at the back door. "Showing me how to position my feet just so for a righty or lefty, like Cobb does for Detroit. Knowing what the pitcher's going to throw so you can cheat a little during the wind-up, and he said Cy Young would show the sign to the third baseman behind his back. Listening careful to the sound the bat made when it met the ball and watching the angle of the bat at the same time, that's what made an outfielder real good, Harry Hooper told him one day in Boston."

Those piercing brown eyes of his would downright glow when he talked like this, and we sat cross-legged right there in the floor amongst the puddles, me listening to him and gazing into his eyes, dreaming of being a ballplayer's wife.

Every day, all of January and most of February, he was running laps, hitting the cutoff man, throwing to the inside of the bag, and hitting, hitting, hitting. Champ, now he'd offer advice on anything Joe

26

did in the field, helping him with the defensive side of the game, but he was silent any time Joe picked up a bat.

"Katie, you just don't mess with what God created perfect. Besides, what could I tell him? He's got a better swing than most of the major leaguers I've seen these past few years. He's different because he loves the game so much. Every part of it he's got a deep passion for. Champ smiled that morning we talked while he waited for Joe to get off work, and I saw how he cared for my man. They were miles apart in temperament, him fiery and quick to fight, Joe even keel and quiet to a fault. But the game brought them together and gave Joe a taste of fatherly attention he'd never been offered before.

Champ was on a train for St. Louis the end of February, heading to spring training with the Cardinals, and Joe was ready for the same with the Spinners. We'd walk past Meminger Park a dozen times a week during the late winter of 1908, and I couldn't help but feel it was going to be a real special season. Who knows, maybe after a year or two in Greenville, he'd get a shot with one of the big league teams like old Champ. But we'd be patient. I did get him to break away and take me to a stage show at the brand new Bijou Theatre. He got a big kick out of that vaudeville stuff.

A week or so into spring training a couple of pitchers came down with sore arms, and we had a game with Wake Forest College. Mr. Stouch didn't have anything to lose and sent his new recruit to the mound. I mean, Joe hasn't been there since he broke a guy's arm with a tight fastball in a mill league game four, five years ago. I sat, wrapped tight in a quilt Mama gave me for my ninth birthday, and tried to fight off a too cold March wind, and watched my man toss a neat four-hit shutout over the gentlemen from North Carolina. But Joe at the plate was different, no hits on a couple of lazy flies to center and a groundout. The cold probably got to his bats.

Scoop wrote it up in the paper, of course, and mentioned about Joe coming from the Near Leaguers and his salary of $75 a month. That set it off and what Papa and I heard directed toward Joe over at Brandon the year before got worse and worse.

"He's from the mill hill, Katie," Papa said quietly, but I could tell he was getting madder and madder. "You and me know that doesn't make a difference in a person's character. Makes it better a lot of times as far as I'm concerned, but these high class bankers and merchants aren't going to see it that way. Keep your wits about you," he said. Lord knows I tried, but when some smart-aleck cut him down, and all his cronies sitting there laughed and picked up the chant, I wasn't above letting this Wynn temper go a-flying.

27

"Don't make the mistake of confusing not being able to read and write with ignorance," I said to them on the bleachers one day, my voice getting louder and stone cold enough for those men and their sassy women to shut up. "And from what you just saw even ya'll can figure out it doesn't take a whole lot of school stuff to help a fellow play ball.

"Just maybe," I said, smoke coming from between my ears about that time, "maybe you can put your brains together and figure out that when it rains you got a good chance of drowning, with your noses so high up in the air." You know, I think I shocked them into silence. They sat there wondering about this pint-sized fifteen year-old soon to be Mrs. Joe Jackson, firebrand and certainly no member of southern gentility at the moment.

"Guess we got us a linthead lover here, boys," one dumpy old bald man finally said. Think I had seen him working as a clerk at Metz and James Furniture Store. "Is you a linthead, Missy?" he finished off.

"Not by birth," I heard Papa's voice behind me, and it was real low, a sure danger signal for anybody who knew him, "but she'll likely be one by marriage before the summer's out. Now I'd suggest, gentlemen," and he stepped a little in front of me, a row above Joe's tormentors, and he was a pretty tall man to be sure, "that the lady's words be accepted as fact."

As those around us, a few Brandon folks among them, started clapping in support, the highbrows stood up and filed out and on down the steps kind of quick. They marched right into a group of Wake Forest players walking off the field talking about the Greenville pitcher and what a fine gentleman he was during and after the game. Danged if that didn't gall the townies good, I'd expect.

Joe came over, accepted congratulations from some of the people, shook Papa's hand and gave mine a gentle squeeze, and asked what all the commotion was about. Before I could sound off, Papa, God bless him, said it was some business he had to get straight with a couple of merchants, and he was sorry if it got a little bit loud. We walked down to where we could catch the trolley home.

Next day my man came by and said he wanted to take me to meet a real special gentleman, but on our way to the other side of Brandon Mill village, all he bellyached about was going hitless against the college boys yesterday.

"Wood on them bats is too soft, Missy, and they just ain't got enough weight. And the handle's got to be thicker - these meathooks of mine wrap around too far and I lose the feel." The faster he spouted his ideas on hitting, the faster we walked, me struggling to keep up, on past the mill, down near to Drayton Street, and then we went behind one of the houses to a small shed. Scraps of wood were everywhere.

"Mr. Ferguson, Joe Jackson." My man introduced himself, and the master mechanic at the mill stood up from behind his workbench, tall, forearms like a mountain bear with about as much black fuzz. His voice was gentle, a lot like Joe's.

"Boy, heard you went the horse collar yesterday and that ain't good with that swing of yours. Here," and he handed a Joe a stick of pine. "Now don't mind about the kind of wood, because what we're looking for is the weight, how it feels in your hands." As Joe started swinging, taking a stance and stepping in to a make believe pitch, the eyes of the older man caught every movement. About the same time both said "too light" and then laughed.

Fifty, a hundred sticks, picked up, swung and discarded, a pile of wood moved from one side of the shed to the other. Then Mr. Ferguson handed over what he called "a hunk took from the north side of a hickory tree last October, on out past your house, Miss Wynn." Oh, but he was a fine man, and I could see why the folks on the hill talked so highly of him.

Joe's brown eyes lit up. "What's it weigh?" like he was asking how much money the bank's got in the vault. "This has got a good feel." Those swings became faster, and if possible, smoother than before.

"About forty eight ounces when we shape it up and sand her smooth. It'll be heavy, boy. Ain't no one I recollect using something that heavy. Not even Champ or them major league guys going to get much whip out of it. But you," and he stared hard at the muscles of Joe's arms and the stride, the follow through, everything Joe did Mr. Ferguson watched, "it'll work for you."

He clamped the stick in the old lathe he had salvaged from the mill and rebuilt, and told us to go on and enjoy the rest of the evening. "Be here late tomorrow, young Joe, and I'll have two of 'em turned for you."

What he did was fashion the pale wood into a thing of beauty, then added a coat or two of lacquer and tobacco juice, knowing my man's fondness for black bats. After Joe added a few more dark rubbings he named them Black Betsy I and II. "Bone 'em good, boy," Charlie advised, "so the grain will get harder. Do that, and my guess is them two ladies will serve you well."

We'll get a good look pretty quick, I thought, considering our first professional season was only a week away.

The Spinners started fast, and Joe was right there in the middle of everything. Funny, I can remember how it looked at Meminger Park, and even when I go over to Greenville General like I have to a good bit now, I see that old ballfield and not parking lots and buildings. It certainly wasn't a sell-out on Opening Day because a cold wind made it uncomfortable, and most of us brought along a heavy coat to wear. But there was still a good crowd, and quite a row of buggies, carriages and wagons stretching from the edge of the grandstand almost to the leftfield fence.

The boys popped Anderson hard that day, 14-1 it says in one of the scrapbooks I kept for Joe. Two doubles and a triple, thanks in part to the magic of Mr. Ferguson's bats, and of course that made Joe happy. What folks remembered for years, though, was the catch he made in deep center, running full speed with his back to the infield, sticking that glove up at the last second and spearing the ball. A thousand hands might have been hurting with the cold, but they clapped and clapped until my man made it all the way to the bench.

It always struck me as funny that the two people Joe was closest to on the team turned out to be college boys. I mean here's this unschooled linthead made fun of and insulted by so-called ladies and gentlemen, and the ones who stood by him were more educated than any dozen of those snakes thrown together.

After the Wake Forest game, Black Betsy I came alive and Joe was considered one of the best hitters on the team and quite a mover on defense. It didn't take long for the *News* to start calling him a second Buck Pressley, probably the best all-around player on the team. Buck graduated from Erskine College, in the town of Due West (and no I don't know due west from what), but his dream was to play baseball and not be stuck in some office. He was a fine first baseman, though with a little soot rubbed on his arms and cheeks and spread through that full head of sandy colored hair, he could have passed for the local blacksmith. Handsome and quiet, Buck was a natural leader who could shepherd his mates through tough times. Wound up going to medical school and becoming a fine doctor, and he returned to his home town and took care of folks there until the day he died.

I need to tell you about one episode that stands out, and of course it was when town folks were riding Joe about being an ignorant cotton mill hand making all that money. One of the tormentors kept ringing a bell and yelling "quitting time" or some such stupidity, but that really was how life was measured down on the mill hill. My man grounded weakly to second base, and the laughter just got louder.

It happened the next time Joe came up, too. "Time to quit!" started up all over again, but this time he blasted a homer to left center. There was cheering and clapping and stomping, but what I remember was Buck Pressley standing up as Joe rounded third, walking a couple of steps so he was right in front of that group, and said to the idiot, "Ring it one more time, you s.o.b., it's time to start again!"

That was just like Buck, and he reached over and shook Joe's hand and held it in a strong grip, and patted him on the shoulder. My man never forgot that, or the thousand other little kindnesses "Press" gave so freely to him and others on the team.

I always thought Joe had more in common with Buck, such a sweet natured man, one you'd want your son to grow up and be like, but it was Hyder Barr that he got thrown in together with, all the way up to when both of them were bought by Connie Mack's Athletics up in Philadelphia. Not that there was a thing wrong with Hy, a Davidson College man from up in North Carolina. Good ballplayer, but a lot more fiery than my man. He was about Joe's height, but maybe twenty pounds lighter, with dark brown eyes, black hair and a handsome face.

I'll tell you, it wasn't beyond Mr. Barr to do some flirting with me, and I'd be less than truthful to say I didn't fight an urge or two wondering what his lips might of tasted like in the moonlight. Thank goodness it was just a girl's passing fancy, and Joe never knew anything about it. I wouldn't have hurt him, because there shouldn't ever be a broken trust between two people who love each other.

Up in Winston-Salem at a game in early May, Hyder and Joe were a two-man wrecking crew. Hy tossed a four hitter and he and Joe hit homers in about the same place, and together they had a half dozen hits in a 9-0 win.

Now a single girl couldn't be traveling with a ball team in those days, so how could I be knowing such details? Mr. D.F. Cason worked at the Telegraph Office downtown, and he got permission to set up in the Opera House and post the progress of the Spinners' out-of-town games as they came in over the wire. There would be a small but right boisterous crowd of us, floating some "hurrahs" across Main Street when Mr. Cason's play-by-play would reveal a Spinners' run or a good catch. Even with those prissy dresses we had to wear, the girls could ram a fist in the air and cheer for our boys as good as any of the men.

Hy and Joe kept up the Pete and Repeat routine a good part of the season, and I think there was a good-natured competition between them. Joe would go three-for-five with a homer and Hy would maybe go him one better, four hits and being the winning pitcher to boot. Then they'd go to the other extreme, like when they beat Greensboro in late June. Hy bunted for a hit and Joe dragged one down the line right after him. Their pitcher threw the ball away and Barr scored, and Joe trotted home the next play on a wild pitch. They had a good time on that one.

But Mr. Barr was one of the most complicated people I ever knew. He'd be laughing at himself one minute, like the day he was in the outfield at Meminger Park, and an Anderson fellow got a hit that rolled up under a carriage way out in center field. Now Hy was dodging

31

hooves and a swishing horse's tail and maybe even manure trying to get the ball, and he just sat right down and laughed until the tears streamed down his face. When he came in after the inning was over and Stouch yelled at him about letting the run score, he started laughing so hard again he tripped over the water bucket, and that started the whole team to hooting.

The very next day he wrote the Greenville *News* about one more in a long line of violations of a city ordinance forbidding the hitching of animals in the street or on a sidewalk. And he listed cows, horses, sheep, goats, pigs - Hy seemed to have a list compiled by Noah himself. When I read the letter to Joe, he laughed near as hard as his friend.

"Ain't he got a way with them fancy words, Missy?" But the laughter died away when my man took the paper from me and stared at it, all black squiggles that meant nothing to him.

Then Hyder would turn and be involved in what he considered a battle of right and wrong, and it didn't matter if the other fellow was a well-positioned member of the local aristocracy. This one time he was madder than I'd ever seen him, and of all things he was defending an umpire, saying that Mr. McLaughlin's calls were fair and just. See, Mr. Mahon the mayor had been using some real explicit language to question the umpire's heritage, IQ level, sexual preferences - you name it, it was said. And Hy used just as strong a language to tell the mayor he had much in common with a horse's backside. Joe and Buck grabbed Barr and pulled him away from the grandstand, and some of the mayor's friends pulled His Honor back as well. I don't much think that chicken wire backstop could have held them apart for very long, and my guess is that Hyder would have whipped up on the mayor.

The most fun anyone ever had at the park was those folks from Brandon when they piled in to watch their home boy play. It didn't take them long to forgive Joe's short stay over at Victor Mill, and his fellow lintheads treated him like he'd never left.

When the Spinners played at home, you could bet the mill village was going to be pretty much deserted because the Pride of Brandon was now the Carolina Confection, one sweet hitter. And more times than not he came through for them. Against Anderson one day, he drove in all three of the Spinners' runs and the fans passed the hat twice, the first time when his homer tied the score, and again when his two run single won the game.

And could they raise a ruckus. Joe homered in a close game that June, and the Brandon folks jumped up and hollered until they were hoarse, threw their hats in the air, stomped on the bleacher boards, and when their boy crossed home plate, made the brass band over behind the first base bench play "Dear Old Joe" five times straight through. Catchy

32

little tune popular that summer, and I'd tap my feet and clap, looking at Joe until he searched out my face in the crowd and gave me the smile that stole my heart when I was just a little girl.

"They enjoy the show," Joe said later, "and it's fun being in front of folks you know. When it's over, they go back to the cotton mill, the long hours and noise and heat, and Missy they ain't going to get away from it in this lifetime, not most of 'em anyway. Me, I'm the lucky one, making a good living playing a kid's game." His eyes would look like bottomless pools, and you know he'd be thinking about Dave, next oldest in the Jackson clan.

The young man had good talent as a ballplayer, but several accidents when he was working in the mill diminished his physical skills. That pitching arm was broken no less than five times. His last injury, when his sleeve got wrapped around a belt running from an E-model loom to the main drive shaft thirty feet overhead, took the boy from floor to ceiling and back down in about five seconds, and made sure his right arm and left leg didn't work any more like they were supposed to. He'd be one of the lintheads who never got away from the mill.

"The Lord's been too good to this old boy. Some of them others could of used a bit of this good fortune for themselves." You had to strain really hard to catch his words, they came out so soft and sad.

The *News* even got into the fun at the ballpark, running a column called "Fan Food", and I'd read the comments at supper. Joe, Miss Martha Ann and the young 'uns got a kick out of it, but Mr. George Elmore did his usual silent act. Or if we were at my house, Papa would do the narrative honors, and I think he and Mama laughed about as hard as Joe and me.

"Now here's a good one," Papa let go another big belly laugh. "'What do you think about sending Joe to the legislature?' Boy, you're way too smart, and honest, to get caught up in such. But here's one that might be more to your liking," and he reached into a pile of stuff on the red couch and pulled out Monday's sports page. "'Thinking it over, it will be best to run Joe Jackson for governor.'"

"He'd be the most handsome man that's been head of this state in quite awhile," Mama said, giving my Joe a hug. That lady always did have fine taste in men.

Another night, at the Jackson household I read, "Though the county convention went for William Jennings Bryan for president before they had the privilege of watching Joe Jackson play ball, it is not too late to run him for Congress."

"My boy the Congressman, now I like how that sounds."

"But Miss Martha Ann, look here," I interrupted, wiping my eyes after laughing too long. "He's called King Joseph I of Brandon! So when we get married, I can be a queen." Looked over to see Joe smile and whisper, "Already are one. Don't need me for that." And he wrapped that big paw around both my hands and squeezed real gentle.

"Uh huh, sure," offered the talkative Mr. George Elmore.

In one game my man was due up in the home half of the second, and Miss Martha Ann was sitting with me, her first time at a Carolina Association game. "Listen, Katie, how they clap for my boy. These uptown folks doing that for a linthead."

"Some of them can still be mean," as a few insults like 'good-for-nothing mill hand' and 'dirty cotton dunce' filtered from two or three mean-spirited morons. Joe then launched one fast ball about thirty feet over the oaks back of right center, answering both the applause and his critics.

"Does he always do that?" Miss Martha Ann asked, and people around us patted her hand and assured her it was more often than not.

"Isn't he just a darling!" One well-dressed townie lass cooed to her companion as Joe touched the plate and doffed his cap to the crowd.

"Handsome as all get out, and so strong!" I was red hot and about to take a step toward the shapely blond waving her little hankie at my man, but heard, "Lady, he's spoke for, and you really needn't rile a wildcat." At Miss Martha Ann's icy words, Truffle Butt and her friend the Dainty Red Rose eased on down the bleachers without ever looking around. Folks whooped it up for "Joe's ma, the champ!" She might rival her son's popularity at Meminger Park before too much longer.

One old fellow there was as much of a character as her, if you can believe it. Albert Jones was president of the Spinners, and he'd sit over in the third base corner of the little "chicken coop" grandstand, wave his straw hat in honor of a timely hit or good play, and gave out a spanking new five-dollar gold piece as a reward for home runs. The furniture business he was part owner of must have been doing pretty good. Since Joe led the Association that year with a .346 average and socked about fifteen homers, we had some extra spending money to see a show down at the Bijou or ride the trolley from one end of Greenville to the other with Captain Martin at the control.

About mid-July we made official what folks had pretty much taken for granted, that Joe and I were going to get married. Guess he figured the team was in a slump, and he'd already broken Black Betsy I and wasn't hitting too good, so this couldn't do anything but change his luck. Leave it to Scoop Latimer to print our nuptials in baseball terms.

"Joe made the greatest home run of his career Sunday," he wrote. "The home run was made on Cupid's diamond and the victory was a fair young lady. The happy couple has the best wishes of all fandom." That was the way sportswriters phrased things then.

So two days after Joe's 19th birthday, and oddly on the 19th of July, Katie Wynn became Mrs. Joe Jackson while standing in Mama and Papa's living room. Reverend W.B. Justice made it all official and here I was all of fifteen and a blushing bride. Lord but I was happy, even if our honeymoon was a quiet walk around uptown Greenville before heading back to his folks' house on the mill hill. Old Scoop even wrote that our wedding night was spent over at Meminger Park as the Spinners were trying to find a way of breaking a slide of two wins and eleven losses and falling into second place behind Greensboro. I'd tell him thank goodness it was spent in our room at the back of the Jackson house, away from prying eyes and ears - we certainly didn't want to disturb anyone.

I didn't know who was more shy, Joe or me, in our first few attempts at making love, and there were more than a few attempts that first night. Likewise, I can't tell you which of us enjoyed it more as all those attempts to have a baby increased over the years. Seems like we never could get enough of one another, and I loved him in every way a woman could love her man, and the sexual part wasn't any different. We may not have known much, but goodness we were fast and willing learners.

That wedding picture of ours, folks must think I looked like the Iron Maiden or something. Had a big old dress hat, high collar white blouse, starched blue coat and matching long skirt, and that coat had the biggest buttons! They were in style, though. And gloves, gloves in South Carolina July heat, can you believe it? Looked quite the woman, even if I was barely fifteen. Of course, that was in style, too, being a woman at fifteen.

Joe, all of nineteen, was getting his first shot at major league baseball, if you could call it that with Connie Mack chasing him between Greenville and Philadelphia. Oh, my man was handsome in his gray suit, white shirt and bowtie, with a dapper gray fedora slid back on his head. Those little boy eyes of his were wide open, and he stood ramrod straight with his hands clasped behind his back. Looks almost kind of scared, doesn't he?

Some folks tried to say this photograph summed up our relationship, me the driving force and brains, him just an ignorant, though athletically gifted, baseball player who brought name recognition to our business. Well let me tell you a little something about my man Joe, and I can feel anger causing my face to flush, like it did when I defended him against such stupid assumptions these people made over the years.

Yes, he was raised over at Brandon. Yes, he went to work at age six sweeping floors in the big cotton mill and didn't get to go to school. No, he was anything but ignorant. Not being able to read or write doesn't erase a mind that can keep up with events going on in the world by listening to conversations around him. It never stopped him from asking the most intelligent questions about new things doctors were doing in operating rooms, about this or that trial that was being held at the moment, about who had died and what kind of family they left behind or how they must have been a right good person and would surely be missed. That was Joe. He couldn't read, but that mind of his stayed in overdrive learning about the world around him.

That picture doesn't tell so much of who was the driving force and who followed along. It tells about two people very much in love, two people who enjoyed holding hands sitting on the porch on a summer evening, content with the touch of soft flesh, and the sounds of streetcars and barking dogs and soft voices of neighbors chatting next door. That was life to us, and oh how very wonderful it was to have him sitting there beside me.

It tells, too, of what we'd be facing in ten years or so, all the heartbreak and ridicule and hate directed at us after the World Series of 1919. Maybe my hard expression anticipated all that, and maybe Joe's eyes saw his mistake and then the betrayal that came his way. Whether it was right then, in '08, or in '19, the greatest thing was that we had each other. Despite what everybody else did to us, or thought of us, or...hated us, and there I go with the tears again, we always had each other.

Chapter 3

Things did change for all of us. Joe's teammates kidded us about being old married folks, and we would grab a bite to eat with them after a game, but more and more we'd politely decline and go our own way. There wasn't offense intended, and none taken by Buck Pressley or Hyder Barr, the other boys or Mr. Stouch. Too, there were other, bigger changes going on as well.

There had been talk for awhile about major league scouts being at games, and that kept things stirred up. See, it wasn't the first time players here had been looked at. Sydney Smith was already with the Athletics that year, and Champ Osteen and Davy Crockett had long moved from Piedmont to those big cities up north. But when the subject of the talk was Joe and Hyder, it was a little bit different. Excited. Scared. Wondering what might happen, how much more our life could change. Dear Lord, how much more could it?

I recognized one fellow from pictures Joe and I had seen in the newspaper. It was Socks Seybold of Mr. McGillicudy's Athletics, who showed up there a couple of games and then was gone. And he saw one great finale to the season, one play folks talked about on into the winter because we came up three inches short of the pennant.

Greenville trailed 6-0 in the bottom of the ninth, scored five runs and had the bases loaded with one out, Joe on third. He took off on a grounder to the second baseman, collided with the catcher, and the ball came loose for one brief moment. That catcher picked it up quickly and tagged Joe out. What happened next I think shaped part of our journey together into the major leagues.

Fans booed so loud, using combinations of curse words that were among the most imaginative I'd ever heard, and threw bottles and stuff in the direction of the home plate umpire. Joe was up, dusted himself off, reached his hand to the catcher and then the ump, said "Good game" to one and "Good call" to the other, and trotted over to the dugout. One man who heard it was Socks Seybold, who had run onto the field to speak with my man. He came over later and talked with me.

"The umpire, Westervelt I think it was, said it was the hardest call he ever had to make, but what I watched, Mrs. Jackson, was your husband." He took the derby off and wiped his forehead with the sleeve of his white shirt. "All this anger and yelling around him, and he's congratulating other people. Then quiet started to spread through the crowd like salve on an open wound. I've never seen anything quite like it." And he walked off, shaking his head and smiling, to send his telegram to Mr. Mack. Funny, but Joe's .346 league leading average was a minor point as far as Mr. Seybold was concerned.

It was a two-week whirlwind. Right after Joe and Hy signed a contract, they played one last game with the Spinners, an exhibition with Greer. Folks up there remembered my man from the time spent with Victor Mill last year, and of course he didn't disappoint them, smoking a long home run way over the centerfield fence. All around people were talking about the two boys, how they'd make good in the fast company where they were headed.

"Connie always told me, 'Go down to Greenville and get this Jackson's brothers and sisters, even his whole family to come back with you if that's what it takes to get him here,'" Mr. Seybold told Joe and me at supper the night we signed the contract. Then he laughed, "But who would have thought that Socks would be sent to fetch Shoeless to Philadelphia." He was nearly as tall as Joe, not as muscled up since his playing days were pretty much behind him, but you could tell they shared a deep love for this crazy game.

Doing the contract with Socks wasn't a problem, and I was there to read everything for Joe and show him where to put that "X" of his. Those big hands shook as he put his mark on the document, but I wondered then and now how much from excitement and how much from embarrassment. Like I said, the signing was cordial enough, but a couple of days later I got a real education on what baseball was really about.

It was a Sunday afternoon in late July when a crowd gathered at the post office, waiting to see the check from Mr. Ben Shibe to Mr. Albert James. Fifteen hundred dollars for two ballplayers, sold to Philadelphia by Greenville, $900 for Joe Jackson, $600 for Hyder Barr. Must have been two hundred people waiting to see the check, figuring it was really something to get that much money for two people. Listening to them, I may as well have been at a cattle auction, and it's a wonder somebody didn't bring up their stud value. My man may always have played the game with a little boy's heart, but my view of the game took quite a jolt that day, and wasn't ever the same again.

To say I was worried sick when Joe left for Philadelphia on August 21st would be saying too little, because I'd been dreading the day since we signed the contract. All my tears were shed by the time the train pulled out Friday morning, Joe waving from the end car on the little iron platform, he and Tommy Stouch standing there, and then I couldn't see them any more. When he got settled in, he'd be sending for me, but I had never felt so lonely. For ten years I'd seen Joe almost every day, and now that we're finally married he goes away from me. My fondness for baseball was being sorely tested.

He didn't want to go north by himself, so Mr. Mack arranged for Tommy to be a traveling buddy, and this seemed okay. "Perfectly willing" lasted all of one day. Miss Martha Ann and I were in the kitchen Saturday popping string beans when David and Jerry tore in from the front porch.

"It's Joe!" the young 'uns yelled loud enough to alert most of West Greenville. I got to the screen door just as he started up the steps two at a time.

One leap and I was in his arms, not caring who saw this barefoot girl, her dress hung up around her waist and underwear showing, kissing him hard and long and wanting to pull myself all the way into his body. Then everyone was around, Miss Martha Ann tugging my dress down, Jerry running off to get his pa from back of the house where he was cutting meat, and the questions started flying. But all I could hear was Joe saying, "I couldn't leave you, Missy. God knows I thought about playing for Mr. Mack and seeing Mr. Seybold again, and maybe no one's going to come asking for me to play baseball up there ever." I looked into those brown eyes and kissed him again. He was still holding me, my feet not touching the ground, finally setting me down only after his mama kept after him. "Maybe nobody up there, but I still got to explain myself to Tommy."

"How?" was about all I could manage.

"When the train pulled into Charlotte, seemed like we'd done been gone a year. Tommy went to get us a sandwich and Co'Cola. And there was the ticket office, and a return train coming through right then for Greenville, and the man at the window let me exchange my fare, and I headed back home. Maybe its wrong, Missy, but..."

"It sure is good to see you," I said and drew his arm around my shoulder so I could walk close to him up the steps and onto the porch. When we got there, a voice from behind offered a gruff, "Damn fool game anyway, boy. I can use help cutting the meat starting tomorrow." Mr. George Elmore got his home grown boy back, figuring, I guess, that the fool's notion of playing baseball for a living was out of his son's head. It was Miss Martha Ann who kept things sensible.

"We'll talk about it, George Elmore, when the boy's rested, and," she leaned over and winked at me, "after we've had a good night's sleep." That lady must have remembered what it was like to be newlyweds.

Morning came soon enough, and Joe was up and gone and I figured he and Tommy were already talking somewhere. I hopped out of bed, threw on my dress, prettied up a bit and ran to the kitchen where Miss Martha Ann was listening to them on the porch. The manager was making his case in real plain language.

"There's things you don't do in the game, son, and one of them is to go against a team that's got you under contract. Damn, it ain't mill ball where you can go wherever and slip on a different uniform and play just because you're good and folks pat you on the back and thank you for coming over." All of that in one big breath. "It don't work like that no more," and me and Miss Martha Ann looked at each other and edged in closer to the front door. Looking through the screen, we could see his arms reached out, almost pleading.

"This is major league baseball, Joe, where folks like the Shibes and the Macks and McGraws spend thousands of dollars deciding which players stay and which get shipped off to other teams. You stay here at home, boy," the big man moved away, lowering his voice, "and you'll be blacklisted from organized ball, and those people can do it."

"What's that?" my man asked, his own voice quiet now.

"It means you ain't going to play for nobody, not major nor minor, for as long as you live. Damn Joe, you got so much promise! Don't bring this on yourself by refusing to report to the Athletics." I'd moved to the door and Tommy saw me and pointed.

"I know how much you love Katie. Hell, that was obvious to anybody who saw you together this past season, and she'll be loving and supporting you no matter what. But don't throw this chance away to build a good life for both of you. You've got so much to offer, Joe. More ability than anyone I've ever seen, more pure love of the game and a desire to have the folks watching you and sharing that love. Damn, boy!" Stouch took a deep breath. "That's all I can say."

Inside Joe, a lot of uncertainty was swirling, I could tell, and he looked over at me. "Missy, I'm mixed up inside." I came out and stood there beside him, taking his hands in mine. You have to carefully choose your responses to the storms of life.

One of Papa's lessons came into my mind while I was trying to think what to say, that your life was only as strong as your commitment to doing the things you were called to do.

"Go. Tommy's right, and I'll be okay here. Soon as you get settled in, I'll catch a train for Philadelphia and watch you play ball and we can walk all over the city and see things we've only dreamed of and eat in fancy restaurants and...Go, make them all sit up and take notice."

He was right about one thing. Word traveled fast and the paper was reporting the very next day how my man hightailed it home, was lovesick for his child bride and all such as that. It didn't matter, because by that time Joe and Tommy boarded a train bound for the City of Brotherly Love, and they made it on through Charlotte. In less than a week he was in the Athletic line-up, starting in centerfield. One for four with a single and an RBI, "one stinking single" I think he said in his telegram home to us, written by his friend Socks Seybold, and we read in Scoop's column how he made a real good catch in the very first inning off one of the Cleveland batters. Folks came around to congratulate us later that evening, telling us that our boy was going to do fine. I just wished it was all that simple.

Philadelphia was hell. For him. For me. We were still newlyweds, and Joe headed off up north on that train. Connie Mack was a good man and tried to do right by Joe, offering to get him a tutor to help him learn to read and write, and Joe turned him down, not wanting to embarrass himself more. But most of the Athletic players took the rookie hazing up a couple of notches.

A picture that Joe kept showed him in a heavy double-breasted sweater while most everyone else was in regular uniform. It must have been early March and still cold, especially for a replanted southern gentleman, but even in dressing for a team picture he was different. Cold, not just because of the weather, but because it was his first time away from home. Scared? He had to be if you set that lonely, boyish face against those veterans who looked hard and mean.

Years later I'd listen to him talk about it, like an old man repeating himself, but you knew it wasn't that. It was so much more. Standing at the window, staring out into the streetlights on Whitner Street as the rain sliced through the glow, he was battling his demons again.

"Damn Katie, I go with 'em and listen to 'em, trying to fit in, and all they do is make fun of me. I can't read, I'm from the south, I'm homesick and to them that makes me some kind of animal in a zoo, to sit there with a stupid look on my face and be laughed at when I drink out of a finger bowl like they told me to in one of them high class Philadelphia restaurants we ate supper at one night.

"I ain't stupid, Missy, I'm smarter than the rest of 'em except maybe Mr. Eddie Collins, but he's the one that treats me okay. And I can play circles around all of 'em, them with and them without book learning. God Almighty, I ain't no side show freak, girl, I ain't there entertaining 'em just because I don't know their fancy ways!"

I'd walk over and take his hand, put my arm around his waist, just stand there and hold him. Couldn't anybody say they knew how he felt, not even me. Some things just won't change, no matter how much we pray to God they would.

Like I said, he loved Mr. Mack, but not the rest of the A's organization, and I can't help but wonder what might have been if Joe had played his career for Connie and not Charles Comiskey. With what was in the papers, both in Philadelphia and New York, fans would never know the truth anyway, because most of those sportswriters said things to make people's minds up for them. Seemed it was that way from the

41

start, except the folks in Cleveland treated him better when we got traded there. Thank God for those few years.

Ty Cobb, he fought the War of Northern Aggression all over again, on and off the field. After the game was over, he'd hit the city streets looking for another battle, and most times there was somebody to give it to him. Joe was different, retreating into himself, and he always remembered it was a game. He'd head out on the big city streets, just like Cobb, but my man would be talking to the kids, playing catch with them, or maybe stickball I think they call it up there. And he'd talk with the street vendors, get him a hotdog for supper and eat and talk with the men and women sitting on the boarding house steps in the evening. Folks in the neighborhoods weren't all that different from those on the mill villages he'd known all his life, and he felt at ease with them.

"You know, Missy", sometimes he'd start back in after standing and watching the rain for several minutes, "when I took batting practice everything in the stadium stopped. Mister Eddie Collins got back 10 to 15 feet on the outfield grass so he could get out of the way of them blue darters, and he'd look in toward home and give me a friendly wave."

All the razzing stopped with the beauty of his swing, and all you could hear would be the sound of Betsy launching that horsehide like a meteor, just as blazing, just as hot. There was freedom for him in the batter's box, and no mean spirits could cross over into holy ground. Free to do what he was best at, and oh how wonderful he was.

The good evenings were when he'd come out of his silence and talk about hitting. The terrible ones were when he'd just continue to stare out the window, not even knowing that I stood next to him. He was grappling with shadows then, some long dead, others long unseen. All very real. Sometimes I'd wonder if anybody really ever cared about how much he, and us, hurt. Maybe it was partly us to blame, like maybe if we'd shared our weaknesses, other folks would have accepted us better.

That fall and winter went fast, and soon Joe was leaving for spring training. I'd be joining him after the swing north and we'd be looking for our first real home together.

I never did make it to Philadelphia, at least not as the wife of an Athletic. Five games Joe played in at the first of the '09 season before Mr. Mack took him aside and said he was going to send him back to the minors, to Savannah.

"I've never seen a more miserable young man," Joe remembered him saying, "and you'll be killing yourself with worry if I don't get you out of here." Just as I was packing to leave, a telegram came, one that Hyder wrote for Joe.

"Coming home. Report to Savannah one week."

So early on I got a real strong taste of what it meant to be a ballplayer's wife.

"Savannah's a nice place, isn't it, Miss Martha Ann?" I said putting my arms around her neck and crying softly, not for me but for Joe's hurt at not sticking in the big time, like I know he wanted to so badly. The boys didn't pay us any attention, excited as they were about just having seen the first car race in Greenville.

"Main Street Hill Climb!" Jerry yelled.

"And we was at the courthouse to watch 'em cross the finish line!" David added. Watching the young'uns enjoy themselves eased my hurt a little.

Not much I remember day to day about Savannah, except we were there for the rest of the '09 season and Joe was the leading hitter in the Salley League, the second time he'd led a league in back-to-back years. And we were happy, but I missed him when he was on the road. Sometimes I'd walk down to the Cathedral of St. John the Baptist, and in the late afternoon quiet I found comfort there. Light coming through the stained glass windows, a click of heels on the marble floor as folks walked by, somebody playing hymns on an organ that had what seemed like a thousand pipes. All that made my loneliness a little more bearable, made me feel warm and safe in the palm of God's hand.

After a home Climbers game at Bolton Park over on Henry Street, we'd walk and window shop to our hearts' content, and every now and then Joe would duck into a store and come out with a necklace or ring or coat or something for me to try on and see if I liked it. Had to learn to say "no" without hurting that boy's feelings, and that was an act of diplomacy worthy of a peacemaker.

That was hard on somebody who didn't have anything much to speak of growing up and wanted to do for his wife what he thought was right and proper. Finally I'd say "Let's just wait awhile, Joe. We're young and got a whole lifetime ahead of us." That seemed to satisfy him, and we'd walk on back to our bungalow up on Abercorn Street. Bay Street, Factor's Walk, River Street, we learned them all on our evening journeys. Even got away to Tybee Island a time or two, both of us fascinated by the lighthouse there. I loved to dig my toes in the sand, stand there with my head on Joe's shoulder, and stare out at the waves coming in. It was the first time he and I had ever seen the ocean.

We heard Hyder didn't last too much longer than Joe up in Philly, and that was his first and last shot at the majors. Twenty two games, only four hits to show, struck out about three times more than he hit the ball. Wired us he was being farmed out to the minors himself, somewhere in the Southern League, and that maybe our paths would cross again. Sad that such happenings were pretty common with ballplayers.

Soon as the season was over, we headed back to Greenville, waiting on word from Mr. Mack whether Joe would be back with the big club or moved up a notch somewhere else in the minors. Useless worry is a big mistake, and the best way to keep from it is staying real busy.

We opened up our first business that fall and winter, a billiard hall down on West Washington Street, and it had a real original name - Joe Jackson's. Had a business partner, Cal Akers, a fellow who used to hang around the Spinners' team, an all right enough guy though his stylish clothes always smelled of cigar smoke. He'd look Joe in the eye, give me a quick bow, and fill our heads with how good this was going to be.

"Not a big venture," he said, "but one with some nice potential." Joe and I worked and enjoyed being around the folks who dropped in to shoot a game or two, or just shoot the breeze and talk baseball with Joe, and Cal handled the public relations, him being so good at getting to know people. He hung around the place at first pretty regular, then not so much at all. After a couple of months, when the creditors started showing up, that was the first idea I had that Cal hadn't paid any of the bills we owed, and that something bad was up. I asked them to wait, and Joe and I took off over to the boarding house where our partner kept a room. And I got what I expected. Cleared out and gone.

"Left sometime day before yesterday, Mrs. Jackson" was all Mrs. Stillwell could offer.

We scraped together enough cash to pay the bills, taking what we saved from Joe's Savannah salary along with what was in the cash register. It was our first lesson at being taken advantage of, seeing hard earned money squandered, stolen by a person you trusted. Down at Brandon some of the mean spirited folks spread it around how the Jacksons would soon be broke again, and that Joe would be coming back to the mill for a buck and a quarter a day doffing. No matter what we did, our status never changed, did it?

I looked at Joe after we cleaned up and closed for the night. "This isn't going to happen again," and I set my jaw like I saw Papa do when he had to fight to save the grist mill up at Paris Mountain back when I was just a little girl.

"We're going to be smarter, listen better, watch every penny and every move made in our affairs." I took Joe's hands, and we stopped for a minute in the cold November night. "And you're going to start learning a bit of reading and writing from me.

"The world's changing, Joe, and we've got to be tough to get along. Cal got our money, but he taught us well." My man looked at me,

44

who understood all about baseball and being tough and honest on the field, but knew little of what I was trying to get across to him now.

"We'll make it, Katie," he said softly. "We'll move up in the game and they'll know Katie Wynn and Joseph Jefferson when we walk into a room, by God in heaven they will." He hugged me tight and we walked on, our breath hanging thick in the night air, a conversation lingering to make exactly sure we understood the promises being made.

"Lord," I thought, "be with us in this world."

There was time for visiting with folks again, and I got a kick out of watching Joe play with his little sister Gertrude, all of two years old and the youngest of the Jackson clan. He'd tote her around Brandon on his shoulders; heck, he'd carry her nigh all over Greenville County bouncing up and down and laughing to beat the band. His voice, it would go real soft when he talked about her, and you saw how much love that big heart could hold.

"Gertie, she was a sweet girl," Joe said. "When I'd come home from playing ball, and that could be a right long time between visits during the season, me and her would take time to just talk. See, there was twenty years difference in our ages, me being the oldest and her the youngest, but that didn't seem to matter all that much to either one of us.

"Sometimes we'd take off and walk uptown, looking in the store windows. Oh, Gertie loved window shopping. And maybe we'd check in the dry goods store for a couple of sticks of peppermint. Sure was different now, people speaking to us and asking how things was going, not like back when I was Gertie's age and the townies didn't want any lintheads around dirtying up their pretty Main Street. Shoot, they used to have special shopping days for mill folks so wouldn't be no contact between us and them what thought they was our betters. Wasn't no need holding to bad memories, though, and watching my little sister's eyes light up when all those well-to-do townies came up to shake my hand and talk about baseball and how I liked Philadelphia and Savannah and all, it was enough for me that she was enjoying it.

"Some evenings we'd sit on the porch at Mama's house, listen to them looms clacking over at the mill, a steady sound coming through long rows of open windows and weaving down the streets and around the houses all over the village. I'd get caught up in that, remembering going to work in that monster of a building when I was six, swallowed up at 5AM and spit back out twelve hours later after sweeping and picking up quills and trash and broken machinery parts all day. When I'd get lost deep in my thoughts, Gertie would climb up in my lap, put her arms around my neck and just hold on 'til I paid her some attention.

"When she lay quiet on my shoulder I'd talk some about when Mama and Pa made the journey from Pelzer to Brandon, about sweeping them greasy floors in the spinning room when my whole body ached to be outside running and jumping and smelling flowers and fishing. And I'd tell her how baseball got me out of the mill, first on to the team at Brandon, and then all the way up to the major leagues. I'd think, too, about them people who never got away from the cotton mills there in Greenville, who took the only life they was given and did the best they could, raised families, laughed and cried, lived and died.

"She'd tousle my hair and kiss me on the cheek, not understanding a word probably, but content to be close. Me, I was loving it more than her, I'd gather. Then I'd tell her about the subways in New York, riding underground to get clear from one side of town to the other, about Philadelphia and the Liberty Bell or the Old North Church in Boston. And them fancy hotels we stayed in, brass beds and a nice place to eat right there in the building. I'd tell her about listening to music from folks standing on the corners of busy intersections, getting hot pretzels from street vendors and gumdrops every color of the rainbow at the confectioner's in one of the downtown neighborhoods.

"Lord, there was never enough time to see everything, to smell and touch all the wonders of that non-stop life, so different from what we got here at home. I'd look over at Gertie, and she'd be asleep with her head on my shoulder, all them stories tiring her out or else old Joe boring her to sleep. We'd sit there a little longer, the clackety clack of them looms going on and the fading light bringing on early winter darkness.

"It was as peaceful a time as I'd ever know, not worrying about the past and the hard times growing up, and not minding about the future either, 'cause playing baseball was making me a good paycheck and there really wasn't nothing my family wanted for. So I just sat quiet, held Gertie and felt her soft breathing on my neck, and looked up at the stars just beginning to shine. Sure was nice."

Watching the two of them, I wondered about me and him having a baby and when it might happen. Wasn't like we hadn't given it a few chances during our first year of marriage - not in excess of most other newlyweds, mind you - and I could lay there in my man's warm embrace afterwards and picture him as a daddy. Oh, he'd make a good one judging from the way Gertie took to him, and when those kids flocked to him at the ballpark, no matter where we happened to be.

"It'll happen when it's supposed to, Missy," he'd say, kissing me and hugging me tight, skin to skin there under the quilts. "Just don't worry. Besides," and he laughed in that deep way of his when he was happiest, "it's just fun being the two of us right now."

Most of the time the only words I ever heard Joe's pa speak consisted of "damn fool game" when he commented on my man's baseball career, but there was a side of him that autumn of '09 that came to light for me. It was the first and only glimpse of his compassion I was privileged to see, but I cherished it for the seed that was nurtured and blossomed in the man I loved, and that was enough for me to start loving Mr. George Elmore, too.

Some of Joe's quiet can be traced to his pa, who I don't think ever got over losing his freedom in the outdoors. See, bad as life was trying to scratch a living on a tenant farm out from Pickens, he had the big woods of the Blue Ridge foothills to tramp, and from what Joe told me his pa loved the hunting and fishing there. Didn't particularly want any company, and if he brought home meat or fish that was okay, and if he didn't that was okay, too. And I've got to tell you about the one picture ever made of the man.

It's in the back yard of the house over near Brandon, and he's sitting there with his arm around Blue, probably the ugliest hound dog it was ever my privilege to meet. And Blue, he's looking at Mr. J., and Mr. J he's scowling at whatever photographer was wandering around the mill hill that day. In that yard, hemmed in by clapboard houses with the underpinning showing, I doubt he or Blue could have felt very much freedom.

"The weeds was high, and there was clumps of grass and bare spots. It was a pretty good make believe ball park for me and my brothers," Joe said. "That is, when we wasn't rounded up and put to work by Pa."

The elder Jackson may have been fairly well versed in woodsmanship, but he was not much for baseball or any athletics for that matter. "If it don't bring home food or money," Joe imitated him, "ain't worth a spoilt slab of fatback, and one what lets fatback spoil is a damn fool."

Joe said he couldn't remember any outward display of love or affection from his pa, not that he didn't feel, but that he was incapable of expressing anything. I can't say that was all true because of something I saw him do one afternoon. A couple up on Abney Street had a baby to die, a real pretty little girl, too, and knowing the photographer would be making his rounds on the village in a day or two, waited to bury the child until after they had a picture taken together so they could remember her. Mr. George Elmore must have heard neighbors talking about this, and cut up some meat to take to them.

Mounting the steps and knocking on the door, he removed his hat, handed the meat to the woman, laid a hand briefly on her shoulder, and went on off without saying a word. Later he was back, having gone

47

to the ice house for a small block, broke it up with his hammer, wrapped pieces in heavy cloth and packed them around the child's body, which was laying just inside the door in a rough wood coffin made up by the mill's carpenter. He and the young father shook hands after they came out on the porch, and again no words were shared. The photographer got there the next day, and the mama picked the child up, washed and dressed her baby one last time, and held her for the picture. Later that afternoon she and her man buried a precious blessing given for so short a time.

I had followed Mr. George at a distance that day, came up way behind him on his first errand to that house of death, and watched his acts of kindness, and loved him for it. It stuck with me, and I never saw him do anything like it again. It made no difference with how he treated his boys and girls or his wife, because for sure that didn't change.

Yet the more I knew Joe, I understood it was a seed, maybe like the mustard seed folks talk about in the Bible that starts small and grows so big. Where it was maybe a one-time thing for the pa, it became a pretty common occurrence for the son, sometimes almost to a fault. There wasn't any way to count the panhandlers who took advantage of Joe, or how many beggars he'd give money to or buy food for. My man had a good heart. He took time for those who were ignored, but ignored those fatheads who felt so important.

Autumn passed quickly, and though Savannah was nice enough the seasons here in Greenville were a wonder to be part of. Before you'd know it, Thanksgiving and Christmas had come and gone, the New Year had rolled in, and we got word from Mr. Mac that our new home for the season would be New Orleans.

"Can't say I ain't disappointed, Katie. I was hoping to be back up, but guess Mr. Mack thinks I ain't ready. I can accept that." He walked off back over to our bedroom after I read him the telegram, big shoulders a bit slumped.

"Don't worry none too much," Miss Martha Ann offered, "he'll be coming around fine. And ya'll got a whole new city to explore down there. Enjoy being together."

And then Mama offered me a hug and kiss on top of the head. "It works out like it should, daughter. Let the plan unfold and follow the path you should take." I just looked at the both of them and marveled at two women I loved so much, wiser probably than I'd ever be.

Chapter 4

New Orleans was good, a lot like Savannah was for us, though it started out a lot rockier. A column on the sports page announced Joe's arrival, spending no time talking about how he just led the Salley League in hitting, and a lot of time calling him high strung, impetuous - whatever that meant - sensitive, easily hurt, and quick to take offense. At least they did mention he brought along a dozen black bats, planning on doing a whole lot of hitting.

But slowly they began to pay attention to what he said.

"Mr. Mack's a mighty fine man, and he taught me more baseball than any manager I've ever had." Those words let them all know he'd set foot in the big show and was planning to do so again.

Didn't hurt any that Connie called him one of the best minor league outfielders in the country. "For batting, speed, throwing and fielding, he can't be beat." Nice things to hear when you've just pulled into town and need a fine introduction.

"Baseball ain't nothing but a kid's game played by grown-ups", Joe said, and when those kids hung around after the game he'd be sitting right there with them. His first time up in an exhibition game in March produced one dinky grounder between the mound and third base, but danged if he didn't beat the throw to first by a full step. And they gave him another nickname, "The Carolina Speed Marvel."

Popular with the players as well as the fans, he loved the game and wanted to please folks so much that he played when he shouldn't have. I watched him throw a ball deep from left field one day, dead on a line to home, and knew his elbow was wrapped thick with bandages from cuts that got infected tangling with that outfield fence on more than one occasion. The manager, Charlie Frank, even ordered him out of the game, but Joe refused gracefully.

"Skip, they came to watch the best team you can put out there, and I think that includes me." He smiled and ran back out to his position, and the old man just looked at the other players and said, "You got to love him." And I think the folks in New Orleans did just that.

A big street parade was arranged for Opening Day, and the line of carriages stretched for more than five blocks, carrying local politicians, the team, and screaming school kids. It was a good team they had to cheer for, with Joe and Heinie Manush and Maurice Rath, and the Pelicans stormed through the Southern League. My man was leading the league in hitting again, three different ones in three straight years, and folks were pouring into those parks and having fun. Joe reached one hundred hits in early July, before any player in any league, and that included Mr. Cobb, Mr. Wagner, and Mr. Lajoie up in the majors, too.

We were up in Memphis playing the Hornets, and got a telegram after the game telling us a big watermelon was being put on ice for our enjoyment when we got back home.

Every now and then on a Sunday morning, the two of us grabbed a mug of scalding chicory coffee and beignets and walked, holding hands, down through the French Quarter, Jackson Square (can you blame us feeling proud?), St. Louis Cathedral and Preservation Hall. We'd be getting up as some folks were just getting in. Maybe we'd hop a streetcar from St. Charles Avenue on to Canal Street and wander along the riverfront. Sounds, smells, tastes like nowhere else we had ever been. After a while I even got Joe to liking shrimp creole and jambalaya, and we sat and ate on the balcony at Tujague's and listened to that city come to life as the sun was going down.

And if one of the players wasn't hitting too good, all of us would meet at Congo Square where the local black folks held their voodoo ceremonies. Figured it was as good a place as any to get the hitless demons out of the wood and commence to go on a tear the next home stand against whoever dared take the mound against us.

Sportswriters got downright poetic about his plays in the outfield. One of them in Chattanooga said "Joe ran hard to get in the comet's path, pulling it down out of the ether by a marvelous leap and stab with his left hand." It didn't eat as good as the watermelon, which by the way I managed to drip all over my toes while we ate it on the back porch of our little bungalow, but they sure were sweet sounding words to Joe when I read them.

He even modified his "show-out" for the Southern League fans. At a game down in Mobile one Saturday, one of their players singled to center and the runner tore from second all fired up to score. Joe got to the ball quickly, but stood holding it until the runner was two steps past third base, going full out. The throw nailed him a good ten feet from the plate, and the folks kind of sat in a stunned silence before a few of them politely applauded.

Next day, it was even better. We were in trouble because a double had already scored a run, and a single to left center promised more of the same. But Joe got a great jump and fielded the hit just as their man got to third. The hot corner was about to boil over. Again my man just held that ball, and waited for Mr. Watson, I think it was, to start home. But after a bluff toward the plate all he did was walk back to the bag with his head down. It was a lot more than polite clapping this time as folks got up and stomped on those wooden bleachers and hollered for The Kid. Didn't die down until Joe came off the field after the inning was over and touched the bill of his cap. My man had the talent to make any ballpark feel like it was home.

They started noticing something else about him, commenting from time to time about how he was a flawless dresser, and he was sporting several pairs of new shoes from M. Pokorny and Sons down on Charles Avenue. Handsome with his clean-cut face and dark curly hair, they thought him a thoroughly likeable fellow. I could have informed them of that if they just listened. When we went out on the town with the other fellows and their wives after a game, maybe to Bruning's Seafood Restaurant out on the lake where the sunsets were almost as good as the shrimp, my man felt truly welcomed and respected. They even called us a stylish young couple, and when we walked by the mansions in the Garden District, didn't anybody try and run us off. None of those nasty hard noses back at Brandon would have believed it, a couple of lintheads from up in Carolina mixing with New Orleans high society, and I wondered which one of them got assigned to Joe's doff box up in the spinning room?

Things began to heat up as the season moved on into late July, and Joe's bat was nearly as hot as Bourbon Street during a Saturday night frenzy. Another of Mr. Mack's scouts, Al Maul, made a stop to check on the Pelicans, and he called my man the sweetest hitter he had ever seen. But he also brought up again how young Mr. Jackson let the tall buildings and the hustle and bustle of the big city worry him and make him lose heart.

"When he makes up his mind to latch onto a major league job," he said, echoing his boss, "nobody's going to be able to stop him."

What Al was doing, we learned about a month later, was working on deals to shore up the Athletics during their stretch drive for the pennant that year, and he needed some veterans. So the deal was cooked up to offer Mr. Rath and cash to Cleveland for Briscoe Lord. Bobby Gilks, the Cleveland scout, already knew about Joe and made him the centerpiece real quick and had the deal changed. Mr. Rath and Mr. Jackson, with the blessings of Connie Mack, became Cleveland Naps at the end of the 1910 Southern League season. It was a good deal for all concerned, I always said, since the Athletics outdistanced the Highlanders and Tigers in the American League race, and then beat the Cubs in the World Series. And Cleveland got two good young players who could fit in right away. Opposite what you might think, those next several weeks rolled by right fast.

After the final home game we celebrated at the Delmonico Restaurant with all the players and several dozen fans, all of them bidding farewell to the new major leaguers. One of the well wishers was none other than Hyder Barr, who Mr. Frank traded for to take Joe's place in centerfield.

"Last time it was me and you, Candy Kid, and can't say I'm not going to miss that." Shook my man's hand firmly and slapped his shoulder. He turned and gave me a kiss on the cheek, which I returned like a good sister, no dreams of moonlight this time around. It was the last time Joe and I ever saw Hyder.

We sure did learn to love New Orleans while Joe was there with the Pelicans, and wouldn't mind coming back for visits now and then.

Got packed up and closed out the lease on the house - I was getting pretty good at this big time responsibility for a seventeen year old - and we were on the move again, me to Greenville for a few weeks and Joe on to Cleveland. When he got settled in, I'd get up there for a couple of weeks to see the city and find a home for us. Thank goodness the Pelicans left for one last road trip that same day, or we never would have seen the majors again.

That sounds strange, I know, but you remember he jumped trains and came home the first time we tried this. On his way up, those same thoughts started up again, like "there ain't enough elbow room in them cities for me", he was always saying. By the time he reached Memphis, he talked himself into jumping the train again, but with the Pelicans playing the Hornets that day, he went to the ballpark first.

"Felt like I was led there, like a sinner to the crying pew, Missy, and the guys came over when I walked into the locker room, congratulated me again and talked about how me and Mo was going to do good things in the American League. Old Charlie Frank, he came by kind of suspecting why I was there, and put his big paw on my shoulder.

"Show 'em, Candy Kid. Show 'em that what every busher dreams can come true, and when you walk on the outfield grass of League Park tomorrow, know that every ballplayer in New Orleans and Savannah and Greenville is pulling hard for you. You'll make it, son, Lord willing, and you'll make it big." He turned and headed out the door, spikes biting deep into the worn planks, the other guys following him out.

My man hustled to the train station and didn't look back. His not wanting to leave the south and report to the big leagues from the time before had already stirred up bad feelings with some sportswriters, and they lit out after him as soon as the trade was announced. One of the Detroit *Free Press* fellas said Joe would lose his nerve when the pitchers started putting a fastball up next to his head.

Idiot only missed it by the distance from New Orleans to Cleveland. My man had already proved himself a hitter in three different leagues, and did it again in his first game as a Nap. In the first inning he took the second baseman's glove off with one wicked blue darter, and then homered in the 8th as the team won 7-2. And those Ohio boys welcomed him with open arms. Joe was so much at ease with them, and it showed with him hitting near .400 for the rest of the season. Yeah, sportswriters sure could judge talent, now couldn't they?

Let me tell you something about when we got there for our first full year in 1911. It might not have been heaven, but it was as close as we'd come in Joe's major league career. After Philadelphia in '08 and the way the veterans made fun of him, taunted him, anyplace would have been better, but Cleveland was more than that. Folks were kinder, and Mr. Lajoie made us feel right at home as soon as we got there. He and his wife had us to supper a few times, and took us down to The Palace on Euclid Avenue to see our first big city vaudeville show. Joe, he loved everything about Cleveland.

It was like being back at Brandon. We moved into 7209 Lexington Avenue, two blocks away from League Park, and Joe, he'd walk to work during the home stands. After a hard workout, he'd sit in the dugout and watch intently at everything that was happening around him. I could tell he was happier as his graceful moves on the field became even more beautiful. Other outfielders would stop just to watch him run down a fly ball, and give a low whistle when leather met leather with him in full sprint away from the plate.

And sometimes he'd even laugh a bit. But there was always that little part of him no one could ever get to, and I'm not sure I ever saw it too often, much less ever got invited there. It's that fearful little corner of ourselves that each one of us keeps so neat and tidy, so we can find every worry and shortcoming and hurtful thing anyone ever did or said to us. In this place, Joe always felt he could never measure up, that he would be what the townies labeled him so long ago, a good-for-nothing linthead, illiterate mill hill trash, and all the baseball talent he possessed couldn't make up for it.

I think because of that, when he'd finish laughing, what was left was not quite a smile. No, it was almost wistful, like he knew the struggle would go on and on. Sometimes it was like he'd push that burden all the way to the top of the hill and almost be rid of it, then he would slip on some loose dirt and that rock would start rolling away and disappear into the darkness below. And then he'd go back down and start over.

One of the veterans who welcomed us was Addie Joss, a great pitcher and really fine gentleman, and oh how he praised Joe as the leader of a bunch of promising young players who would bring new life to the team. During spring training Addie was there to encourage him, though Joss didn't seem to feel all that well, and Joe called Addie his friend, first time I'd heard him use that word toward another player in the big leagues.

There were good times right off. All of us laughed early in the season when the Senators' Al Schacht pitched against us. See, he disobeyed Mr. Griffith's orders and threw a fastball to Joe with a man on.

"I remembered two sounds," he said in the paper the next morning, "the crack of the bat immediately followed by the crash of the ball into the outfield fence. Jesus it was loud, and then I was hightailing it away from Skip before he could get his hands around my throat!" Joss read the account in the dugout during warm-ups for the second game in the Washington series, and tears rolled down the face of nearly every player sitting there. Al always was the Clown Prince of Baseball.

Before April was out Addie was dead of tubercular meningitis, just that fast. Joe didn't let too much emotion show through all of the mourning, though tears rolled down his cheeks when he spoke to Mrs. Joss after the funeral was over. I mean, Billy Sunday already had most of us crying when he finished his hour-long sermon, because you sure couldn't call it a eulogy.

When bad things happened back then, everybody got together to try and help out. Kind of like a "pounding" back at Brandon Baptist Church when folks got food together for a family going through tough times. Of course, this time it was a baseball game to benefit Addie's widow.

Good bunch of men they brought together, too. Some players we were getting to know and form friendships with, and some it was necessary to learn to steer clear of. I think Tyrus Cobb was everybody's first choice as a drawing card, and can you believe the son-of-a-gun forgot his uniform? Clubhouse boy rustled up a Cleveland jersey and pants, but there wasn't a Nap fan all that happy about the Peach desecrating holy cloth.

Mr. Lajoie, wasn't anyone about to leave him off that list any more than they were going to overlook my man. Mr. Eddie Collins, Smoky Joe Wood, Home Run Baker and a host of others agreed to come. Hal Chase, he got invited, too. Didn't trust him then because of some stories about his shady play, and all I can add is that the years proved my first impression was the right one.

League Park was nigh onto full for the game, and the folks were generous, raising $13,000 for Mrs. Joss and the little kids. Bet you not one of us remembers a thing about who won, because it was all for Addie.

My man went back to that private corner of his, and maybe wondered if everything he cherished wouldn't be taken away from him too soon, but he used Addie's death to drive him on. Joe stood silent and alone at the plate, slamming daylights out of the best American League pitchers could offer. That .408 he hit for the whole year, best average in all his major league seasons, highest ever for a rookie, was a testimony to how much he cared for the man who was his friend that 1911 season.

Joe came right off that great average and led the league in triples the next year, the most exciting play in the game in my book, by the way. It seems the folks associated with baseball all of a sudden had an opinion on my man, some nice, some downright mean, others just too screwed up to make any sense at all. Cobb, who lied and made Joe out to be a fool during that batting title chase the year before, was telling anybody who would listen that no one ever hit the ball harder than Jackson.

"A level swinger, and sometimes they just carried out of the park even if Joe wasn't going for home runs."

Our own skipper, Joe Birmingham, made it real simple, figuring he wouldn't trade Jackson for Cobb straight up. "I consider Joe the greater asset to a club." And you can bet Mr. Cobb was off cursing up a storm over such blasphemy. Right on the heels of a compliment in the paper, though, would be his worst enemy in the press, Joe Williams of the New York *World Telegram*, who took a real joy in degrading my man as a dumb southern hick.

Of course, another southern hick, Scoop Latimer down at the Greenville *News*, asked Walter Johnson how he pitched to Joe.

"I used to give him the best I had," Walter said real serious, "then I'd run over and back up third base!" Now Joe liked Walter a lot, and I'm sure he got a good chuckle out of that one.

But it seems a fact that for every bad person who weaseled his way into our world, there were two good ones put there by the Good Lord. When Williams or some other idiot would begin to spit poison, and I'd see my man getting a bit down, I'd pull out two stories and read them out loud while we sat on the steps at home on an early summer evening. I think the neighborhood kids got as big a kick out of them as I did, and pretty soon Joe would be smiling and pretty much his old self.

F.C. Lane, in one of his *Baseball Magazine* pieces, said "to sum up his talents is to describe those qualities of the ideal player, the greatest natural gifts any one player ever possessed."

"You tell 'em, Mrs. J!" one of the kids would yell. "See, Joe, you're the greatest! Everybody here thinks so."

And Bill Evans, great umpire that Joe had utmost respect for, got real specific. "A smart ballplayer with the intuition to do everything right - hitting, running, fielding, throwing. He never did a dumb thing on the field."

The kids, as close as our own sons and daughters, they'd be cheering and rubbing his hair and shaking his hands or hugging him.

"Oh," he'd say, "some folks are just nice, Missy. And these guys know I just swing, and if a pitch looks good enough to hit I go for it, low, high, inside or out. If I get the hit sign from Mr. Birmingham, I'm going to go for it."

"Let's go for it now, Joe!" every one of those kids yelled, and they'd take off, sneaking into League Park for a game that ended after dark, because neither Joe nor the kids was going to quit as long as they could see the ball.

We'd still travel home for the off-season, and always have an adventure or two sticking close to us, let me tell you. Happy, unafraid when it was just the two of us, somehow finding ways to get in trouble.

We struck a pose—now can you believe this, Joe and *me* in baseball uniforms—just inside the center stair tower at Brandon Mill. Had to be on a Sunday afternoon when the mill wasn't running, because I don't remember any of that rumbling of the heavy machinery shaking what seemed the very foundation of the earth.

Joe was his usual handsome self in his Cleveland uniform, standing proud with hands on hips, looking down at me and smiling. He had a heavy double-breasted wool sweater on, all buttoned up and neat as could be. But I don't think the club could ever find one that would cover those long arms of his, and typically this one stopped a good two inches above the wrist. So sticking out from those dark blue sleeves were those big hands of his, big enough that he could swing three bats in the on-deck circle, and I mean wrapped clean around all the handles, too.

Of course, I should have realized even then, though we hadn't been married very long, that those big hands were guided by a bigger heart. Joe grew up not having much, but once he started making money playing ball, he'd buy candy and give it to kids, get clothes for his brothers and sisters, and help put food on the table at his mama's house. And if there was a beggar on the street, or if a local church held a "pounding" for a family that was having to struggle, my man was there with a few crumpled bills or sacks of flour and potatoes, or sometimes both. Yes, those hands were so big because they held so much good will to be given away to others.

Now the folks with the Spinners made me up a right nice fitting uniform to kind of go with what Joe was sporting, though I have to admit the pointed dress boots I wore looked a bit out of place. The gray flannel togs fit well enough and the black stockings showed off my legs nicely. Heck, sometimes I figured these legs were what that old mill boy married me for. Just kidding, but Joe and I were probably a little ahead of our time, making no bones about enjoying one another's physical beauty, with clothes on, and yes, with them off, too.

They gave me a matching gray sweater, not that sharp double Joe had, but comfortable and nice looking. And I put my hands on my hips just like Mr. Jackson, and I stared back at him, real stern like, but the photographer snapped the picture about when I was starting to crack up. Almost stepped on one of the baseballs that fellow had put on the floor for this shot, and I was laughing hard and got off balance, but then those big hands of Joe's just shot out to catch me. Those hands, so beautiful and strong, steadied me. I just fell into his arms, surrounded by powerful muscles, and at the same time enveloped by gentleness, and I looked up into his eyes, deep with wonder like a little boy's at Christmas, drinking in all the goodness and hope and love flowing so deep in my man, and I thanked God that I was Mrs. Joe Jackson.

We were young, so in love, so lost in each other, and finally I think that photographer got a bit embarrassed, or maybe he was just being a gentleman, and he packed up and tiptoed out the double doors. Joe and I just stood there in the stair tower, in the quiet of a Sunday afternoon, and let a sweet kiss linger until, hang it all, my neck started getting stiff and I couldn't stand on my toes any longer. Before we left, I turned around and looked back up the first flight of the stairs.

Did you ever notice how the wood got worn down more quickly in the middle than on the sides, though you'd expect folks would get to the wall and use the handrails? They hit them regular every morning at shift change and again in the evening, or reversed it if they worked third shift. Six days a week, except for the July 4th week and maybe sometimes at Christmas for a few days. Most of them spent their lives there, like the generations before them, with never a hope of leaving. Joe and I were different, luckier, and walked out of that cotton mill, not just that Sunday afternoon, but forever. We had places to go and big cities to explore and cars to buy and living to do.

But you know, those mill folks had deep roots and family, and we began to envy that before our journeys brought us back to them. And most of them opened their hearts to us when we returned to Greenville, after our souls had been about sucked dry. After we'd been called every bad name in the book by high-minded northerners *and* the southern gentility.

Couldn't any linthead ever make good, they'd sneer at him, and knew he didn't have any morals, and only got where he was by having gamblers take care of him. Excuse me, but damn I hated every one of them. Couldn't ever let down my guard or take off my mask, not ever, around people like that.

Mill folks, they mostly hugged us and asked what we needed or what we were going to do. They welcomed us home. I think I understood better about those worn steps in that center stair tower at

Brandon or Poe, or Monaghan, or Judson or anywhere else. The well-worn paths spoke of order, and they always led home.

One rainy Saturday afternoon, on toward six o'clock, Joe had caught up with Webb Cashion, a baseball-playing buddy from over at Brandon. Joe and me, and him and—name just went right out of my mind—anyway, his girl, traipsed up and down Main Street, window shopping, drinking a Coke and eating peanuts along the way, not worrying about a thing. Dodging raindrops and laughing was mostly what we did, and it was a fine evening.

We had come up on the city jail at Broad and Falls streets, and I could just see this idea go off in Joe's head. His brown eyes lit up like a kid watching Mr. Conduras fill a nickel sack of gumdrops and handing them over, and Joe said to Webb, "Let's go see what it's like to be in jail!" Not exactly a normal Saturday evening request, but it was an offer of adventure, and Joseph Jefferson Wofford Jackson, never-grow-up mischievous kid, wasn't about to be talked out of it.

"You two boys can go through with this, but you'll forgive two proper ladies for just watching," I said, and popped him in the ribs and smiled up at this man-child. How could I ever help but love him? "Go on in, you two. We're right behind you." By the time I finished, Webb and Joe were already clean to the top step and heading through the door. The girl and I climbed the stairs, dodging puddles, and caught up soon enough.

Constable McAbee was there, a nice fellow who used to watch Joe play ball back in '07 with the Spinners. "The easiest job I had was to keep order at the ball games, tone down the loudmouth fans and an occasional drunk, and watch Joe Jackson and Hyder Barr whale into the visiting team's pitching. It was easy money," he said. Being a slow Saturday night, even by Greenville's standards, he saw no problem in going along with the boys, and agreed to put them behind bars for a few minutes.

That old jail was a dungeon, and folks called it "Little Siberia", said it was cold and lonely like what they read about in Russia. But there was something strange that happened when the door slammed, and the heavy padlock slid into place and clanked shut. The door was fashioned in 3 x 3 inch grids, made out of heavy iron and riveted at the corners of each square. The only bigger opening was a six-inch wide slot for sliding food through. When Joe and Webb turned around, in that moment their mouths were hidden by one of the iron bars, and the look in their eyes didn't seem to be happy at all. With the fingers of both hands draped through the spaces, Joe looked like he was just hung on that door, locked away for good. Even the turnkey had a grim look on his face. The joke had given way to something almost evil.

"Let's get on back out, Joe," I said, trying to kid around and doing one poor job of it. "You two promised to take us to a show." When the door creaked open real loud, we said goodnight to Mr. McAbee and hustled on out.

Coming down those steps in a light misting rain, none of us said anything for the longest time. "Hell, Webb, wasn't near what I thought it would be. How 'bout you?"

"Nope, and don't guess I want to be finding out what it's like for real. Not ever."

"Agreed," Joe said softly, slipping his hand into mine as we turned down Main. "How does supper down at The Mansion House sound about now?" Those were the last words spoken until we sat down at the table, and honestly, can't much remember any of us were all that hungry.

Another great thing in our lives happened while we were with the Naps, and that was Joe's friendship with one of the new kids in the league, George Ruth up with the Red Sox. I'm pretty sure it was in the summer of '14 when he got his first pitching assignment with Boston. Joe was in right field that day and got a couple of hits. There was something different about the way that young man watched Joe in batting practice before the game, and every day after that when the two of them were in the same ballpark. Like he was memorizing every movement Joe made at the plate.

"Guess I was able to help him a little, Missy, get him away from that old spraddle-legged stance he used that couldn't generate any power no matter how hard George tried." He took a sip of iced tea and leaned back in his chair. "I taught him to turn into the ball, and he's the only one who ever listened close enough to get the basics and make it work. He's gonna be okay, and he's an alright kind of guy."

You know Joe had to feel good about him, because on a couple of occasions he even loaned Black Betsy to George. Then it turns out the two of them became the only hitters to ever knock a ball clear out of the Polo Grounds up in New York. Doesn't sound like a big deal now, I know, but I remember the buzz around the park the day Joe did it for the very first time. He launched a low outside pitch off the Highlander's Russell Ford, and that ball flew several feet above the highest section of the upper deck roof, landing in the middle of Manhattan Field next door. Folks sat stunned, then offered polite applause like they wanted to acknowledge a work of art with the dignity it deserved, not rowdy like what greeted most homers. George managed to do the deed a few years later almost in the same spot, to a thunderous ovation. He was like that, able to wring every bit of emotion out of anything he started.

59

Over the winter, Joe toured all around the south with a group of actors in one of the old vaudeville shows we all used to enjoy. My man, shy and southern, getting out there with the smell of the grease paint and the roar of the crowd. Hard to imagine, isn't it? He was enjoying himself, I could tell, so I came on back home to Greenville to get us settled in. It was going to be about three more weeks on the tour before Joe got home, and that wouldn't be long at all. Turned out it was way too long.

Seems my temper got the best of me when it concerned Joe, and this time it was partly over another woman. Not like nowadays, when you read about all the infidelity and hush hush affairs in Hollywood and New York. No, this was more like they were just good friends. But it happened. And I didn't like it. And Joe knew it when I found out. And there wasn't anything like it ever occurred again.

The show debuted in Atlanta before heading out to several cities in the south. Joe did a monologue on how he hit the ball—batting stance, keeping your eye on the ball, that sort of thing—and found out he had a fondness for life behind the footlights. Plus, he was getting a weekly salary to do this.

Another one of Joe's stories was about turning down a three year contract from the Federal League in 1914, which would have paid him $20,000 a year. They were luring players with the promise of big money, and that was more than we ever dared dream about, much less have offered to us.

"Chased the two agents away, flailing at 'em with Black Betsy. Oh, I didn't hit 'em. Guess my swing wasn't level that day. Closest I ever came to the Federal League was a visit to Wrigley Field when we played in Chicago one day."

Anyway, my man stood in the glare of the theater lights and told the audience there were things in this world to be regarded above money. Keeping faith with your friends and upholding your word were two that came to mind. One of the sportswriters up in Cleveland picked up on that, and wrote that you didn't need to know how to read and write to be a man of principle and conscience.

Funny, but throughout the rest of Joe's life, there weren't many people who remembered this, much less gave him credit for living it. Even folks who said things in his behalf damned with faint praise, always talking about his lack of education like he was some sort of deformed cow or something. Couldn't they see Joe was anything but dumb? He was a good businessman, an ordinary guy who reached out and helped other people any time he could, and it didn't have to be close kin either. He was a man of conscience, and he never played to lose, no matter what part of his life folks wanted to pick apart. Didn't they know that? Didn't anybody care enough to find out? Couldn't they see?

Problem was, there was idle time on the train between shows, time for talking and card playing and the like. Folks, men and women, got thrown together, and Joe and a young lady became good friends. From all I was ever told, by him and others in that troupe, that's as far as it went, but he was married to me and I have to say it didn't sit well at all. Even she told me he wasn't anything if he wasn't always a proper gentleman. See, we had our one and only conversation at the train station in Greenville the day Joe came home.

"I can believe that," I said, "but I'd be obliged if you might find another amiable traveling companion, because extra temptation can't do a young man any good when he's on the road." My words were kind of icy, I suspect.

"Yes," she muttered, and hurried away. I never saw her again. And to my knowledge, neither did Joe.

Joe, he just looked at me.

"Katie, wasn't nothing to it, you know that." I did, but when it came to Mr. Jackson, I was one jealous woman. And you know what they say about hell's fury and such a female.

Our failings always seemed to be on display for all the world to see, and wasn't much of a way to keep the rumors of "domestic troubles," I think they labeled it, out of the papers or off people's lips. Folks looked at us a little different, whispered after we walked by, and you'd better believe it hurt. For a long time I'd lie in bed at night, and listen to the sounds coming through the open window in our bedroom, wondering just how much Joe's vaudeville lady was a friend and if there was more. Then I'd turn toward the wall and pretty soon would feel the tears rolling down my face in time with my man's steady breathing. I can come closer, you understand, to controlling these words more than the hurt and anger they brought about.

"Joe, Joe," I'd whisper, knowing somehow we were going to have to put this behind us.

It didn't happen until we returned to Cleveland. It wasn't drastic or anything. We both woke up early one morning to the sound of that big old city getting started, and my man reached over and held me close.

"Missy, ain't no need to cry like that ever again. You ain't alone. And," he stroked my hair and face and neck, "there ain't never been no other lover. You're the only one I ever had, only one I'd ever want." His kiss was soft and gentle. Mine, too, at first anyway. It was a wonderful morning of lovemaking and nibbling and touching. There wasn't another mention of Madame X, and we started to smile back at all of the whispers, and walk on past hand-in-hand.

61

But I don't think we kept anything right in '15, all sorts of stuff falling flat no matter what we tried. We got our differences behind us and then the car accident out east of the city threw us for a loop. Here we were riding along when the Chandler began acting up, and my man gave the driving duties to me as he climbed out on the running board to listen to the engine. Here comes a passing wagon that proceeds to sideswipe us, knocked Joe off, and he got dragged nearly a hundred feet before I could stop the car. He injured his right knee pretty severely, and I could only sit there, crying and shaking. It took him a long time to get me calmed down. Longer to get me to sit behind the steering wheel again.

"Had visions of being through as a ballplayer," he confessed at the hospital, and even later when we'd walk so he could strengthen his leg, he'd still bring it up. Baseball was all Joe really knew, the one job he could ever love, and I think he sensed how fragile it was and how easily it all could slip away. His hitting sure enough fell off that year, and like in any good baseball town the rumors started flying.

"Joe's through," you'd hear on the street walking to the park.

"'All that girl chasing, and then the car accident, a double stroke of bad luck for the team" from behind as I'd turn into Mr. Zantoni's store for some fresh vegetables and kielbasa.

More and more the talk was he'd be traded, and what we dreaded happened in mid-August. Mr. Somers got to thinking he had damaged goods on hand, I guess, and we were moved over to the White Sox. You know, the day before I read to Joe from the Cleveland *Plain Dealer* that the Sox had gone out and got another outfielder, Oscar Felsch, from Milwaukee in the American Association and spent some $12,000. Seemed a lot of money until it came out what Joe cost them, more than $30,000 and three players. Back to the fairgrounds and the cattle auction, that's what I felt. Guess old Mr. Somers was getting richer by the minute, but I was wondering if he wouldn't miss Joe, and if his loss wasn't Mr. Comiskey's gain.

So it was Joe going on to Chicago, and me packing and following behind. We wired everybody at home that things were fine, which they were, that Joe's leg had healed and we were like newlyweds again, and here was another big city to explore. Let us through, folks, the Jacksons got places to go, and we're in a hurry to get there.

Kid Gleason sent one of the clubhouse boys with Joe to an apartment house down on Grand Boulevard, owned by Henrietta Kelly. A good many of the players and their families lived there, so it was a nice place for a newcomer to be. She was a real fine woman and treated us like we were her own grandkids while we got used to Chicago.

Didn't get to see Joe's first start in centerfield with our new team, but I wasn't more than a week behind him. Baseball wives learn the ropes real quick about paying up the bills, and getting the lights and water turned off. What we don't get used to is saying good-bye to each other when a trade like this happens, and farewells to Mrs. Lajoie and the wives of the other players were tough when folks started dropping by.

I turned and gave one last look at the empty house, felt the tears starting to well up, and I asked myself, would there ever be another place like Cleveland? Every step I took on the hardwood floors echoed off of bare walls. And what kind of people would I meet where we were going? Guess we always fear too much because we trust too little, huh? I got the taxi down to the train station and headed to Chicago.

We began looking for a permanent place to stay the day after I got to that big old town, but one thing I definitely wasn't used to was the stockyards. I swear I think every big herd of cattle from Texas all the way to Montana was driven there to be slaughtered. We decided on the Trenier Hotel at 40th and Grand Boulevard, and I was happy with our choice, especially when the desk clerk greeted us with an enthusiastic, "Welcome to the White Sox, Mr. Jackson, and you too, Miss Katie."

In the lobby, Joe introduced me to a rather small gentleman except for big ears, quiet and very polite. "Katie, this is Mr. Eddie Collins, our second baseman," patting his teammate on the back. Eddie and I exchanged a few pleasantries and then the little man was on his way. What Joe said that day, and all through his life about Collins, stuck with me.

"As fine a man as there ever was in baseball." Just like Hyder and Buck back home with the Spinners, Joe counted another college man among his acquaintances and friends.

To celebrate our arrival, the Jacksons pounded the Chicago streets on a shopping spree. I got my man to try on shirts, shoes, suits— oh, he looked so good in everything. And we got him double-breasted blue pinstripes and two-tone black and white shoes. My man had as much fun watching me model the latest fashions for him, and we decided on one real pretty blue dress trimmed in white with a white collar. He even went and bought me a fox wrap and it was the prettiest thing I ever owned. Got to wear it on several occasions too, around a lot of American League ballparks and even back in Greenville.

Now the craziest thing we bought that day was a multi-colored talking parrot, and I'm to be thinking that bird had been owned by the raunchiest sailor on the waters of the Great Lakes. It was one foul fowl, and the string of cussing and insults it could launch into would embarrass even John McGraw and send straight-laced Connie Mack into a tizzy. Used word combinations I have never heard, and couldn't begin to imagine. I think the only thing that bird was better than was a snake, and you know how I hate slithery critters. Had some of them in the pet store, too, but I was particular to steer to the far aisle away from them.

But you know what my man did? When magazines or even newspapers came to our rooms over in the hotel, Joe would look through them and if he saw a picture of a snake, he'd cut it out with scissors. It was sweet of him, though I can't tell you the number of stories we never finished, because the ending, or an exciting part in the middle of *American Field*, a weekly magazine about pure bred sporting dogs, or the *Trib*, had gotten clipped and shredded along with a rattler or boa constrictor.

Shopping wasn't limited to buying stuff in Chicago. We talked about it, and bought Joe's ma the house in Brandon where she was living. I'm sure it was the first time home ownership was a reality for anybody on that mill village. Miss Martha Ann and all the chaps were excited as could be.

Folks in Chicago seemed to take to us right away, and it wasn't too long before "Give 'em Black Betsy, Joe!" started ringing through Comiskey Park, and it was just like being back at Brandon or Meminger Park. I was there pulling for my man, and Weaver, Felsch, Williams (had to show support for a fellow southerner), Schalk and all of them. Pretty soon I was The White Sox Girl, and even got to share a private Pullman with Joe on a couple of road trips toward the end of the season as long as we paid my part of the fare. You know Mr. Comiskey wasn't exactly free with his loot.

"He's putting together a good team, Missy. Ain't paying us near what some other players around the league are making, but still...getting paid for playing baseball is like living every kid's dream." That smile and those big brown eyes shining told us all how much he loved the game and everything about it. Fact was, the Sox weren't going anywhere in '15, and I could only hope he was right about future prospects. Try as we did in Cleveland, we never saw a championship, so maybe this was our chance at the top of the world.

One thing happened at the end of the season, and it was about the only time I ever heard anyone talk about changing the way Joe Jackson hit a baseball. Cobb, Lajoie, Wagner and Lewis, there wasn't one of them ever tried to mess with my man's near perfect swing, but I respected the man who did after I read his letter to Joe. Mr. Hillerich, president of that company down in Louisville that made bats, sent three to my man by Wells Fargo Express, wanting him to try them before the end of the year. He'd heard about that year being Joe's lowest batting average in the majors, I could tell.

"I hope you will get good results with these. If you will continue to use this weight bat, you will find you will get much better results." It was so simple and matter-of-fact, and I can remember Joe sitting there in our apartment on the sofa, leaning forward with his chin cradled in his hands as I read to him, then grabbing the nearest stick of lumber and jumping right up into a batter's stance, moving his hands and arms through the swing. Lord, it was going to be a long off-season. I could already see it, him and Champ and thirty kids shagging balls from first light to dark most days.

"He's right, Missy. How could I have been so stupid?" The swing and the stride worked together smoothly, and he lectured me all the while. "Too much weight I put on them bats, over forty eight ounces, and that's too much. Slows the bat down through here," and he showed me where the bat barrel would be when his arms were fully extended. "But with maybe thirty eight ounces, the whip comes back! Lady, he's right! Smart man, ain't he?"

"Mr. Jackson, could you be as passionate in bed with your wife, on this cold and rainy fall afternoon when the game's already called off, as you are hitting a make believe baseball and talking to a man a thousand miles away?"

I smiled mischievously as he swept me up in his big arms, my slippers falling off and plopping on the floor. He could, he definitely could.

It continued that folks had a way of either loving Joe or putting him down, and really I don't guess that changed a bit from the first time he set foot on the ball field at Brandon until now. Only more people were lining up on one side or another since he was somewhere on the sports page most of the time, and those opinions usually heated up.

It bothered us - me, anyway, because Joe never brought it up even when his teammates did - that somebody like Grantland Rice could choose the best outfielders playing then and leave Joe out. He picked Cobb and Speaker, and anybody is able to understand that, but then Ed Roush in Cincinnati? I don't know, maybe Granny talked with the townies back in Greenville when he was stationed at Camp Sevier up by Paris Mountain during World War I, getting all the stories about the worthless cotton mill boy who never went to school and couldn't read nor write. By the time he was through, you would have figured old Joe was hobbling about the field, "his skills on the decline, especially his speed on the base paths", I think was one of the phrases he used.

Then you turn around and read where another writer, Tim Murnane I think, explained how no player is more conscientious and loyal to his manager or team, or works as hard for its success as Joe. Let me find that over here, because I always kept it tucked in this little music box my man gave me one Christmas.

"Unlettered and unlearned in the ways of the world when he broke into the limelight, he is today a person in whose company one finds pleasure, a gentleman of manners at ease in any gathering, his down home wisdom a delight to hear, his honesty and straightforwardness a relief in these sordid times in which we live." Those words, they are something else, and I treasured them because they spoke the truth about what Joe had become, a real gentleman. But even with that kind of writing, most people just kept believing him to be an ignorant, tobacco-chewing man with cotton between his ears to keep his head puffed up.

Speaking of Murnane, the players around the league had an all-star benefit for his family a few days after he died suddenly up at his home in Boston. It was late September 1917, and a whole lot of people got together to honor the memory of Mr. Tim. George Ruth, Ty Cobb, Tris Speaker, Walter Johnson, now how's that for a good start? Will Rogers was there, doing rope tricks for the crowd, one of them twirling a thirty-foot loop around both teams. Fannie Brice and some other girls from the Zeigfield Follies sold scorecards, and former heavyweight champ John L. Sullivan did a little catching for the Red Sox team. George's team bested Joe and his mates that day, but the great thing was the thousands of dollars raised for the Murnane family. They were good folks.

Joe won a trophy that day for taking first in a throwing contest, and he told how.

"I was sitting out by the flagpole out in centerfield, when Cobb and Speaker signed me up and I didn't know it. So when my name was called by the PA man using a big megaphone, I picked up the ball and throwed it toward home."

Ruth, Speaker, Duffy Lewis, Cobb, couldn't any of them come close to what my man said was an okay effort at best. The only thing in that ball's way was the backstop, so they called the throw 396 feet. When folks back home heard about it, they asked if Joe's arm had been a bit sore since he used to throw them a lot farther down at Brandon.

Sometimes in my jealous moments I'd sit and try to figure out who he loved better, baseball or me. Now Joe, he would never have said anybody but me, as you might expect, but still I'd think it just the same. And at some of the oddest times, too.

Like one day when the Sox were at home against the Senators about 1917. I remember it was early in the season, because it was so miserably cold in Chicago. It wasn't Johnson he was hitting against, maybe Doc Ayers or Jim Shaw, in the fourth inning or so, and my man got a low outside pitch. I could see it coming, the realization that Joe was going uncoil on this one with everything he had, and it was just a beautiful thing to watch.

There was this pop that hung in the air, sort of settled in over the field just like the cold, and the ball traveled a high arc way up over the right center wall. Landed somewhere in that coveted south side real estate way beyond Comiskey Park. What I remember most, though, is Mr. Jackson standing in the batter's box, swing completed, staring out to that point where the ball disappeared. There was a majesty about him right then, like he was the center of the whole world, and everything else was revolving around him.

It wasn't arrogance that kept him standing there, and in fact it took awhile for me to realize how fast that ball got out of the park, it was hit so hard. Then he started that easy gait around the bases, tipped his hat as he rounded third, and winked at me. What woman wouldn't be jealous when she watched her man so in love with something other than her? Well, I might have been his first love, but baseball sure was breathing down my neck a close second.

That year ended with so many good things happening that we felt like we were grabbing the brass ring every time the calliope made a circle. Being invited to Boston as part of the league's best to take part in that Murnane benefit game was good enough to top off most seasons, but the Sox marched right on to the World Series. Here two lintheads make it to the biggest show on earth, and it's against McGraw's Giants.

Started October 6th in Chicago and it was a seesaw affair all the way through. The Sox took the first two games at home, turned around and lost two shutouts in New York, took the third in Chicago and wrapped it up with a close 4-2 win at the Polo Grounds. You'd have to call Mr. Eddie Collins and Red Faber the real heroes, since College Boy batted over .400 and stole three bases and Big Red nailed down three of the four wins. Oh, it was great, World Champs in baseball and me cutting loose in the stands, clapping and yelling and crying all at once. My man did himself proud, hitting over .300, all singles if you can believe that, and he was always in the thick of every rally.

We did most of our celebrating on the train back home, not hanging around New York too long after the last game was over. And Lord you should have seen—no, you should have been part—of the celebration once we got back to Chicago. Festivities just kind of started and then didn't let up for a couple of days. Everybody stayed to soak it all up before going our separate ways and heading home for the winter. Didn't know it then, not a one of us did, that we'd come back next year forever changed, our innocence cut to shreds by the Great War, and by some personal tragedies and betrayals along the way.

Things had been heating up over in Europe most of 1917, and every day in the papers they had stories of battles with real strange sounding names. Messines Ridge. Passchendaele, where there were terrible casualties in the mustard gas attacks. Caporetto. Joe, he'd make me read them over and over to him, and one reason was because his old Brandon teammate Henry Stokes volunteered for duty in the Allied Expeditionary Force. Joe was so proud of him. For us, it was a different kind of decision that weighed heavy.

They had what was called a "work or fight " order for all men between twenty and forty five, and that meant registering for the draft or finding work in a war industry by July of '18. Joe and I discussed it riding back to Greenville on the train, and continued to hammer it out when we walked from home at 4 Bryant Street and headed around the mill village as November evenings gave way to Christmastime and the air got colder. Sometimes, when the wind whistled through the bare limbs of those oak trees, it was like the world whimpered in pain for what was happening to it, being torn apart by hate and greed and evil. I'd hug my man close as we walked alone, the echoes of our steps on the frozen roads swallowed up by the night and the wind.

One of us would manage to step the wrong way and get a foot caught in those iron-hard ruts left by wagons or an occasional flatbed truck or tin lizzie. We'd trip and be falling, but one would catch the other, stop the fall, and we'd regain our balance and be on our way. That was always how we made it, one of us strong when the other seemed not to be.

See, Mr. George Elmore died back in February of '14. I remembered it because we had to report late to spring training with the Naps, and since then Joe had become sole supporter for his ma, brothers and sisters. He was Class 4, meaning dependents to support, but then he got re-classified and went to Class 1, "fit for duty", by good old Local Board #2.

Finally we signed up for the Civil Defense Corps, Wilmington Delaware. Joe had a hard time with the decision.

"I know I'm about supporting my kin, Missy, and I know others are taking Civil Defense jobs for reasons lots less proper than mine." He'd clasp and unclasp his hands, over and over. "But I still just ain't feeling like it's all proper for me. Look at Cobb and Christy Mathewson, and my buddy Henry Stokes, they're over in Europe now." Christy got caught in one of those mustard gas clouds and it about did his lungs in. That fine gentleman wasn't listed as a war casualty, but when he died so young, and from breathing problems to boot, I always felt he was deserving of military honors and burial and all.

For this "treachery", dear old Mr. Comiskey ridiculed Joe in the papers as a draft dodger, and of course it didn't have a thing to do with losing the services of his prized commodity that year. It seemed Commie ever had very little of substance to say to us anyhow, so this fit right in. Joe, he'd ask me what "ridicule" meant, and when I told him he said it was a word that just about spit evil in your face.

"They ruined me when I went to the shipyards," he said to me years later, anger in his voice, and it was true after the press got involved, as always. And as always it seemed there were those who would defend him, and those who would damn him to hell and back. By the time we left the White Sox in mid-May 1918, the war of words was going full blast in the sports pages across the nation, and I'm sure everybody had an opinion of us.

Joe was defended in an article in *The Sporting News*, but *Stars and Stripes* singled him out as what was wrong with our country when ballplayers could avoid the draft by working. Comiskey's boys over at the *Trib* called my man a slacker at heart, saying he would make a good fighting man, except he preferred not to fight. Damn! What did they want from us? Why were we held up for ridicule - and I learned to regard that word the same as Joe - time and again when we did what was right?

Some nights we'd just lay in each other's arms, the dark seeming to be the only friend we had, the silence the best comfort we could ask for. I sensed Joe staring at the wall. Hot tears slid down my face, no sobs or anything to give me away to my man. Right then it was like we were the only two people in the world, and I think we were both afraid of letting each other down. We never cried together, though sometimes I wished we had. Thought we could handle it all by ourselves, but now I'm not so sure.

Now my anger could come on like a Walter Johnson fastball when folks tried to crucify Joe and stopped short of condemning other players keeping stateside duty. Comiskey, Ban Johnson, Mr. Mack, McGraw, wouldn't one of them come too close when the White Sox Girl got riled. See, George Ruth took off to Lebanon PA to play ball with one of the war industries there, and I do believe half of Connie Mack's Athletics hunkered down at the shipyards in Philadelphia. But it was dear old Joe who got pounded.

We packed up and left Chicago, heading east to Wilmington and the Harlan Shipyard of the Bethlehem Steel Corporation. We left Comiskey ranting and raving against the linthead draft dodger, and without Joe the Sox were out of the running for the pennant real quick. Couldn't do any better than a sixth place finish out of eight teams, and George Ruth's Red Sox captured the flag.

We found a little house not far from the shipyard, and I set about making it home for us. I scrubbed it down real good and then turned it over to Joe to give it a fresh coat of paint. Good practice for him, since painting ships was going to be his job down at the yard. We'd sit in the kitchen, with a red-checkered cloth on the little table and white curtains fluttering when the wind came through the open windows, and sip coffee real early in the morning before my man headed off for work. With him I could find a little piece of heaven just about anywhere.

We were happy, and the folks at Harlan seemed glad to have us around. Joe wasn't able to jump in and start playing ball, because Steel League rules made you wait two weeks before suiting up. The first day he wandered in, shook hands all around with the fellas, and sat on the bench in his work clothes, chomping at the bit to be in the game. He was also politely ordered from the bench and into the stands by Sergeant John Devenish of the Wilmington Police Force. Everybody got a big laugh from the show, even Sarge, as Joe came up and sat next to me, but what I was remembering was him and Webb looking through the cell bars back in Greenville that night years ago. What started as fun then ended up scaring me more than I'd admit to anyone, even my man, and I tried to give him a smile now to cover the sick feeling all over me.

Forty bucks a week for his work, forty bucks a game to act like a little boy. They put him in charge of a crew painting ships, and you can believe he worked as hard or harder than the folks along side him.

"Painting is pretty easy, Missy, a whole lot less sweating doing that than doffing them filling frames back at Brandon in July, maybe even easier than walking barefoot over them rough spinning room floors pushing brooms as a kid." Soon we'd be listening as the quiet settled in now that the day's work was done.

"You know, Mrs. Jackson," Nick Permente said to me one day, "this yard needs more men who got brains like your husband." He was a local boy who was on Joe's crew, and did the scorekeeping and waterboy chores and doctoring duties for the team. He and his girl Jennie would come over and have lemonade and fresh fruit with us in the evening now and then.

"Never gets loud, just goes and starts work and tells us how he wants us posted that day. Hard as he goes, not a one of us would dare let him down. He's quick to praise us for a good job, just as quick to offer help or advice. If he has to say something about one of the fellas slacking off, why he handles it in private, and I've heard tell in a quiet and easy way. Never had to take nothing any farther than him, because he'll get it set right. Yep, be nice to have more Mr. Jacksons in the world." His face just glowed when he talked about Joe, like a younger brother looking up to the eldest of the brood.

70

Remember he said the work was easier than back at the mill? But there was a stretch when dear Mr. J wouldn't admit to that at all. In late July the crews started in at 4AM or so. It was a rule the men had to complete a day's work before they could practice, but when the high reached 122 degrees, wasn't a soul concerned about baseball. Good thing, too, because it was called off quicker than if there was a gully-washing thunderstorm.

In a lot of ways Harlan reminded us of being back on the mill hill. Folks were known to get loud at the ballpark, and we'd meet to rehearse our songs and yells. When the crowd numbered two or three thousand, why we just had ourselves a grand old time creating misery for the visiting team. All the employees got together and produced a minstrel show that we later performed at one game against Steelton from up the road a ways. I got asked to join in because some of the wives heard I was a stage entertainer. About the only thing I ever entertained on stage was pretty much inviting Joe's lady friend to take up residence in some other area of the country. I smiled and thanked them for their generous offer.

Like he always did, my man played all out, crashing into the fence trying to run down a long fly, almost taking right fielder Patsy Gharrity's head off in a collision going for a liner in the gap. Such efforts as those made him look something akin to a Red Cross poster boy, wrapped up in tape and bandages, but he didn't know any other way to show his love for the game and the fans except to go as hard as he could. Not long after, in a game over at Fall River, he stole second, third, and home, one right after the other. He was a favorite, even on a team that had twelve other major leaguers, and I like to think it went way beyond his hitting .390 something. Joe worked hard, at the plant and on the field, and folks knew it and respected him for it.

And he'd take a 4 a.m. shift so Harlan could loan him out to a Red Cross benefit game, everybody knowing that Shoeless Joe being there would mean a bigger crowd and more money for the cause. He got loaned out on a pretty regular basis as a drawing card, and he got his rewards for all the extra time he put in. Like when he hit two homers against Sparrows Point and the fans stomped and cheered and made up a large sum of money to give him, just like passing the hat back at Brandon that Jerry and David used to do right after a Saturday Special. All the papers talked about his knowledge of the game and how quick he could think, so you don't have to wonder why we were happy up there. Comiskey and Chicago and bad talking sportswriters were only distant memories, at least for a while.

When the Steel League team didn't have a chance to win the pennant, he got loaned out one last time to their other team because they were playing in the Coxe Trophy Series for the Shipyard League Championship. This wasn't small potatoes either, with the final two games being played in Shibe Park. It was another trip back to damnable Philadelphia, which I'd tried to steer clear of since 1909 when they treated my man so bad.

Couldn't have ended better, even if I'd written it out myself. Joe hit two home runs, the second one a blue darter zooming out and crashing into the right field bleachers. And the folks from Delaware went wild and threw dollar bills at him as he trotted across the plate. I can still see him with that smile, not bragging or anything, but proud he'd done his best and it turned out good. He came over to where I sat behind the first base dugout, and handed me a fist full of greenbacks. Folks cheered even louder when I wrapped my arms around Mr. Jackson's neck and gave him a big old kiss.

If it could have ended there, Harlan and Wilmington were about near as perfect as Savannah and New Orleans and Cleveland. When we got back to the yard, though, a telegram from Scoop Latimer waited, wanting us to know that Henry Stokes had died of bronchial pneumonia while serving in Europe. Henry and Joe had formed such a deep friendship that lasted from when they were kids up to that moment. And now Stokey dead, coming home like thousands of others, a funeral rather than a parade, mourning instead of celebration.

I watched Joe as I read Scoop's words - "a good boy...Joe will remember...we're all sad...so close to the end of the war...he will be missed..."—and tried to figure what this was doing to him. An evening or two later, walking on the beach hand in hand, both of us barefoot even in the October chill, it all broke loose inside him.

"Everything I've ever had come hard, Missy, except I guess for you loving me." That was enough to start the waterworks for me, but the mist was thick and there wasn't much light at all, so he didn't see my tears.

"Not having much growing up on the mill hill, a pa who I could never be sure loved me, trying to help ma with food and clothes money for me and the chaps because nobody could depend on what George Elmore would bring home. Taking care of my brothers and sisters and being a pa to them when he was off hunting and fishing with his buddies at the mill. The only chance I ever had to be a kid was on the ball field.

"You know that better than anyone, and understand it, too." I was so tired of wiping my eyes, my arms hurt from raising them so much, and he caught me once or twice when I stumbled, and put his big arms around me and drew me up close. "My only friends were there, the Stokes, Cashions, Turners, Richardsons from the mill, and then Hyder and Buck on the Spinners. One by one they seem to drop away, and what with all the moving around me and you been doing, it ain't no wonder.

"But now Henry dying, and me standing here alive because I didn't go and fight over yonder..." We stopped walking, just stood with the water running across our feet, the sound of the waves breaking, the wind whipping sand against our bare shins. And we cried, and not even the darkness was big enough to swallow up the sobs and the tears. We didn't try and stop, letting the grief wash over us again and again, and how long we stood there I can't tell you. I felt the wet sand up over my ankles, and the waves started to come up quicker, and the mist got thicker thank God. We were protected from anybody seeing us and we clung to each other for everything we were worth, like we were the only real thing in each other's whole world.

We walked back to the bungalow, almost exhausted, took off our wet clothes and got into bed naked, not for making love but to feel one another's warmth and be reassured that we weren't alone. Got to sleep just at sunrise.

It was noon when we stirred back to life, an October Sunday, cool and the sky so blue it just about hurt to look at it. Joe's assignment was up day after tomorrow and we'd be heading back home, then rejoining the Sox in spring training in February. I rested my head on Joe's shoulder, satisfied to lay there with my man the whole afternoon.

"Missy," he said, leaning down to kiss me, "I ain't got no world but you and baseball."

"First place!" I yelled, jumping up and prancing around the bed, laughing at his startled look. "Pennant fever hits as Katie Jackson takes the flag!" And we laughed and loved the afternoon away.

Didn't take the train back to South Carolina. No, my man had other ideas, telling me it was time I had something real nice to call my own, and he showed up at our bungalow that Tuesday in a big, new Stutz Bearcat Coupe, with real alligator skin on top.

"Joe, it's beautiful!" I ran and jumped into his arms.

"Least I could do for the prettiest girl in the world. Now, Mrs. Jackson, there are ladies who could wear a thousand dollar outfit and still look a tramp. You, dear girl, wear a pair of overalls, barefoot just like back home when you was little, and look like a million bucks, total class, always a bit too pretty to be on the arm of a old linthead who can't read nor write too good!" He laughed easy enough at that, but it still ate at him, despite everything he'd learned and everything he'd accomplished.

"Mr. Jackson, I'll not listen to any man put you down, and I certainly refuse to listen to you do it to yourself. Now let's throw our stuff in the back and light out for home." He kissed me real soft, opened the door for me, then piled the stuff about us, wherever it might fit. Most of the other folks on the team had already left.

Nick and Jennie came to tell us goodbye as Joe was putting the last of the bags in. There were hugs all around, and Nick spoke some of the nicest words anybody ever said about my man.

"You were a real leader, an inspiration, and yet more like a big brother who was looking after all of us," the young man struggled to keep back the tears. "You're not somebody easy to forget, Joe. You and Mrs. Jackson are the finest folks we'll ever know," and he and Jennie and me and Joe all stood there like fools with tears running down our faces. Don't think the Jacksons could have taken very many more friends dropping by.

Back through West Virginia, Virginia, the Carolinas, talking and even singing sometimes, Joe made up a tune to a little poem I'd read him from the paper. One of the local writers up in Delaware gave notice to my man's hitting ability:

> When Jackson steps up to the plate
> To hit the horsehide ball,
> The fielders get so far away
> They really look quite small.

That was always one of his favorites, and at least brought back a gleam to his eyes once in awhile, so much better than the emptiness I saw more often these past few weeks.

We stayed in hotels the three days it took us to get home, and folks in the towns made such a fuss over Shoeless Joe, talked baseball with him at the supper table, or when we stopped and got gas by the pint at the drug store. Wherever we were, they seemed to be waiting. They'd wish him good luck, shake his hand or slap his shoulder, and you could hear daddies telling sons and daughters, "there sat the greatest hitter who ever swung lumber."

"Better'n Cobb?" one knee high asked.

"Better" was all his pa said as he shook Joe's hand, and leaned over so that little boy he held could hug my man's neck. Of course the contract from the Sox was waiting for us on Miss Martha Ann's kitchen table when we arrived, old Comiskey shooing Joe back into the barnyard for one more year. Six thousand dollars, same as '17. Both of us felt there wasn't much reason to haggle on this one, seeing as we'd been missing from Chicago almost a full season and wasn't a thing gained by getting folks mad at us.

A quiet winter, my man working out with Webb Cashion and Sid Smith, all of them running and throwing and hitting and whooping it

74

up at Brandon Field. Sunshine, rain, wind, even a couple of snowy days, they stayed at it, acting like a bunch of fool kids who didn't know any better. Me, I learned to drive the Bearcat.

Now driving around Greenville in that car of Joe's, with the top down, was more fun than you could ever imagine. Me all decked out in a white, wide brimmed hat and white scarf, long white dress with blue polka dots, and laced high-top boots. I enjoyed that. It was just him and me, owning what no linthead ever should have been able to afford, and us making sure to wave to the townies who thought as much.

A lot of folks would still crowd around the machine to talk baseball with Joe, and he'd do his best to answer their questions. All the while he held my hand, his big rough fingers caressing my skin. It was his way of knowing he wasn't alone. My man drove that car as gracefully as he ran after long fly balls in the outfield, smooth and never a bit concerned because he knew he was in control.

"Want to drive, Missy?" he'd ask after we got down past Brandon where there wasn't any traffic more than a wagon behind a team of horses every half hour or so. Folks would smile when he used that nickname, remembering from when we were kids. Then I'd wait for him to come around and open the door, take my hand while I stepped out on the running board and then to the ground, and waltz me to the driver's side. Unless there was a mud hole, and then he'd put them huge hands around my waist and carry me. Son of a gun never even stumbled. How I loved that man!

So I'd be trying to work the clutch, gas, brakes, and starter all at once, and it seemed my feet slipped so much off those pedals that it was like being barefoot on the creek bank behind the house, except I didn't have to worry about falling. Only about making a fool out of myself. But after four or five lessons I got the hang of it, and did a pretty good job if I do say so.

If Joe was there with me, folks would be real polite as we drove past, the men touching their fingers to the brim of a fedora or skimmer or straw hat. But if it was just me, why they'd go with the "look out, woman behind the wheel!" and make like they were hightailing it out of the street for the nearest covered storefront. One time, though, it was me and Joe's ma who had one fine laugh at their expense.

We were coming down Academy Street, heading away from the girls' school, and there were puddles everywhere from the rain the night before. October day, just beautiful and the wind blowing fresh. Of course, it would stir up leaves and cinders, and there was no telling what would fly up over that little square windshield and splatter on your face. One of the loudmouths saw us heading his way and started his "look out! look out!" laughing and pointing at us.

75

Now the elder Mrs. J, sitting there in the back seat decked out in her Sunday finest complete with a mosquito net veil hanging from her hat down to her chin, leaned up, her hands clutching the back of my seat so hard all her knuckles turned white. Just as we got near, the loudmouth fool, who was backing up, tripped over a clod of dirt and fell back spread eagle into the deepest and muddiest hole the entire length of the street.

I stopped the car as the old guy lifted himself out, and then I just busted out laughing. Mrs. Jackson joined in, along with everyone else close enough to have been a part of our little comedy, and standing up in the car, she looked at our tormentor and announced, "I'd move quick if I was you, Mr. Taylor, 'cause I'm not beyond requesting my beloved daughter-in-law to back this thing up and run you over right where you're a-laying!"

Well, dear Mr. Taylor moved quicker than I ever saw Webb Cashion hightail it on the base paths for the old Brandon Braves. We laughed all the way back to the mill village, shaking and rattling and rolling at an incredible 20 mph.

With the Jackson's, life was never dull.

Chapter 5

The doughboys were back home in time for the 1919 season, and everybody was excited about things getting started. But there was something strange that kept teasing my mind, just enough to make me uneasy, but nothing I could get hold of.

'Maybe,' I said to myself, 'it's the bad stuff you keep hearing now and then about Joe and the others who kept stateside during the war. Or maybe Henry Stokes' death keeps hold of him stronger than I realized. Or maybe a hundred more things. Or maybe nothing.'

"Snap out of it," I said one morning in the bathroom, "there's not a thing wrong. Ought to be ashamed, girl, for taking a good life and trying to mess it up."

"You needing me, Missy?" Joe's sleepy voice carried from the bedroom.

"Up and going, Mr. J. You're needed at the ballpark for Opening Day!"

Funny how I don't remember much at all about the season, at least until things wound up in a tight pennant race. Joe, he had a good year hitting, but as usual it wasn't enough to come close to Cobb, and our fellow southern boy Lefty Williams won twenty-three games. Four teams were in it all the way to the end, and we finally got by them all—Cleveland, New York, and Detroit.

It was quite a battle, and folks were talking like this was one of the hottest races in quite a few years. It went pretty much down to the wire, too, with the Sox clinching in late September at home. Now, that's nothing easy to forget, since my man singled across his good friend Nemo Liebold in the last of the ninth for a 6-5 win over the Brownies. That season might still be a blur, days and games melting into one another until you can't figure where one ends and another takes up, but this I can tell you. There is no forgetting what we got swept up in when the Series came to town, though the dear Lord knows I have tried.

"It's been there all year, Katie, and anyone who watches us play can tell." His voice was soft and I had to lean forward on the couch to make sure I heard. "We been two teams all year, with me caught somewhere middle ways, pulled this way and that until I'm just about all fed up. Gandil and Risberg, they don't like Collins and Schalk, and the rest seem to fall on one side or the other. Of them all, guess Mr. Eddie Collins is the one I like and respect most, but most of the other fellows with him think I got cotton where my brain ought to be."

He sat quiet, looking out the window as all those city lights started gleaming, fighting off the darkness about to swallow Chicago up.

And here I was, wondering if we would ever fit in, just be accepted for being Joe and Katie, with nothing else attached.

Things couldn't get any stranger, right? You soon find out how wrong you can be, and in this case I missed it by a mile. I would watch the workouts as the boys tuned up for the Series with Cincinnati and see the two sides form right on the field, and I knew as well how carefully Joe watched all this unfold. I mean, there was Swede at short and Eddie at second, and they never looked at each other, never spoke, nothing - not exactly what you'd want happening on the eve of a championship.

When they took a break, sure enough here would go Swede, Chick, Lefty and Cicotte and a few others. Heading the other way were Collins and Schalk, Dickie Kerr, and Liebold. How sad to see it.

The next day at practice I noticed something else, and I've never forgotten it. While the two groups split up, Buck Weaver picked up a ball and tossed it to Joe, who was still on the field, probably thinking like I did that no good was going to come of all this. He and Buck just stood out there about thirty feet apart and tossed the ball to each other, a simple game of catch like a million kids played in the streets and on vacant lots and on fine ball fields. They smiled, and the pop of leather on leather was a rhythm nearly like a lullaby you'd sing to a fussy baby. If anyone else noticed, they never said anything about it.

One day there was screaming and commotion in the dugout, and this was after everybody left and I was waiting for Joe. The voice belonged to Kid Gleason, and it was obvious he was yelling at my man, and that was odd because the two of them got along well and Joe said many times how much he liked playing for Kid. The only words I made out were "You'll play! You'll play!" Then Joe left and walked across the infield, not lifting his gaze from the ground. I didn't say a thing all the way home.

"You asked what?" when he said something about it after supper, almost swallowing my teeth. My voice was not exactly a lady-like whisper. It was late, and the restaurant was empty, thank goodness. "Say that one more time for my benefit as well as your own. What in the name of...what has gotten into you?"

"Benched, Katie. I asked to be benched. For the first time in my life it ain't a game. They done made it something else." He rested his head on the back of the stiff chair, eyes turned up toward the ceiling, and they were closed.

"They? Joe, who are you talking about? How can they make baseball something bad? How...?" But there was no use asking more questions, because I don't think he ever heard me. Not that he was being mean or ignoring me, but his thoughts were so much deeper than I was going to reach right now.

Names and places started popping up, most of them not associated with baseball, and that was so different from what I remembered from two years back. Places like the Hotel Ansonia in New York, the Warner in Chicago. Folks like Nick the Greek, a local gambler, and Abe Attell, a boxer, got talked about a lot. Bill Burns, too, a pitcher Joe remembered playing with Detroit. When we walked into the Sinton Hotel in Cincinnati just before the games there, folks were gathered around a man, standing on a chair in the lobby, like a fool, thousand dollar bills between the fingers of both hands, yelling that he would cover any Chicago money.

"Who's that, Joe?" I asked.

"Don't know," was his answer as we hurried by.

Maybe nobody should have been surprised, because there was a lot of gambling going on in baseball at that time, and I'd seen it at different parks around the league. But then the word "fix" snaked into conversations and that made me nervous. I remembered my man wanting no part of playing ball, and it would take something like stacking the deck to drive him that far.

"Oh God," I prayed as sincerely as I knew how, "don't let any of this be true." But it was, and got deeper and nastier so quickly that it swallowed up anybody who was close.

When Joe came back to his room after the fourth game there was money lying on the bed, what I learned later was payoff from the gamblers, delivered by Lefty Williams. He grabbed me and told me we had to talk. We set out walking the Chicago streets until nearly dawn, leaving the Lexington Hotel and moving on down Michigan Avenue and out into the night. By the time Joe was through, tears ran down my face. I was both scared for my man and ashamed at how his so-called friends tried to drag him down. What maybe stung the most was Chick and Swede and Lefty laughing at him when he told them to take back the money.

"You poor simp, go ahead and squawk," Joe's voice cracked from a lot of emotion as he told me what was said. Part of it was anger, so unlike him. "We're all gonna say you're a liar, and you're just out of luck."

"All those meetings, and you never went. All these games so far, and you've watched the misplays and knew the accusations were getting louder. Joe, you kept playing to win, and you only need to take the dough and go to Comiskey and give it back and tell him what little you know." I surprised even myself with words that were cold as ice and all fact.

"It'll be done soon as morning comes, Missy, but you got to know I'm afraid of the people mixed up in this, and it ain't just Chick and Swede and small time thugs like Nick. We've seen 'em all before. No, it's folks from New York, and I even heard Capone was dealing heavy, too. Guys who make money ruining lives and killing, making sure the story is always in their favor." There wasn't a way to slow him down, so deep was that well of emotion.

"Hell, Missy, I wondered if they might come after me, but that didn't scare me near as much as how I feel on the inside." Nothing else was spoken as we made our way back to the hotel, except for the cops walking the night beat who recognized my man and yelled, "Go get 'em, Joe! Give 'em Black Betsy, and let's pull this thing out!"

"You betcha, we'll be getting back at 'em!" He smiled and waved as we walked on past. We were grateful for the darkness.

There was a lot on his mind when he went to Comiskey's office early next morning and told his secretary he wanted to see the boss. Harry Grabiner said Mr. C was busy and my man sat down and waited. Lord how I wished I'd gone with him, because we'd have walked on past prim and starched stiff Mr. Grabiner and sat the old Roman down and had our say. But Joe insisted on going this alone.

He never counted what was in the paper bag stuffed with fifties and hundreds, figuring Williams said $5000 because that's what was there.

"What do you wish to see him about, Mr. Jackson?"

"Personal and important."

"One moment." And Joe said Grabiner disappeared into the next room for a few minutes and then came back out.

"He won't be able to chat, Mr. Jackson, a lot going on with the Series, you know. Perhaps I could help."

"No, sir, I'll come back. Thanks."

And he suited up for the game and played. Everybody pretty well knows, and has a strong opinion, of the outcome of that Series, but funny how all of them closest to it never talked much.

"I've said some things I shouldn't, and some I didn't mean, just to get them to leave me alone, and I got to handle this, Missy." He walked out quietly, standing straight and tall. He went back to see Mr. Comiskey again, taking the money.

Grabiner stopped him and kept him away from Commie, and again it was a mistake of mine not to be there so Joe would have a witness to all this. He finally gave in and showed what was in the bag to Starchy.

"He said there was $3500 there and that I should keep it and go on home. Wondered about that total he come up with but maybe he was right, and I just wanted to get out of there and get back to you." And that was the last my man said about the meeting that never took place.

Knew that I should have been there, but then I did what Joe asked. After Lyria Williams told me what happened to her and Lefty, maybe my man understood the dangers of all this better than any of us. See, the gamblers got word to Lefty, who was in deep, and told him he had better be making sure Cincinnati came out on top his next start. They made it real clear the threat was aimed at Lyria and the children. My Lord, how she cried, how I cried about things that could get so screwed up and out of control.

"When Lefty told me the story, Katie, I knowed I done the right thing keeping you out while I tried to set things right. All I want them to look at are the hits, the home run, no misplays in the outfield. But even when I told Lefty that, still believing the records would be enough, that old boy just give me a sad smile, saying we'd all be bundled and shipped out together. His face looked so old, and his eyes had no spark left. That scared me."

He pulled the window shade down in the Pullman as we raced across the dark land back south. The Reds took the championship, five games to three. We took the heartbreak, then and now.

"But I had to play, and I did play," he said as we held each other and tried to sleep. "Look at the record, and Buck Weaver's too, and you don't need any more proof that we played to win." The rocking of the train, and those strong arms around me, were as comforting as a lullaby. I'd need all that, and more, these next few years.

I've come to believe that we sow the seeds of our own damnation, and despite all our efforts to set it right we still water them with our tears and make them grow. One of Daddy's old Bible verses came to mind that he recited to my brothers, sisters and me, trying to teach us kids what our actions could bring.

"He who sows the wind shall reap the whirlwind."

Probably got it in one of them hotter-'n-hell July evening tent meetings, but it stuck with me, like the infrequent but long remembered pop of his belt across my bare legs when I misbehaved.

We had no contact with anyone from the Sox other than Lefty and Lyria, and we stayed pretty close to home that winter. But how Joe drove himself in his workouts. He and whoever he could get to catch his pegs from deep center. Or pitch to him, Black Betsy seething with anger as she whistled through cold air to find and flatten already ripped and scarred baseballs. And he ran the bases, cutting the inside of each bag, sharper and sharper until the angle was perfect. Then I timed him - thirty seconds at mid-December dropped to twenty-five then twenty-two by January's end.

81

That body, always trim and beautiful to me, now was hard with muscle and those beautiful brown eyes glinted with determination stronger than I'd ever seen before. Whatever doubts and rumors were left over from last year he was going to beat out of existence.

Between him and me, there was no more discussion of those events. It was as though the '19 Series was off limits, that it was frozen and removed from time. The only thing he did was tell me to write a letter to Comiskey using his exact words, which I did, offering to come to Chicago to talk, and that letter was never answered. All I can say is that when it came to the 1920 season, Joe Jackson declared war on the rest of the American League, and he was there to play the best baseball of his life.

Dear old Harry Grabiner showed up at our house to talk about the 1920 contract. Supposedly. That man had the best timing in the world, showing up when I wasn't around, and he and Joe discussed the $5000 or $3500 or whatever it was. In addition to the "X" on his contract, he wanted Joe to sign some other papers, when nobody was there to read them and let my man know what he was putting his mark to. More stuff to protect the boss. Can you tell that I'm not exactly wild about Harry?

"It was the contract for this season, Missy, and some papers he said Comiskey needed from me, saying I played to win in the Series. I guess," and he stopped and looked at the floor where we were sitting on our couch in the living room, "guess I didn't want to and then he asked if I didn't trust him, and..."

"And you should have said no." I was doing my own seething now, my jaws hurting because I'd been clinching them hard. "Joe, couldn't you have waited, just a little bit, until I got back here and read the papers to you? I'm learning you aren't able to trust very many folks at all, not if they have something to gain by hurting you. So what is the contract for, or did dear Harry forget to tell you?"

And I was sorry I said it soon as the words left my mouth, but couldn't find a way to take them back, even when he raised his head and I saw the hurt in those brown eyes.

"Six thousand dollars, same as last year." I heard him say it as I hurried down the front steps, walking fast as I could. Just out, and it didn't matter where. I moved through a blur of tears and messed up thoughts, and wound up at the ballfield.

"Where is this all going to end?" I looked up at the stars and screamed. It was late enough, thankfully, and no one was around to hear the crazy woman baying at the moon. Finally, I got myself quiet inside and made my way back to the house about an hour later. My man was still sitting on the porch where I left him.

"I want to win this year above every year I ever played," he said on the way to spring training, "want to get back in the World Series and try to beat some National League club to death. That's what I want to do, Katie." He slipped his arm around me as we rode the train, muscles strong after his off-season running and working out. Maybe, I thought, looking out the window and watching the countryside move by in the settling twilight, maybe we can make it all better again, put all of last season's bad memories behind us. Just now, it all seemed possible.

After one of the games early in the season, I remember hearing an umpire talking to a reporter, saying he never saw Jackson miss a signal or a hit-and-run play, or a steal, or any sign at all.

"Just never did anything stupid," he said. And the way things started out in 1920, that seemed about right, because my man went on a tear and never let up. Twenty triples and twelve homers that year—the most times he ever was able to lope around the bases.

He and Black Betsy were quite a pair, tearing up league pitching no matter who was throwing. I think some writer asked Walter Johnson how he was trying to work Joe when we were playing Washington sometime in early May, and the Train said," I give him my best stuff, and then I go over and back up third base!" Good fellow he was, a real quiet gentleman who was always most gracious to us.

And really, it was a thing of beauty to watch Joe at the plate, gearing up at over a .400 clip and staying there until...until everything crashed down around us, first Ray's death and then the accusations about what went on in '19.

We heard about it, how Ray Chapman, Joe's old friend and teammate from Cleveland, was hit in the head by one of Carl Mays' submarine pitches in a game with the Yankees. Somebody later told us it sounded like the ball hit the bat, and it rolled all the way back to the mound. Somebody may as well have carved out sections of my heart. It was so hard to picture Ray close to death, and when you love somebody too much, losses always hurt more. We stayed up most of the night; sometimes praying, sometimes sharing a funny story about him, most times holding each other and feeling silent tears mingle in our shared grief.

Mr. Lajoie's telegram the next morning let us know it was over. The young man's death weighed heavily on Joe, but in a strange way it took his mind off the fix being gabbed about on every street corner, and focused it on more important things.

"Does God take away every good man, every decent thing, I've ever touched, Missy? Friends in the war, Ray—is He going to take you away, too?" It was almost quiet desperation, like there wasn't anything much left to hold to.

We made arrangements to be gone from the team, took the train to Cleveland and attended the memorial service, a little less than ten years after doing the same for Addie Joss. A couple of the guys came up and spoke to us as the crowd was breaking up, but I noticed most of them kept their distance. Talk travels pretty fast in baseball circles, so here we were again, linthead trash tolerated as an inconvenience. We didn't stick around too long, said goodbye to Mr. and Mrs. Lajoie, hugged Ray's fiancée, and shook Walter Johnson's hand. And didn't look back.

Some folks, they lose when someone close to them dies, but my man seemed blessed to be able to take the best memories folks left him and weave them into the fabric of his own life, making it richer and fuller than before. That was Joe, getting through the worst and then making good grow from the ruins.

A couple of weeks later, all hell broke loose. The tight pennant race with Cleveland, Detroit, and the Yankees all of a sudden didn't matter. The last game Joe played in '20, he was one for four, "one stinking single to show," he said. Funny, it was the same thing he did in his first game back in '08 for Mr. Mack's team in Philadelphia. Accusations and "what-if" games had been going on for weeks in the paper, especially when the focus turned from a Cubs-Phillies game in '19 to the World Series itself, and things turned real hot real quick. We took a lot of long walks in the evenings after the games. Chicago was good for that in late August and early September when the air could get a chill to it now and then. Sometimes, the click of our heels on the sidewalk seemed the only sound that lingered in the night.

"Wasn't nothing the same, Missy, not after the first mention was made about getting extra money." He stared straight ahead, and I could only imagine what those eyes locked on in the distance. I listened, moving closer to him and feeling his arm tighten around my waist.

"They had meeting after meeting, one hotel or another, New York or Chicago or Cincinnati, but I wasn't there. Then the money showed up in the room, and I think by then it was out of Chick's hands and into rougher territory, if that was possible." We slowed under a streetlight, lingered there against the chill, hugged each other to fight off the loneliness closing in. The dim glow was better than the unmoving darkness beyond.

"And there wasn't anyone to listen to you," I said.

"Only you," he stroked my face and I kissed his fingers when they passed my lips. "And I was afraid they would try and hurt you, because it got to being a rough time, like Lyria told you. But I'd have taken my chances against 'em with Black Betsy in my hands if it had come to that." His voice was quiet, a strained rhythm that made you absolutely sure he wasn't kidding.

The evening after that game it rained, a cold and steady drizzle that set in. Then, three days before the end of the season the suspensions came down from Comiskey in a letter addressed to Joe and left at the hotel desk. When I read Joe the words, it might as well have been eternal damnation to him. Think about two people sitting alone in their hotel room, one trying to read, her mouth just not willing to pronounce the words, and one trying to listen, his ears refusing to let the sound in, and you just about have us figured out right then.

"Your suspension is brought about by information...If you are innocent you will be reinstated...If guilty you will be retired from organized baseball the rest of your life...I take this action even though it costs Chicago the pennant." One thing for sure. If we were thinking that what went on before was bad, it got tougher, and people got nastier. Lies were accepted as truth, and the truth itself was blown apart into a million little pieces.

First it was Fullerton's story in one of the New York papers, you remember, the "say it ain't so, Joe" with the little boy tugging at my man's sleeve and at every heartstring in the country.

"Same guy who told me back in my rookie year that I would fail in the big leagues because I was ignorant." Joe shook his head and gave a sarcastic sniff. "Was old Hugh and them other New York writers wrong then, or now? 'Course, I guess it doesn't matter. They're all laying one brick at a time and building a wall between me and the game." Sometimes the prophet does not always understand the full significance of the words he speaks.

"Not everybody is, Joe. There are people out there who believe in you, good folks who are willing to stand with you, with us, and one day soon we'll be giving all this a good whipping." I could hear myself, and hoped I was convincing him and me that maybe there was that chance.

I was wrong. First there was a lawsuit filed by Charles Nims, a fan from Chicago, saying he lost $250 by use of a confidence game. Not something I understood, but it was in all the papers nearly every day so you couldn't avoid it. Then there was the appointing of baseball's commissioner, Kenesaw Mountain Landis, and from the first I saw of this federal judge wasn't much I liked. Joe once called Swede Risberg a hard guy, and that was exactly my term for this little white-haired man. As things headed toward the Grand Jury proceedings, an article by Joe Williams quoted Landis.

"There is no chance for any of them to creep back into organized baseball. They will remain outlaws. It is sure that the guilt of some of them will at least be proved." Now doesn't that sound like it ties pretty close to what was in Comiskey's letter? And what about innocent until proven guilty, the way the law says? It was like icy fingers clutching at my heart. Something was going to be bad for my man, and I wouldn't be able to change the outcome, hard as I may try.

"Cicotte, Jackson Confess" was headlines across the country, so it all had finally broken loose. Let me say something here about the confessions everybody put so much weight on, since it couldn't hurt anything now. My man met with Comiskey's lawyer, Alfred Austrian, just the two of them, and that arrangement was always no good where Joe was concerned. Part of it, yes, was that he couldn't read, but more of it was that he always wanted to believe the best in each person he ever met. Mix into that being scared of what he was hearing was going to happen to him, both by gamblers who figured they had been double-crossed and by the high lord of baseball, and who knew what he was thinking. It was a situation that couldn't turn out good. It didn't.

"He told me signing the confession, and the waiver of immunity would be in my best interest. I had at least seen him around the ballpark at some games, so yeah, I trusted him."

He knew Joe couldn't read, and didn't bother reading either document to him, my man said. What happened you all know, because instead of Joe being only a witness like Austrian promised, the lawyer turned those papers over to state prosecutors. Old Alfred coined the phrase "conspiring to do an illegal act," words that formed the damning indictment against Joe, Eddie, Swede, Chick, Hap, Fred, Buck and Lefty. But the guy must have been good, because Cicotte and Lefty *could* read and write, and they did the very same thing Joe did, signed the papers and all.

Time just started crawling, like it was meant for us to bear every insult, feel every pain two or three times, get chewed up by regrets over and over, and all the time wondering how it could ever get this bad. Sometimes folks did try to be sympathetic, and particularly I remember dear Walter Johnson saying in the paper,

"I'll never believe Joe was a bad fellow at heart. He was easily and terribly misled by his associates." Doesn't sound like much, but there weren't many ballplayers who had guts enough to say one iota in Joe's favor.

When I read that to Joe, he sat at the kitchen table, hands folded, and stared out the window into the busy Chicago streets, a world where we didn't belong any more, and certainly where we felt no welcome. He spoke, his voice barely rising and falling at all, about like you remember folks talking when they visited the family of somebody who died - didn't know much what to say, and what came out was only meant to spare folks any more pain.

"I should have just run, Missy, run the hell away from 'em the first time they mentioned selling out for money. It wasn't enough that I stayed away from the meetings at the Buckminster Hotel in Boston and the Sinton in Cincinnati. Or that I took the money back to Comiskey that Lefty throwed on the bed." Voices filtered into the room from the busy street below, and they seemed a million miles away. He looked at me for a moment, then dropped his gaze and kept on talking.

"Hell, we'd heard of gambling in baseball for years. You remember going into parks and hearing all the yells about 'I'll cover that' and 'Give me some New York action', and it only got worse because pretty soon they was marching right up to us after games and trying to get us involved. Chase, McGraw, even Cobb, there were rumors about so many.

"Missy, I played my heart out. I got no apologies to give, don't know a way to ask for forgiveness when I tried to set it right by taking the money back. What do I do? Tell me, what?" He looked to me and I felt like a little girl, lost in the woods and not able to get back home, though I knew home must be close by.

Guilty knowledge? People inside and outside the game knew about it, gamblers, sportswriters, owners, and players. Baseball routinely pushed aside players and managers who reported shady plays and bits of curious conversation. Everybody must have thought if ordinary folks knew about that stuff then the game would suffer.

"Christy Mathewson, a man of great integrity and one of the best ever to play, he couldn't get nobody to listen to him about the wheeling and dealing of Hal Chase. If Big Six got brushed aside as so much of a bother, must have been a lot of rotten apples they wanted to hide at the bottom of the barrel." Joe likened Christy to Eddie Collins, God just didn't make any better than them.

It was an uneasy winter at home, folks keeping their distance from us, not many of the mill players coming round to ask Joe's help on hitting, especially those Scoop had written about as having a chance of breaking into the minors. People who did come by to talk down in Brandon, or who stopped us on the street when Joe and I would be uptown, they kept the chat a respectful mile or two from the '19 Series and from the suspensions. Wouldn't have done them much good to push, because it was something we decided wasn't going to be talked about until the trial started sometime the next year.

Beginning in July of 1921, our world existed in the Criminal Court of Cook County, Austin Avenue, and Dearborn Street, Chicago. There were papers served which ordered my man not to leave the state, and we had to meet $3000 bail. So here we were, more familiar with Sheriff Charles Petus and his deputy Walter van Horn; with our lawyers Crowley, Short and Gunther; than we were with our own family.

"Couldn't go nowhere," Joe was fond of saying," and I'd never been one for idle wasting of time. So I opened a pool room, sort of a sports center at 55th and Woodlawn, right across from the University of Chicago. Kids from the college dropped by, shot a few games, and talked baseball and stuff. It was good having 'em around."

I dropped by a time or two and he was so at home with the kids who had so much more book learning than he did. Just like with Hyder and Buck, Joe was as much at home with the college boys as he was chatting with folks at Brandon, or stopping on the Chicago streets and greeting folks as they shook his hand. Bad as the accusations and proceedings, good people had a way of making things seem not quite so hopeless.

"Buck was the only one," Joe would always say those few times the Scandal was ever brought up between us, "who had the courage to go to the ballpark and talk with Comiskey, to explain that he played to win, too. Finally got in one day, but at the end of the visit he left with his head down and didn't talk to nobody about what was said."

Joe was a lot more right than I was as he watched everything going on around him, just like he was so good at doing on the field. Nothing got by him, his instincts just as razor sharp as his skilled reflexes. He saw how the deck was stacked, and I missed it or either never wanted to believe it.

That summer was as hot as anyone could remember, and it brought back thoughts of those sticky days in New Orleans eleven years before. Seemed more like 11,000, when we were just kids, newlyweds lost in love and the world at our feet. Now I felt old, and me all of twenty-eight, with my strength used up trying to protect my man. Folks said my world was shattered and torn, but that both Joe and I bore that sorrow with dignity.

"She has a big heart," Joe said one day to Lefty Williams, "and ain't nothing I could do without her next to me. She's been there through all this hell and ain't never flinched the first time. No man could be luckier than me." Lyria told me later how his eyes just shone bright every time he mentioned me, and I'll say it again - how I loved that man!

During the trial, spectators and witnesses, the jury, the accused, court officials and lawyers may have thought they had latched onto a little of hell's blazes. Shirtsleeves and no collars was the order for everybody except those who had to take the stand. And the proceedings would have been a real education to a small town girl if there wasn't the fear of watching my man stand accused.

There were more charges and counter-charges, finger pointing, and denials than you'd ever be expecting to hear. What always got me was the names the prosecutors and defense attorneys would be hitting the witnesses with, and whether who spoke to who else through the Series.

"Did Joe Jackson know Sleepy Bill Burns and did he ever conduct business with him?"

"No," Joe said, "just greeted him in the Sinton Hotel in Cincinnati and that was all."

"What about Hal Chase?"

"No," he said, "knew him only as a player, and had never known him personally," and he stared them straight in the eye.

"Then what about Rachel Brown or Abe Attell? Didn't you know that they were associated with gamblers?"

"No, never heard of any of them, and do not know them at all."

The lawyers would set off real fireworks now and then, like one special Thursday night session. Mr. Replogle, one of the folks acting for the state, called a bunch of the team, including Kid Gleason, Eddie Collins, Cracker Schalk, little Dickie Kerr, and Ray Williamson. When asked where the accused were on the morning before the first game of the Series, all of them stated there was a team workout at Redland Field. Interestingly, it was the same time Bill Burns said he met with the players and completed the deal for the fix to happen. You figure that would be a strike against them trying to destroy my man. I watched Harry Brigham, foreman of the Grand Jury, as he listened very carefully, leaning forward and resting chin in hand, now and then shooing away a fly, or patting a handkerchief to his forehead and neck.

Another time they asked Joe about his hitting and fielding in the Series and the regular season, and he recited those stats like some people do the Lord's Prayer or Pledge of Allegiance. Proud of what the words he said stood for, proud they showed he played to win. And when Mr. Short or Mr. Gunther asked him about some of the other players, and Joe couldn't pull their numbers off the top of his head, why our lawyers reminded the jury that nobody on Cincinnati came close to him, and even Mr. Eddie Collins hit about 150 points lower in the Series than my man.

Sometimes when there would be a recess, somebody would try to break the tension and get a laugh. One day my man, all dapper in his navy suit and black shoes, kept the courtroom in an uproar explaining

89

how he got two bailiffs drunk one evening. And yes, some people managed to turn that laughter into a nasty piece of work, sorry as it is to say. Especially when there were things more dangerous, more evil, going on right under their pious noses.

Can you imagine the confessions, the ones everybody made a fuss over when Cicotte, Lefty and Joe gave them, those sacred pieces of paper just up and disappeared right under the noses of the whole Chicago judicial system? Just like playing "Red Rover" when we were kids, except nobody ever got caught and kept on running forever. Dear old Mr. Austrian, Comiskey crony and all, couldn't explain what happened to them, either, but I can tell you every other person in the courtroom had an opinion. "Lost" doesn't exactly describe things truthfully, you understand, since the documents managed to turn up at all the right times for Landis and Comiskey and whoever else wanted to badger the players.

There was talk that Rothstein and his men planned the theft, and some said old Commie was part of it, but of course no one ever bothered to follow up on it. Even a high up baseball man said Arnold paid $10,000 for the confessions, that he came to Chicago and went straight to Austrian's office. Does anybody want to do a little two-plus-two here?

"We was tried instead of the gamblers," I heard Joe say to Benedict Short one day, "and if gamblers ain't tried and convicted, then game fixing is going right on. Others had knowledge of this stuff, didn't come forward, and not a damn thing was said or done to one of 'em." Oh, folks talked and made much of the fact that Rothstein was not on trial and the players were scapegoats. An opinion, plus a nickel, would get you a Co'Cola down at Bolts' Drug Store, too, and that was about as much attention as anyone paid to an idea not fitting with baseball's nice and neat conspiracy theory.

The Sox players, when all this started, wanted to go on trial right away, and it was the state and baseball that sought to slow stuff down. What they wanted was to leave the players under suspicion, ruin them that way. Let lies and half-truths eat away at their hearts and souls, and of course it was "new evidence forthcoming!" when there was a complaint. I got so tired of hearing that, probably another cute phrase dreamed up by Austrian or Grabiner or somebody. Weaver's attorney, Tom Nash, and Mr. Short, weren't having any of it, and opposed even a short wait, saying Buck and Joe were ready to beat this thing and get back into baseball before the season ended.

Maybe the best talk we heard in the courtroom was from Mr. Frumberg, a lawyer for some of the small town numbers players from out in Iowa who got mixed up in all this. He waded in with both fists swinging at the high-minded prosecutors, asking questions that turned them tomato red with anger. My favorite, "Why do you let the instigators of the Scandal go free and crucify underpaid ballplayers and penny-ante gamblers?"

There wasn't anybody, not Replogle, or Austrian, or even Judge Friend, who dared answer or dared stop him. And oh boy, Frumberg could get wound up tighter than Billy Sunday in a tent revival, shirt sleeves rolled up, jacket thrown across the back of a chair, handkerchief in hand mopping his face.

"How could Arnold Rothstein, Sport Sullivan, Rachel Brown, Abe Attell, Hal Chase and all the others never even be brought to trial?" Sometimes you could see the veins sticking out in his neck, his teeth were clenched so hard.

All you could hear was folks fanning with whatever paper or cardboard they could lay their hands on. For nigh on to an hour he had the defenders of the less-than-holy game back on their heels, and wasn't anybody coming forward to challenge him.

I wished it had been in favor of the players, but the things that happened were like waves on the ocean. One minute you'd be on top and the next slammed under. No sooner had Fromberg's oratory ended than Mr. Replogle moved things back in the state's favor.

"We will have more indictments in a few days, and before we get through we will have washed organized baseball clean of everything that is crooked and dishonest. We've got the goods on the gamblers now, and we are going the limit." There was a hardness to him, like someone who wasn't going to shy away from anything until he got what he wanted. With my man on the stand, most every question was about the money.

"Weren't you mad when you got only $5000 instead of the $20,000 you expected?"

"No, I was ashamed of myself."

Joe, explain! For God's sake, tell them more, about the threatening phone calls and taking the cash to Comiskey's office. In his honesty, he answered as he should have, but didn't say enough to let folks know that he never played to lose, to let them know he was simply in over his head.

"Who gave you the money?" I wanted him to offer 'Lefty put it on the bed, saying there would be more when I delivered the goods. Then Risberg threatens to kill me if I squawk and that's why I don't get far from the bailiffs until this whole thing is over. Swede is a hard guy.' But all Joe said was, "Lefty Williams put it on the bed in my room."

About as close as I got to my wish was Mr. Short getting Joe to recollect a conversation with Gandil, not nearly as dangerous as Swede,

91

and the scene he painted wasn't close to being as powerful as it should have been.

"I'm not going to be in on it. I'll get out of it all."

"You're in it already and might as well stay in."

"I can go to Comiskey and have every damn one of you pulled out."

"It wouldn't be well for you if you did that."

"Any time you want to have me knocked off, go ahead and do it."

"Yeah." And Chick walked off laughing.

The lords of baseball even had a detective going around as the Series went on, a Mr. O'Farrell, and he followed about every lead and every character that came his way, from Rothstein in New York to gamblers in St. Louis and Iowa. He traced them to all the meetings they were supposed to be having with the players, and he said many times, including once on the witness stand, that my man couldn't be placed at any of these locations. Oh, it was a fact, an important one to me and a lot of other folks, but you didn't hear it being a big part of the trial. It was hardly mentioned at all, and took a back seat to what I felt baseball was always after - protecting itself at the expense of everything else, even the whole truth.

Funny the little things you remember. Like Buck Weaver, sitting apart from the other seven, not speaking to them when he came in or left. Joe, he sometimes turned and watched as the big third baseman took his seat, and I know their eyes met once or twice, but there was not even a nod from one to the other. Years after, Joe would talk about him, always quiet and respectful.

"Buck, he was the most noble. Played hard, took no money, upheld the man's code of silence about ratting on his mates. Wouldn't even hear of barnstorming with us as the Black Sox Traveling Diamond Show. Never did one thing wrong, and wouldn't a soul listen to him insisting that he was innocent. Everyone knew, everyone, those of us who stood accused and those protecting the righteous game, that Buck should have gone back into baseball."

The trial dragged on, but if you watched carefully you could see that the prosecutor's case was coming undone. Charges against some of the small time gamblers were tossed out, and Judge Friend thundered out an ultimatum.

"Unless further evidence can be provided by the state, I'll be considering acquittal of at least some of the players." The last man to testify was Jean Dubuc, a pitcher from the Giants in '19, and all he added was that Bill Burns told him to bet on the Reds. So after fifteen days as guests of Cook County, the judge sent the jury out to get their thoughts together and present the verdict.

I sat, squirmed, got up and walked around, not wanting to be too far away when the twelve good men came marching single file back into the courtroom. Believe the dress I had on was navy blue with white trim, and I can tell you my cotton stockings and underwear were wet with sweat. It was life hanging in the balance, for Joe, for me, for the other fellows and their families. Turns out the wait was a little less than three hours, and then Mr. Brigham was asked if they had reached a verdict. When the words "not guilty" got out of his mouth, you should have heard the cheers from a hundred people.

Oh, the boys were up and slapping each other and laughing. Weaver, he jumped over a row or two of chairs and came up with the other fellows for the first time since all this legal beagle stuff began. Folks patted my arm and whispered how glad they were, and one kind gentleman loaned me his handkerchief, because all of a sudden I was looking at the courtroom through a blur. Dear Lord, I don't know when I had cried so much, and I was thankful I didn't ever take to wearing much make-up. I did hear Judge Friend congratulate the jury, telling them he felt it was a just decision, and that brought another round of hearty applause. By then I was standing on a chair, looking for my man in the midst of all that excitement.

There he was, sitting quietly, strangely apart from the noise and celebration, and it was like he was invisible as he surveyed what swirled around him. I realized that he was weighing, stacking and then restacking all he heard and saw, understanding the verdict from every angle he could. It was that wistful, almost sad smile I had come to know that played at the corners of his mouth.

"Joe!" I yelled and jumped down from the chair, fighting through folks and finally reaching him. He pulled me close and gave me one of those sweet kisses that still melted my insides and made me giddy as a schoolgirl stealing her first smooch.

"We did it! We're back in the game! Safe at home! Safe at home!" I expected him to give me a great big hug and whirl me around like we were at a victory dance, but my man stayed quiet, not letting go of the smile.

"Maybe, Missy, just maybe you're going to be right. I hope and pray it's so." Weaver busted through and gave him a bear hug, and whirled me around, all the while laughing his fool head off. One by one the other guys made their way over, but they were so wrapped up in their own joy not a one of them noticed how differently Joe took it.

On the day the verdict came down, the singer Caruso died, and that helped to take the headlines away from the boys for a little while as the world mourned the great tenor. Soon enough, because of baseball's new commissioner, they were right back in the center of the storm.

Remember, he was the one who spelled it out, "that the guilt of at least some of them will be proved," and I just sort of felt he lumped the guilty and innocent in there together. Folks, some of them anyway, would ask how I felt about Landis, and don't think I made any secret about it.

No, there's not a reason to dredge up the word "hate" because that never played a part in things. When he worded his response to the verdict, it became clear to everybody that neither my Joe nor any of them would set foot inside major league baseball again, and he was a man hell-bent on setting an example no one would ever question. I credit him for being right on that point.

Remember the words "regardless of the verdict of juries"? He was going to be judge, jury, and executioner to everything that applied to baseball, and the rest of the world be damned. Now, I've got to slow down, quit talking so fast, and being a mite louder than I normally am.

Calling him dictatorial is accurate, I believe. Now, inconsistent, that's got to be in there. Landis could sentence a man to jail for violating Prohibition, go home and sip bootleg liquor, and never see his hypocrisy. What bothered me most was that he didn't give any weight to Joe going and trying to talk with Comiskey and return the money to him. So "guilty knowledge" seems pretty widespread, wouldn't you think, since baseball executives knew about the fix, too? But then, he didn't give any weight to strangely disappearing confessions, or to Joe's play in the Series, and he never objected to the fact that every gambler went scot free.

Sometimes, there is talk about a conversation he had with me. Got to stop again, slow down, smooth my dress or something, because I'm getting too wrapped up in this.

"When all this blows over, Katie, Joe will be back." Words like that? I'll just have to let folks wonder if it ever did take place. But you know I always thought something bigger than baseball was at stake here, and letting a linthead and a few of his buddies take the fall was the simple way out. Making sense out of Landis' ways is as hard as trying to prove Joe's innocence after we got on the outside looking in. Saying that it was impossible is offering up one huge understatement.

I don't think any of us were prepared for the way fans and players and owners rallied around the Commissioner, and he did have that personality that dominated anything that came close to him. Anyone, that is, except for George Ruth. Folks want to talk about somebody saving baseball, if there was anything to save, it was George Herman. But Landis did rally the public against the Black Sox, as they were now being called, and if any of us thought we understood what it was to be ridiculed and shunned, why, we were just getting our first good look at it.

"Remember what Hap Felsch said after it was over, Missy?" Joe said as we were closing out everything in Chicago and getting ready to leave for home. "'I'm out of baseball, and would have got as much money on the level if the Sox won. What am I going to do? I don't know, go to hell, I guess.'"

"Ain't never thought I could feel so low, girl," and he leaned over and put his head on my shoulder. "Always said the only things in my life was you and baseball, and that's cut in half now." He didn't say anything else, and I didn't have any answers. He never complained, accused or blamed anyone, not then or at any other time. He agonized alone. And though some newspaper writers said he left Chicago in disgrace, he certainly never acted that way. The way they carried on, it was almost a daily crucifixion, but there were good folks like Judge Friend, who went so far as contacting baseball officials on my man's behalf, and tried to let them know some of the underhanded methods used by the state's attorneys. I'll give you a handful of guesses as to which ones got listened to and which was the voice crying in the wilderness.

On our way back home we pulled over and spent the night somewhere in Tennessee. They were having the county fair, and guess who's got to go and walk the midway and eat cotton candy and candy apples and be a little boy again, all the way down to a tummy ache later? But maybe if we spent an evening with different sights and sounds it might ease our hearts just a little. Of course, that meant staying unrecognized, and Joe didn't.

"Folks, we got us a great ballplayer right here!" yelled one of the hawkers on stage just up from the freak show. Fat and sweating in the summer heat, he slipped a shiny quarter to one young man who beat a path to all corners of that modified cow pasture and reported our whereabouts. "Gather 'round, everybody, and let's see what Shoeless Joe has to say."

"He's a crook!" I heard a big old farmer shout back, holding the hands of his two young sons. Joe looked at the boys, one about six, dark haired and tall, the other blond and no more than three, and they stared back at him.

"Katie," my man started, "this wasn't no good idea and maybe we better leave." But then we heard other voices.

"No! He was set up! Joe don't play to lose!" That was offered up by a well-dressed older fellow.

"He ain't no crook, he's one of us, and they done tried to hang it on him and the other players." The lady behind us said the voice belonged to Preacher Canfield from over at the Methodist Church.

More and more people were speaking up, some still voicing opposition, but so many more blessed southern folks hanging with us, giving us hope, and yes, even courage.

The hawker came back with words cutting through the uproar. "Shoeless Joe, come on up and talk to us!" Pushed, dragged, floating, I don't know, but we got down front and Joe was hustled up the steps. I sat on the edge of the platform, and as he spoke I watched the people, eyes that never left him for the ten minutes or so he talked of baseball, the men he knew - especially George Ruth, though folks hereabouts said "You mean Babe!" - the recent Series, and the trial. He finished up the only way he knew how, in the midst of the game he loved.

"If Landis sees fit to put me back in, I will appreciate it, but if he does not, it won't change anything. As long as God gives me strength, I will play the game, even if I have to do it by myself. I love it that much." We started down the steps hand in hand, and the dark haired boy we saw a little earlier with his pa tugged at my man's sleeve and said, "Don't have to play by yourself, Joe. I got a glove, and a ball Daddy made me with twine and tape from over at the mill. We could have a game now, if you want." Oh, the crowd loved that, cheering maybe not as loud, but so much more from the heart, than I'd ever heard in a major league park.

Greenville wasn't as kind when we got back there, the townies letting us know pretty much soon as we got in earshot that it was about what they expected of a linthead. Insult heaped on insult seemed to follow, like when the papers came out with the story that he might have to pay $1200 income tax and penalty on the $5000 he was accused of taking from the gamblers. Funny about paying this new fangled tax on what you never kept in the first place, don't you think?

"Did you ever tell anybody where the money wound up, Joe?" I remember asking him one night several months later, sitting on the porch at Miss Martha Ann's. It was still warm, though edging toward early October, and I leaned my head against his shoulder.

"Business manager on one of the teams I traveled with a couple of weeks ago up to Forest City to play in a couple of games. Wasn't much to do riding the train up there except to look out the window, and we got to talking. Nice fellow, but don't remember his name. Had a lot on my mind." He took my hand, lifted it to his lips, and kissed it so soft.

"His question cut through all that was swimming in my head, not catching me off guard exactly, but making me think straight again. It was one I was wishing somebody might ask. Told him I gave it all to a hospital hereabouts where they might help kids. So many of them died of flu back in '18 and more not too long ago from cholera. Told him me and you loved kids. I leaned back and closed my eyes then, quiet for several minutes before I finished up. Said I'd done tried to give it back twice before so this time I was going to put it where it would do some good."

"Joe," I said after several minutes of my own quiet. "Let's go try and make a baby one more time. It's been a while." I reached up and kissed him, his hands beginning to work down my sides, and he lifted me up and carried me inside. We let the screen door to, locked it, and I whispered, "And I'll be real quiet, too," and laughed. Still, I was glad for the back bedroom, just in case.

We stayed on for awhile in Greenville. Then after getting our things packed, and saying goodbye to Miss Martha Ann and Mama and Daddy, we took Lefty and Lyria up on their invitation and headed down to Savannah. What we were going to do to make a living in this world I didn't know, but we'd be getting by.

Chapter 6

Joe could still latch on with teams about anywhere he traveled and pick up a pretty nice sum of cash, and he started doing that. I was happy to follow my man wherever he played ball, just like always, but there was one trip I refused to make, thinking it was a big mistake then, same as I do now. It was one of our few arguments, and except for his show girl thing, probably the most heated.

"Barnstorming like in the old days, Missy, when we'd pack 'em in." Sunlight swirled through the kitchen window on a fine spring morning at 409 East 49th, Savannah, and Joe was practicing his stride into the ball.

"It's not the same, Joe. You're going as a member of the Black Sox, and listen, if you think Weaver's going to join you, you're crazy. Dear God, think! The world's already labeled the lot of 'em crooks, except that for you and Buck the jury's still out." Hands on hips, I was staring right through those brown eyes of his, which I did real well when I was mad.

"Folks, they'll turn out, and we can talk to 'em, make 'em listen and maybe..."

"There's no maybe, Joe. It's not a game any longer, don't you see? Landis has them on his side, made them think the unholy lot of you threw dirt on the sacred game he is sworn to protect. Can't anybody break his power, Joe. Now listen to me!"

He was going to turn and walk away, the first time it ever happened, and the only time it ever did. Dear Lord, I could feel my heart break. And I think his broke with the words I sent following him out the door into the back yard.

"I won't be coming with you, Joe, not when you're about to make the biggest mistake of your life. And don't tell me it's because you don't want to hide. Joe, wise up. Chick and Swede are going to use you again, just like they did in the Series! Joe!" I could feel the tears running down my cheeks, splashing down on the hardwood floor and glittering there in the bright sunlight.

"Joe!" But he was out of earshot, around the house and heading up the street, a cigarette in his mouth, and back straight as a ramrod.

I was right. I really didn't want to be, but I was. Joe packed up and left early the next morning, the first time he didn't give me one of those fairy tale kisses on the lips. The ones you kind of remember between waking and sleeping, then you barely open your eyes and see your lover close by and you know it was sweet for sure.

No, he touched my shoulder and was gone. Soon we started seeing reports about the barnstorming, from New Jersey to Ohio, down to Arkansas, back through Louisiana and Alabama, up into Georgia. What they found was an indifferent world at best, mean at worst, and capable of turning a game into a riot. More than once a game was stopped, and sometimes never even got started, as the cries of "Cheater!" and "Benedict Arnolds!" and "Judas to a man!" filled the park in place of cheering.

Joe came home, not playing north with them, and without Shoeless, as I suspected, the whole charade collapsed. But damn if Chick and Swede hadn't succeeded in playing us for a sap again.

Anybody who got close to the Black Sox got sucked in, and there were good folks who wound up on baseball's wrong side. Dick Kerr was a hero after winning two games in the Series when Cicotte and Williams fell flat, and look at how he was treated. In '22 he refused to report to the White Sox because Comiskey was going to pay him next to nothing, and the little guy with the big heart went off and played semi-pro ball out in the midwest. Trouble was, he tossed an inning or two against his former mates and earned a one year suspension from the majors by our friend Landis, who I'm sure got a big thank you from Commie.

I don't really believe Joe was the same toward baseball after he got back from that round of games. It was like black water stood between him and the game, and there wasn't a bridge that could reach across.

"All of us knowed we would always be on the outside looking back in. Even Buck, I think he felt it, too. I wasn't prepared for what we got from the fans. I mean they went from cheering the verdict to just about worshipping Landis when he kept us out." Don't think I'd ever seen so much hurt in anybody's eyes when he stopped talking and looked at me.

"Listening to 'em yell at us, even spit on us when we walked close to the grandstand, damning us to hell for all eternity if it was something they could of pulled off." He turned and walked out to the porch, and said it so soft that I about missed it. "Maybe I'm just the walking dead, never being a part of no place again." I bolted three or four steps to get in front of him, put my arms around him and we held each other.

"Let's walk the whole town, Joe, window shop like we used to do, go down and listen to the ocean the way we did up in Delaware. We're not ever going to be alone, Joe, not ever. We have each other, and that's got to count for something even if the rest of the world turns its back on us."

We took off for our night on the town, me holding on to his hand for dear life, like the darkness would snatch him from me if I was to let go even for a second.

For whatever reason, we settled on opening a dry cleaning business, and I always thought it funny that one of the Sox who refused to wash his uniform, to spite Comiskey's demand they pay for it themselves, was now agreeing to keep other people's clothes clean.

It wasn't a chore to go in and run the store every day, the way you hear about some people hating their jobs. For us, it was working side by side like when we ran the pool room in Greenville, or the one up in Chicago when we couldn't leave during the trial. Most mornings we'd walk from home, holding hands, maybe stopping for a cup of coffee. The spring and fall mornings were the best of all, when the air was still cool and the colors were busting out all over. He and I liked to call these times our short secret honeymoons.

We'd be getting there just before Holden Johnson, and of course Slim and Jessup. Days started off pretty much regular at 7:30, getting the lights on and the fans turning, cracking a window or two to get a good cross draft.

"Morning," my man would say, and start his customary handshaking tour around the store. More than once I saw the men wringing a hand Joe squeezed a bit too hard without even knowing he had done it. "Lots to do, fellas, so let's get to it," and with that he reached up, loosened that tie, pushed the skimmer back on his head or maybe even just took it off, and hopped to work with the washing and pressing.

Now Johnson, his tie and vest never came off, no sir. He was some kind of distant cousin to Joe, and did the tidying up and greeting customers as they came in. Got the feeling more than once he might like to run the till, but that was under my direction and no one else's.

"Hsss. Hsss." Those big pressers sounded like snakes coiling up to strike, and that steam gave you a sweat moustache even in the dead of winter. My man and the two Negroes pretty much turned out a day's work before lunch.

The old National Cash Register weighed nigh as much as me, and had raised gilt edges that reminded me of my grandpa's tombstone. A little girl's hand once moved over the rough edges of that Confederate corporal's last effort to explain his life,

> He Lived Honestly
> And Did His Best

and now I was running this business with Joe the same way, trying to slap the world in the face and make it take notice that we were as good as anybody. And we knew it would take the rest of our lives to do it, with never any let-up. My work dresses, dark browns and blues capped with white collars I had sewn around an open neckline, that was my prim and proper uniform. I'd be bending over the ledger, entering numbers with a precision I was proud of.

Joe toted a stack of pressed shirts up front, big hand unrolling the brown paper and in the same motion tearing the length just right.

"Missy, these belong to Mr. Parsons, what Slim tells me. Pull the order, please ma'am, and we'll have it ready and waiting!" The package was neatly wrapped as he finished speaking, and he gave me a wink. Sophisticated system, tacking orders on the wall behind the counter, taking them down when we were through. Worked good, too.

The most elegant thing about the whole building was the stamped tin ceiling, like the dining room in the Ottaray Hotel up in Greenville Mama told me about once after her and Daddy ate Sunday dinner there a long time ago.

"Why's it like that, Miss Katie, all fancy patterned and all?" Jessup asked one day.

"Damn sight hard to keep clean and painted, we all know that!" Joe came up and grabbed the chubby black man from behind, picking him up a good foot off the floor. Had to beg Joe to set him back down, much to the delight of Slim, who was used to that position with Jessup as the joker.

"Come on, Mr. Joe! I was being serious, least for a second or two!" And that was about right as the place filled with laughter. It was my man's way of signaling break time, and he'd head to the drugstore two doors down, Co'Colas for everybody. We had a reputation of being tight with a nickel, near squeaky from what I had overheard on more than one occasion, but no one around us, or who worked with us, was ever wanting for anything.

Interior decorating was courtesy of the Jacksons, early twentieth century American, such as it was. Joe had a photo of the 1917 championship White Sox team, I think the thing he was proudest of in his baseball career. The players that year were presented a small medallion for winning the World Series, and he had it fashioned into a ring complete with a diamond in the middle and his name inscribed on the back. Left out the "Shoeless" part, though, because he never did like that nickname. My contribution was an advertisement for a Mary Pickford movie, *Amarilly of Clothes-Line Alley*, a nice little comedy that Joe and I saw up in Delaware not long before the shipbuilding assignment was over. Both frames hung as crooked as the April calendar and the "Not Responsible for Articles in Case of Fire and Theft" sign. A regular museum of fine art.

Pretty soon most everybody put aside us being the outlaw Jacksons, to be talked about like trash, and at least accepted us for being hard working folks who did a good job getting their cleaning back to them.

"Hell, Missy," Joe said one day, "just tell them we stay open late because I'm still washing my socks!" Slim and Jessup had a fine time with that one, but dear Holden, I don't think a light ever did come on in the attic.

Of course, Joe played ball. He got a letter one day from the Armstrong Clothing Company, "requesting to have you play a series of games on our diamond next week. We'll be glad to hear from you." I smiled at my man as he packed to go, because this was a baseball request, not some carnival sideshow where he'd be a resident freak or out-of-place curiosity.

"This is real, baby. They want you to play ball because you're good and you can help them win. There's folks out there who haven't given up on you, who are going to cheer you again when its for all the right reasons. Not," and I took a deep breath and spoke a bit softer, "like the tour with the Black Sox. I just can't get my heart broken like that again." Much as I fought, the tears started sliding down my cheeks. When he held me close and kissed me, I could taste his tears as well.

Even with the money Joe got from traveling around playing exhibitions and such, and throwing our little bit of savings in, starting a business took more than we had, no matter how hard we worked. We moved to a small apartment down on Abercorn Street to try and save money, and we painted it up with lots of light blues and yellows to make it a right pretty place for the two of us. About the same time, we got a letter from one of Joe's lawyers, Ray Cannon, that sent us spinning off on another crusade.

Joe had me write two letters back in the winter, one to Comiskey asking for his pay in 1920, money which he never received, and one to Landis, which was Joe's one and only personal appeal for reinstatement. My man told me how he wanted things said, and I was good and honest and kept to his words, though God knows there were some choice phrases I wanted to slip in. Like I said, the words that made their way onto paper were what Joe dictated. I did answer the one letter to Mr. Cannon, whose response set a lot of things in motion.

"I want to trim Comiskey," the lawyer said, "and I am sure we'll be able to do it." With no response from the White Sox on the money they owed Joe, it was going to be up to us to force the action.

102

A couple of months later we did get an answer from the commissioner's office on the appeal, and if you ever heard words that spit contempt right in your face and then laughed at you, it was in what the Judge wrote.

"The signature thereto does not appear to be yours, and beyond this communication to you no action will be taken thereon." While I tried to keep hate out of what I thought baseball was doing to Joe, here was Mr. Baseball himself showing it for me and my man. It made the answer to Ray Cannon an easy one.

"Go hard." Once you grab on to the truth, it carries you through everything life throws your way.

Nobody really expected Joe to quit running around, playing baseball just because there was a big trial staring us in the face? He took off way down south for a couple of months, and I pretty much kept the home fires burning, though I did slip away for a weekend or two to spend with my man and watch him play ball.

"Made the tour of Bastrop, Louisiana (came out Loosana)," he was telling Slim and Jessup one morning soon after he got back. "Nice town, called itself the 'Home of Better Baseball', and by the crowds we packed in there wasn't no disputing that. Besides, one of the owners was the sheriff of the county..."

"Parish," I added, just letting them know I was keeping up with their leisure time.

"Yes'm." He smiled up at me, and Slim and Jessup hooted and punched him in the shoulder and slid that old Panama down over his eyes. "Mr. Carpenter had the means of keeping the ballpark real neat and fixed up, mostly with his guests down at the local jail."

I pictured him hopping off the train, toting only a suitcase and a leather bag holding his bats.

"More than $200 a month they was paying," and his two friends offered up low whistles of disbelief.

"Good place to play ball, that 'bout right?" Jessup asked between swigs of Co'Cola and mopping his sweaty face. Joe got real quiet for a minute, like he always did when he was weighing things out.

"Good and bad, Jess. Lots of good players, and pitching was above maybe what you'd expect. Had some real good games, and even shined up my 'show-out' a little bit, copying how Slim does it sometimes when we play up here." The tall Negro smiled as Joe looked up and winked.

I knew what he was talking about, not even being there. See, it meant Joe would throw this curve ball from deep in centerfield, starting it over toward third base before it sliced back left and slammed into the catcher's mitt just in front of the plate.

"What was bad, Joe?" Slim wanted to know. And so did I.

"Me, I guess. Fella really got on me one day when we was playing on the road. 'Look under the plate, Jackson. You might find something there,' bringing up the Scandal all over again. I was ashamed of how much it got to me. Stepped out of the box, and had that bat in one hand with a death grip about halfway up..."

Joe got up and took a couple of steps before he could get control of himself, even here among friends. I noticed the big hands trembling, but the fury passed in a few seconds. He sat back down.

"About halfway up the barrel, and headed out for the stands. I was going to make the loudmouth take back what he said, no matter what I had to do." His voice got softer, and he reached up and rubbed his eyes. "Thank God I stopped after two or three steps, shut down that hot anger, and walked back up to the plate."

"If you was thankful, Joe, think what that other boy must of been feeling!" Jessup gave that deep laugh like only he could do, and Slim and I chuckled, too. "You shut him up, and that had to feel good."

"Yeah, it did, 'specially the way it happened. Hit a home run on the next pitch. That ball rattled in among the train cars stopped out past right field, a place folks said ain't no ball ever been hit."

"Break over," I said. Slim and Jessup walked past Joe, slapping his shoulder on their way to the presser.

"No remembering Gus Johnson?" I offered after we closed up and were walking home. It was the name he signed under when he got to Bastrop, and of course it didn't fool anybody. Wasn't throwing it up to Joe in a bad way. I just wanted to know.

"Wasn't no need," was all my man said the rest of the way.

With all the preparation going on for this second trial the last half of '23, asking for Joe's 1920 salary that he never received, and letters flying back and forth between us and Mr. Cannon, my man was his happy, good-natured self. He'd load up nieces and nephews for a Sunday drive in our Oldsmobile, and along the way we'd stop at a gas station to get a Co'Cola to wash the dust out of our throats. We were way out in the country just as the sun was setting, and the kids, knowing what was coming, started.

"Uncle Joe, let's don't go back! There's lots of road out there we ain't come close to exploring, and we got a little while before dark!"

"Got to turn back, kids, get you home so we don't make no mommas and daddies mad, and so we can get their okay to do this again." Then we'd be coming into town in the cool of the autumn evening, the last rays of sunlight falling across the ocean. With the soft shimmering of the first stars, it was easy to picture the doorway of heaven looking just like this. I slid my hand into his, and we proceeded to drop off a car full of sleepy chaps.

We talked about Mr. Cannon's questions, how much to ask for, and travel arrangements to Milwaukee, where the trial was going to be held.

"Why so far away? Why not Memphis? Or Cleveland? Somewhere we'd feel a little more comfortable?" I asked. "Why Milwaukee?"

Joe stood by the window and looked out into the night, more concerned, I think, if he was going to play baseball this weekend. When he spoke again, I knew I was right.

"Slim and Jessup asked me to come and play with their team Saturday afternoon, Missy, and I told 'em okay." He laughed and came over, gliding across the floor, picked me up out of my chair and gave me a big hug. "They're good folks, and we talk baseball all the time at work. They play in a vacant lot over near the edge of town close to where they live and...hell, I couldn't tell 'em no."

I was laughing now. "Joe Jackson, here we've got all this work and all you think about is going off to be the only white man on a Negro team! Don't you ever think of anything but baseball?" This time it was him doing the deep kissing.

"I think of you," he said, carrying me away, and I kicked the door shut to the bedroom. Work, as you may have guessed, was done for the evening.

That game was more than talk can do justice to, and being there with my man was as perfect an afternoon as we ever spent. Sharing the food was special enough, with fried fish, clams, shrimp, and all sorts of vegetables cooked up spicy. About all I was good enough to do was slice watermelon and cantaloupe. Lord, kids running everywhere, loving every minute of being together.

You learn pretty quick that no one remembers the final score of the games too much after the bottom of the ninth closes. My man, he was the one having the most fun of all out there, and if the magic had ever left, it was back on this Saturday afternoon, starting in warm-ups and never even thinking about letting up. Joe, he only divided the world up one way, those who loved baseball and those who were cursed by God and didn't. If you loved it, you were his kin. Black and white, that didn't mean a thing to him at all, no more than if you were a rightfielder, third baseman, or pitcher.

See, Joe was against the Factory Law in South Carolina when it was passed about 1915, that prohibited cotton mills from employing workers of different races in the same room. I think he saw that lintheads was doing exactly what the townies had done to them for years—find someone to put down and feel good about themselves while doing it. Wasn't Joe's way.

Slim and Jessup, they were good folks just as my man said, hard workers he could be shoulder to shoulder with and still laugh when they were sweating up a blue breeze in the back of the store. They'd talk about picking cotton, and oh the two of them would laugh when Joe said he was only a fair cotton picker and never took to the task. But they all agreed there just wasn't any harder work than picking cotton. We paid them same as everyone else in the store.

"They earn it, they get it, Missy," he said, mopping his forehead where the hair was getting to be a little thinner.

Me and the other wives, we sat in the September sun and sweated, cheered double steals and double plays, hit-and-run bunts, taking two bases on a sacrifice fly, home runs and blue darters. And laughter, bantering back and forth good natured like we hadn't heard in the mill leagues or the majors. This was it, the game just polished up perfect, being what it was meant to be down to the littlest detail. Some folks, they say we weren't with our kind, but for my man, his kind was the honest sort who loved the game, and that was all he needed to decide if a man was good or not.

There was one Christmas Eve down in Savannah, at the party we had and all of us at the store exchanged gifts. There was one there "To Katie, From Joe".

"Joe, did you wrap this up all nice and neat, without help from Slim's or Jessup's wife?" Couldn't help but be surprised, such a nice present here at the store, set under the tree that was tall enough to partly obscure Miss Pickford.

"Joe Jackson, you...!" I screamed at the top of my lungs when the paper fell away to reveal a jar of earthworms he made up especially to scare the living daylights out of his loving wife. You might understand that I draw no differences between snakes and worms, and that the present from my loving husband got thrown back across the room in his general direction on a beeline.

"The throw made him proud, Miss Katie!" Jessup said between fits of laughter that had him doubled over. He and Slim were in on the gag, I am sure, since I remembered them slipping off to toward the back before I was through unwrapping my present.

"Though it almost knocked my brains out." Joe said as he grabbed me around the waist and hauled me under the mistletoe for one long kiss, amidst the cheers from everyone except the humorless Mr. Holden Johnson.

106

For all the memories of those good days, preparing for that trial got more and more particular, and not all of the proceedings I was agreeing with. Especially when it turns out that Happy Felsch and Swede Risberg were getting into the act of suing for their back pay, too. I swear, nothing good ever came when any of the group tried to ride what Joe was doing. I tried to keep my mouth shut, because my man had his hopes up that getting the money we were owed would help in running the business.

We had a picture taken in Greenville when we went there for a visit, and at first glance you could have figured we were a successful middle-aged couple waiting for an evening out on the town. A few of the folks walking by even commented as such. We were sitting on the top step of the porch at Miss Martha Ann's, faded brown clapboard house with darker brown shutters starting to peel after rough winter weather and a hot early spring. Geraniums and pansies bloomed in clay pots at the corners of the steps and on the bannister tops.

Joe, he's sitting there with his dark blue suit and bow tie, fedora slid back on his head, laced hightop shoes spit shined to a glow. I matched him for the occasion, light blue dress and high-laced black boots, my fox wrap draped across my shoulders and my dress hat cocked stylishly to the right. But my man was a lot more comfortable, because that corset was eating me alive and the stockings made my legs sweat. Let them call me Shoeless Katie, because I'd a sight rather be barefoot and skipping about in a cotton dress than being stifled and formal.

"Looking forward to the evening," we smiled and waved, or something just as empty and meaningless. This was anything but social, heading over to see another lawyer, Mr. Price, who had written Mr. Cannon on our behalf about a couple of questions we had. Joe was going be heading to Milwaukee before too long. My man kept his emotions and thoughts locked away, but this trial was a rallying point, a stand against what baseball had done to us, against all the "Dirty Joe" comments that we tried to swallow with as much grace and class as we could, against everything that wanted to destroy us.

But sitting there that evening, all we could muster were sad smiles as we looked at one another and held hands. Joe, he reached back and gently broke off a stem of red geranium and put it behind my left ear, and then he kissed me just as gentle on the lips. The Hupmobile chugged to a stop in front of the house, and Mr. Price jumped out, came around, and opened the door. He nodded and offered "Miss Katie" to me, and he and Joe shook hands.

It was like everything froze in place, and I was the only one alive. I looked long and hard at the sunset, the rays burning through white clouds like you see on the McAfee Funeral Home fans. Stared back at the house where we'd shared so much, and let my eyes sweep over the mill hill, this wonderful place where we'd grown up together. Watched Joe and Mr. Price with jaws set hard and eyes looking off towards eternity. Everything was so quiet, and I heard myself breathing it all in, thinking,

"What else, dear Lord, can the world throw at us?"

Joe climbed in and slammed the door. "Let's go, Missy. My time to bat," and still all he could offer was that sad smile. We drove off.

Another letter came from Mr. Cannon in mid-January of 1924, saying that there was another offer of settlement from the Chicago club - $2500, way less than the amount Joe's contract called for, and he turned it down. Did you know that right away Austrian said they'd probably offer a few hundred more before the trial got started next month? Then there was the statement which sent a shiver through me, like when you know something's not going to be alright but you won't be able to move fast enough to stop it.

"It won't be necessary for Mrs. Jackson to be here." I read the line over and over. Why? Because I might say or do something wrong? Listen, I sat through the 1921 Inquisition, complete with the burning at the stake of the innocent, and the lawyer says it isn't necessary for me to be with my man?

"No need to get all worked up, Missy. Mr. Cannon's a good man, and he'll be there every step of the way. Ain't nothing going to happen that him and me can't handle. Besides, you got to be here to run the business and all. You're the only one who can do that." He took both my hands in his and kissed my fingers. "It'll be fine, Missy."

A week later he boarded the train with the ticket Mr. Cannon sent, and he was off to Milwaukee. And the lawyer did work on Joe's behalf, one afternoon hopping a train himself and heading to Chicago to bring back the article old Hugh Fullerton wrote for one of the papers during the '19 Series. It was the one that said if the Sox wanted proof of a fix, all they had to do was get in touch with Sleepy Bill Burns down in Texas, and Mr. Cannon was going to use it to show that club officials knew all was not well. Can you believe, and much less understand why, the presiding judge refused to have the paper admitted as an exhibit, and that Mr. Austrian said he had no recollection of seeing it?

I should have understood it was bad then, and that it wasn't about to do anything but get worse, because the whole trial stunk of a set-up. Low and behold, those missing Grand Jury transcripts from back in 1921 miraculously re-appeared in Alfred Austrian's briefcase. Now, he used those to say my man was lying, and Joe always told how Austrian waved the pages in his face, how even the judge sat there with a smirk on his face.

But Mr. Cannon put old Alfred under oath, and asked if any reports from the detective agency hired by the Sox to turn up evidence against the eight players ever mentioned Joe Jackson. When the answer was "no", that piece of evidence was ignored by the court. I wondered, could the whole system of law in this country throw decency and evidence and truth out the window when the powerful and privileged geared up to crush their handpicked scapegoats?

Guess I got a pretty good idea how crazy things were getting when the lawyer's telegram arrived. "Ticket waiting at station. Get here fast. Ray." All hell was breaking loose and falling in on my man just like three years ago, and I was too late to help.

All the way to Milwaukee I must have asked myself a thousand times,

'If Joe hadn't been caught up in the Scandal, where would we be today? Would I be happy?' And as I drifted off to sleep now and again, I dreamed of the answers. Our kids running in the backyard and their dad pitching them baseballs so they could swing a sawed off bat and hit them into the beds of rose bushes he and I had planted. The two of us sitting on the front porch before he'd be going down to coach the boys in an afternoon game. Such as that, you know. But waking up, all I'd see was the landscape getting bleaker, more like real winters we remembered in Cleveland and Chicago, until the snow finally covered the ground. As far as you could see and feel, there was only snow and biting cold.

Sometimes you just have to wonder how many people got involved with this thing, what with testimonies reappearing just in time for the defense, a judge that was as much for hanging as any of them out in the old west, and Comiskey's lawyers that hightailed it soon as the trial was over because it was such a mockery of justice.

"The jury was just leaving for deliberations," Joe said as we drank black coffee with Mr. Cannon, soon as I could get settled in at the hotel and join them. "Then he called me up to the bench. I was smiling because I knowed how good a job Ray here had done, and I felt we won. Then Judge Gregory said, 'You are ordered arrested for perjury'.

"My jaw dropped and I couldn't even talk for a minute or two. Then one of the deputy sheriffs took my arm real gentle, like he really didn't want to follow the order, and led me out of the courtroom and down to the jail. Even had Hap Felsch arrested because he was a witness for me." Six o'clock it was when they put the cuffs on my man.

He reached over and touched my face, like he always knew when I was about to break down, and I watched my tears run down his fingers and onto the back of his hands. Things always look worse when you're worn out.

109

"Mrs. Jackson, I have no explanation for the proceedings." Mr. Cannon spoke quietly, but I could see he was trying to control his own rage. Seems he was a streetfighter in a gray pinstripe suit, and it was easy to see why Joe liked him so much.

"That jury was led clean out of the building, over to an annex, and once they entered the door was locked and guards posted. They never even knew Joe had been arrested. And why? Because when he spoke the truth tonight, what he said didn't agree with three-year-old coerced grand jury statements!" He brought his hand down hard on the table, spoons somersaulting through the air and clattering to the floor, heavy white coffee mugs bouncing against each other and the sugar bowl. We had quite an audience then, but all of the mid-westerners staring at us didn't slow him down one bit.

"Judge Gregory posed the question, 'Did the plaintiff unlawfully conspire with other members of the White Sox to lose any of the 1919 World Series games with Cincinnati?' And, Mrs. Jackson, you only thought you've seen men lose all sense of reason until you witnessed the judge's tirade at this jury who voted 11-1 in favor of your husband!"

In no uncertain terms Mr. Cannon told how the jury awarded more than $16,000 to my man, but the judge immediately reversed it. "'You failed to discharge your duty!' he yelled.' "Ray was up now, mimicking the way Gregory looked and sounded, and despite all the heartbreak, Joe and I had grins on our faces.

"'How you could answer the questions in the manner you have, the court cannot understand.' Hell, there wasn't but a few who couldn't understand, he and Comiskey's lawyers mostly. And me, I was guilty of sitting there, staring in total disbelief at what was going on around me.

"Foreman of the jury, a Mr. Sanderson, kind of quiet, tall and rather thin, he had more guts than all of us lawyers in that courtroom. Stood up slowly as the judge got louder and louder, stared at him until old Gregory paused, and said with simple dignity, 'We the jury felt we did our duty, based on the testimony and our common sense.' Judge Gregory didn't look his way again as he dismissed the proceedings."

It's like you're moving in and out of a dream, trying to figure where your sleepwalking ends and when you're wide awake. "How?" I finally managed to get out after taking a long drink of strong coffee and offering a few stares back at our audience, and oh yes, they glanced away real quick. "How could you and Joe come up with $5000 of bail money to have him out of jail only four hours later. Commie's lawyers weren't counting on that, I'm sure."

Mr. Cannon patted my hand as he stood to leave. "There are a few good men left in this world, Mrs. Jackson, like our friend Mr. Sanderson. Even among my lawyer brethren, an honest man can be found without a lantern. Joseph Padaway and George Dammon signed a real estate bond for Joe's release as soon as wind of the court proceedings hit the streets.

"You see, Milwaukee is not without its heroes, who believe that what has happened to Joe is wrong and are not afraid to show where they stand." He shook Joe's hand and offered us a ride back to the hotel.

"No, sir," Joe said, slapping his friend on the arm. A lot of admiration they shared for one another, that much was sure. "If it's okay with Missy here, I'd kind of like to walk back."

"Hovering around zero, folks," Ray cautioned as he turned and shook my hand as well.

"Mr. Cannon, Chicago taught us a great many things, not the least was how to survive cold, dark nights." Perhaps my words were a bit too crisp. And perhaps not, as he lifted my hand and kissed it gently.

"Ma'am, I can understand better now where your husband's strength is grounded. You are a good woman, and your husband a fine man. This battle is not over just yet. One thing, though. Be prepared for reporters by early morning." He was gone through the door, down the sidewalk, and disappearing into the darkness.

Oddest thing. Watching Mr. Cannon leave, I remembered that time Joe and Webb Cashion got locked up as a joke at the Greenville jail, and how that fun loving jaunt turned sour. Now I saw it in light of what had happened to Joe, spending two nights in jail for real, one during the Black Sox inquiry and now here in Milwaukee. Those are not the kinds of memories you exactly cherish.

We made our way back to the hotel, thankful for the heavy coats but not all that concerned about the wind and the cold. We walked in silence, Joe taking my right hand and, still holding it, putting both his and mine into his coat pocket. Back to him and me again, at least until morning.

The vultures arrived right on schedule, newspaper reporters all wanting first crack at Mrs. Joe Jackson.

"What did you feel about your husband being locked up the night before?"

"Was divorce an option?"

With Joe already gone to an early meeting with Mr. Cannon, I asked the floor maid to sit with me while the interview went on. Wasn't going to give them a chance to call me a liar, improper, or a southern hussy, no sir. Grace stayed with me the whole time, and I gave her a tip for it later.

They started off writing about how I looked: curly bobbed hair, long lashed blue eyes, and a trim girlish figure. About what I wore: a taffeta breakfast coat. About how I felt: mad, betrayed, hoodwinked. It had to be kind of obvious that I was standing by my man all the way.

"I've been in love with Joe Jackson since I was a little girl, and no charge of perjury will change me." They took a little step back, I think, after my tone of voice showed them I wasn't running scared of their like.

"It's almost sixteen years since we were married, and we've been in a lot of good and bad times together. But I never get tired of being married. Never wanted a divorce, and don't guess I ever will."

One deep breath to compose myself, and I was off again. "I believe you take your mate for better or worse, just like the vows say, and that means you stand by them." There was some small talk after I finished, kind of pleasant really, and I give the men credit. They printed it pretty much as it was said. Most mid-westerners were good and honest that way, and maybe I judged this group too quickly when they came in.

It didn't take more than a day or so to see where things were heading. Mr. Cannon, true to his word, went right back and filed an appeal, and he talked to us about it over breakfast the morning we were scheduled to head back to Savannah.

"It'll scare them, at least, because they expected all of us to turn tail and run. Now they see Jackson standing like a stone wall," we all got a nice laugh at that appropriate connection, "and I really don't think they have anywhere left to mount another attack. Except..."

"That baseball is powerful, and has got my man, above all the others, set up as the scapegoat in this, and it looks like they can't be stopped. Does that about sum it up, Mr. Cannon?" My voice, I am certain, betrayed my white-hot anger. "Well, you can go and tell baseball we'll be waiting. We aren't very hard to find."

"Damn, another stone wall." He looked at me with what I took as a good bit of admiration, too, took a drink of luke-warm coffee, and continued. "That about sums it up, yes, Mrs. Jackson. What I believe is that the White Sox will offer some means of settlement before the appeal has the chance to see the light of day. They cannot risk embarrassment like they just experienced, especially having two fine men like Padaway and Dammon stand up for Joe and basically tell our whole judicial system it was wrong."

"You're getting at something beyond all this, Ray," my man said just after finishing up his potatoes and eggs, and like so many times since we were married, I witnessed his keen mind cut straight to the heart. "We've pushed it about as far as it's going to go. That's right, ain't it?"

"It is for certain that I can tell the world, Mr. Jackson, that you are a perceptive gentleman. It will be in our best interests to accept the offer, for that in itself is a major victory. Others will know it, sooner or later. If truth were on their side, sir, they would not offer settlement." He called to the waitress for more coffee all around.

"We'll be thinking on it," Joe beat me to the punch, "and me and Katie will come up with the path what's best for us. You have been a real friend through this, all the way to calling and getting your lawyer buddies to post bond for me. No, I didn't know it for sure until just now when your eyes give you away, but I am touched that you can believe in me so deeply. I am grateful for that."

He turned to me and smiled. "We'll need to make that train, Missy." Joe reached across the table and offered his hand, and Mr. Cannon took it for a long moment. I could see tears welling up in his eyes, and after a bit he spoke in a voice cracking with emotion.

"You, sir, are the truest gentleman I have ever known. Mrs. Jackson, and Joe, take care of each other, for what you have together is so special in a world going crazy very fast. God bless you both."

This time it was us leaving Mr. Cannon sitting at the diner, and a few of the customers looked familiar from our last meal there. Hand-in-hand we headed out into the cold morning glittering in sunlight, heading home. Ray called out after us.

"You were only half right about the bond, Joe. I was going to ask the two of them for the money, but they handed me checks even before I had the chance. You have a lot of folks pulling hard for you." He smiled and waved goodbye.

Our train stopped in Cincinnati, and browsing through the paper I came across one of those *Ripley's Believe It Or Not* drawings. Joe always liked for me to read them to him, but my eyes about popped out when I saw that my man was the subject.

"Don't kid me now, Missy. There ain't no way Mr. Ripley would write about that."

"Here it is. Gives all of those statistics of yours for the Series, and finishes up by saying, 'No one with such numbers could be accused of throwing a game.' One thing about it, Joe Jackson, baseball's learning you just won't go away and be forgotten." Somehow, I wished I hadn't added that last little bit as we were pulling out and heading on toward home. What was almost a smile when I got through reading Ripley's piece turned into a far away look, and for the longest time he watched out the window as the countryside flew by us.

We settled back into our work routine at home, getting up and going in to run the store every day, Joe sometimes getting together with Slim and Jessup after work to throw and hit down at the field the Negro teams used, me answering mail about offers Joe was getting to play ball.

A couple of telegrams came on back-to-back days, one from Mr. Cannon.

"It was as expected. Offer of settlement came. Not as much as jury awarded, but still substantial for you. Recommend we accept. Wire reply as soon as possible. May God bless. Ray."

"The money will get us out of hock on the store, Missy, and that's what we hoped to gain from all this mess," Joe said as we were locking up one cold and rainy Thursday evening that February. Winter wind blew pretty hard off the ocean and you could taste the salt in your mouth. In his voice there wasn't anything but a matter-of-fact acceptance of what was, and an understanding that he was willing to live with that. Abiding by his wishes, I wired Mr. Cannon back that we'd accept.

The second one came a week later, and about shocked me to death. "From The Office of the American League" it said.

"Congratulations on beating Comiskey and his boys. Good luck. Ban Johnson."

When I read it to Joe, his reaction was not what I expected, because instead of a laugh, or even a smile, he walked out on the porch, lit a cigarette and leaned against one of the small rounded columns. He just stared out at the quiet street.

"Joe?" I didn't know what else to say, and I let the screen door shut quietly behind me. I stood there with my arm around him, heard his slow and measured breathing. "Getting to where you're holding too much inside, Mr. Jackson." He drew me tight against him. He always bore his afflictions with a quiet dignity.

"Don't you see, Missy? It's just that we beat Comiskey in this. Not because we were right. Not because it was something that should have been done. Not even because it could have been a way to crack the door and get back to the majors. No, it was because Mr. Johnson so disliked Comiskey that he would have cheered anyone beating him. Even me." He let go a deep sigh, not sadness exactly, more like this was something he just had to make the best of, too.

"We've got a life to get on with, girl," and he gave me one of his kisses that usually meant we were in for an evening of enjoying one another, body and soul. He picked me up and charged back to our bedroom. Always said I couldn't help but love that man.

We may have lacked for money a time or two in our lives, wondering whether we might be able to finish paying on a house or keeping the business in the black. But one thing I can promise is Joe Jackson never ran out of places to play baseball. And of course I got to see a whole lot of the country following him around, usually smaller towns and crossroad communities after the Scandal. Like Americus.

114

My man got a letter sometime last of May, dropped off at the store like most of our official correspondence, and with Americus Baseball Club on the envelope we opened it only to see when they wanted him. Beginning in July he'd be off again, and for $75 a week would be the manager, rightfielder, and clean-up hitter for the team. That was awfully good money, and we could use it. Games would be scheduled for Friday and Saturday afternoons, so it would do for me to leave out on the morning of the first game and make the 2 p.m. starting time.

There were folks in lots of places still running Joe into the ground, like dear Morgan Blake of the Atlanta paper.

"Benedict Arnold of Baseball shouldn't be allowed to sully the good name of the South Georgia League, and it would be just dandy for Albany, Bainbridge, Blakely, Dawson and Arlington to thumb their noses at Americus and vote them out of the league. Some crimes," he finished up, "just cannot be forgotten."

When I explained about Benedict Arnold, my man didn't like it one bit, and took real exception to feeling he was endangering the well being of the whole league.

"Hell, Missy," he threw back over his shoulder as he headed out the door, putting on a white Panama with a red band, "ain't doing nothing but making a tempest out of a teapot." He slammed the door, and I was glad for the bell ringing because it covered up my giggle at his mis-ordered words. Slim and Jessup were getting as big a kick as I was, though not a one of us would let on to him.

The first game was at old Barlow Park, down next to the Americus swimming pool, a rainy Friday afternoon, and six hundred curious souls showed up to see what old Joe could do to lift the spirits of a last place team and get them going. Some folks had read Blake's article, that was for sure, and they let old Benedict have it when he stepped on the field. Funny that when you hit a three bagger your first time up, and a double on your second, just how many people you can shut up.

"Give 'em Black Betsy, Joe!" one old graybeard yelled, sitting down in front of me. "Ain't lost nothing, I'm telling you!" he said to a young barefoot boy next to him. Found out later the old guy was Gilly Pervis, self-appointed head cheerleader for the local club. By the time the game ended, an Americus win by the way, most of the folks were shouting and stomping and running down on the field to shake his hand, slap him on the back, just wanting to be near the man.

"Ain't gonna be no last place team long," a young man said to his wife, his shoes covered with mud as he climbed back into the grandstand, her standing not too far from me. "Team's going to take off, wait and see, Julia. It'll do this town proud."

They played good ball in late summer, and around that league an appearance by Joe Jackson was treated as an event, not just a baseball game. I mean, there would be advertisements in the paper weeks ahead of time talking about the upcoming band concert and barbecue associated with the game. "This Is The Day You Young Married People Can Tell Your Children About!", one placard said, nailed up on every pole within the vicinity. Everybody had a revival fire in their hearts when the boys captured the second half flag and prepared to meet Albany for the title of the South Georgia League, and even old Blake down at the *Journal* was calling it Georgia's Little World Series.

Now there might have been only six hundred at the game the day we showed up, but we downright shook the foundations when two thousand plus roared in for the playoff opener in Americus. We won that one, and pretty soon we rode to four wins in six games for the championship. My man? A smooth .500 average with two out of the park, enough for a passing-of-the-hat through the stands adding up to about three weeks' worth of salary. Like everywhere he ever put on a uniform, Joe gave the paying customers a good show, and most folks weren't stingy about expressing their gratitude.

After celebrating with a big barbecue and dance right there on the infield the night after the clincher, there was talk of next year, Joe coming back and all, of course. He even talked with Mr. Ayers, manager of the Windsor Hotel there in town, about leasing his pool room. Everybody was so happy that evening, we just wanted it to go on forever. My man held me tight as we danced the night away, him near as elegant two-stepping as he was going from first to third on a single. He kissed me, and when folks caught us they cheered and laughed and whooped it up.

"Watch it there, Joseph! Such things been known to wreck a man's batting eye!"

"Or worse!" Lots of laughter floating up in the summer sky. "With a pretty woman like that, you may never get your mind back on the game!"

We strolled out just as the courthouse clock popped eleven thirty, and a big moon lit the way to the Windsor. But like a lot of things, this bit of heaven didn't last either, because the league didn't re-form for '24. 'Just not enough interest' was the party line, that the other teams were feeling that Americus, with Joe firmly in hand, couldn't be beat anyway. What was whispered was Landis was watching now, and anybody with major league hopes had better not be caught playing against an outlaw.

You couldn't ever say that life just dragged on for us, because we were always busy and into something. It could be the long hours at the store, or going down to watch the Savannah minor league club at Bolton Park. It was the same team Joe played for after the '08 disaster in Philly, and there were still folks who remembered him and came over to speak. And a like amount who remembered but wanted nothing to do with my man now. Hero and villain. It wasn't unusual to see us sitting by ourselves.

Now, when we went down to where Slim and Jessup played, we were welcomed right in.

"Social outcasts, by color and by deed," I heard Joe mutter to himself as we walked into the park one fine spring Saturday in '25, and I just looked at him and marveled at how much he saw in this old world.

"Me, I should of just run when Williams and Gandil came into my room, Missy," he said as we took our seats in the creaking grandstand, and he helped get the shawl around my shoulders since it was a mite cool.

"Me not being welcomed, hell, that's all my fault, but for these folks, being rejected is almost a birthright, ain't it? Fine people down here, just like Slim and Jessup and their families. Most times I'd rather be here, because the warmth is real. And," he smiled and kissed me, "food's a damn sight better than in them places we eat in the other side of town."

"Joe Jackson." It was Slim trotting up, and oh Lord a uniform rolled up under his arm, and Joe's cleats from the store in his hand. "We short one, and me and Jessup done said you'd be in left field for us. What say?"

"Slim, you ever heard my man say 'no' to playing this game?" I couldn't help but laugh, and Slim joined right in, followed by Jessup and the other guys who had run over. One more game, one more chance to thrill folks doing what he loved doing most. Jealous? Sometimes, but I always knew he was coming back home with me.

"No'm, but always like to make sure. Folks down here sure love to watch him play, and Miss Katie, they cheer for the man and not just for the hits. You got to know that."

"Thank you Slim, Jessup, and all you fellows," and wiped away a tear or two. "Dust coming off the infield," I offered.

"Yes'm. Like that sometimes." They smiled and went over to join Joe, who was coming out from under the grandstand, changed into those baggy gray flannels and ready to play. Slim, about the same height, late thirties and just as elegant in his movements, punched my man in the arm and they laughed. Jessup, pudgy and a good half a foot

117

shorter, about what you'd expect from a catcher, laughed as both men reached out and rubbed his bald head, their pre-game ritual for luck. You know, Slim and Jessup were the only folks who ever invited us to church all the while we were in Savannah? It was their Baptist church on Montgomery Street, and we went a few times. Enjoyed it, too.

We cheered, laughed, and ate away the afternoon, everything nigh on to perfect at the old field. Pretty soon we were all acting like kids at the county fair, you just couldn't help it if after watching my man, Slim, Jessup and the other guys probably having more fun than what was legal.

"Ain't that just about magic!" He whooped as we headed home, sweat and dirt mixing, to mark him with war paint from some secret tribe, initiated and accepted. "Just can't get no better than good folks and good baseball, now can you, Missy?" Sounded like a pistol shot when he slapped me on the behind and whooped again.

As we walked up toward where we lived, people started looking back over their shoulders and snickering after we passed them by. My man with cleats tied together and draped around his neck, walking in his sock feet with that baggy uniform still on, me carrying his rolled up clothes under my arm. One fine southern lady made a nasty comment or two about how we looked and where we'd probably been.

"Yas mahm," I mimicked her Savannah uppityness as best I could. "White trash Jacksons down amongst the coloreds again! Had a real fine time with folks who at least can be decent and welcome us in!" I turned and whirled away, grabbing my man's arm and skipping down the sidewalk. Even stopped and took my shoes and stockings off, so we truly were the shoeless Jacksons on a fine spring evening in the city of Savannah. The azaleas sure were pretty there in Forsyth Park, prettier than anything I remember from home.

"Joe Jackson," I said, putting my arms around his neck and kissing him as we reached the porch steps, "I'm all dusty and thirsty. Grab us two glasses of lemonade, light the big candle, and let's sit in the porch swing until midnight." There wasn't any need for words in those quiet hours. Sometimes when we didn't say anything was when we felt the closest to each other.

Once in a great while there would be something nice written about Joe in one of the big papers, and it would find a path to our local gossip sheets. One of the nicest, I think, was an interview George Ruth gave. On a slow Tuesday morning at the store I read it out loud at Slim's request. Him, Jessup, all of them there had schooling except Joe, but wouldn't one of them ever make him feel bad.

"Tell us 'bout Ruth, Miss Katie," Jessup said in that deep voice of his, "least I get to hear him talk about himself and old Joe. Him

hanging around Babe, and still letting Slim here outplay him in center!"
Slim and Joe laughed hardest of everyone, my man putting his friend in
a headlock and rubbing knuckles across his head.

"Picked the greatest hitter I ever saw to watch and study,"
George said, "and that was Joe Jackson. I watched his stance, how it
gave him a better chance to turn, a better chance to make the bat whistle
through the air because his hands and shoulders had more room to work
in."

"You mean Jackson of the Black Sox?" The sportswriter quoted
himself, typical of most of his breed, stirring it up, trying somehow to
make it his own sizzling story.

"Kid, that's Mr. Jackson to you, and me, and anyone who ever
played with or against him. Yeah, I know its supposed to be zipper lip
where he's concerned, according to the lords of the game, but I'm telling
you the truth. Have sense enough to listen to old Babe. Joe Jackson is
the greatest hitter I ever saw, and he's a fine man on top of that." When
you just hit 59 home runs in one season, you can say what you want, to
who you want, and Landis could stick it if he didn't like it.

There was more on the hitting theory and all, but there wasn't
any need to get into all of that. Jessup slapped Joe's arm and walked
back to the presser. My man, he was a bit embarrassed, and tried to
lighten things up.

"Probably had two hot dogs in one hand and a Co'Cola in the
other, don't you think, Missy?"

"Or two beers," Jessup bellowed, and that did it. When prim and
proper Dorothy Taylor walked in to pick up her dress blouses,
announced regally by the door bell, I'm sure she had no clue about all of
us in there laughing louder than was accustomed in proper Savannah.

Whether it was George Ruth, or some kid at either Bolton Park
or the Negro League field, Joe was always answering the call to teach
somebody how to hit, never asking for a thing in return.

The team down in Waycross, Georgia, wrote to him with an
offer to play and manage down there the next summer, and that meant
me heading down on weekends after closing up the store Friday
evenings. They had the money, being sponsored by the Atlantic Coast
Line Railroad Shop, and were willing to spring for two hundred a
month. It may sound like a lot of money, but remember, the boys were
playing about a hundred games that season all over south Georgia and
into Alabama and Mississippi. But they could probably have gotten him
for a lot less.

Joe, he went at it with the same enthusiasm as always, the little
boy who was never going to grow up, pulling out Black Betsy and
hitting what the stats say was .475, and playing a real slick outfield.

Must have done pretty good in his playing and managing, considering there was one stretch that summer when the guys put together a twenty eight game winning streak.

Did Mr. Jackson ever say one word about that except, "The boys is playing pretty good, Missy. Too bad you can't see us every day"? No, not one bit. And I learned about it only when Slim read it in the paper before I did. Think he had been alerted by some of his kin down that way how good a ball Waycross was playing. It took a kindred spirit to put it into words for me.

"He ain't meaning to slight nobody, Miss Katie." His friend offered this in a quiet way that reminded me of Joe sometimes. "It's the game what matters, not wins or losses or batting average. That's why he ain't never gonna get old. None of us do who play baseball just for the love of being on that field. And when you can find one or two others who feel the same way, like me and him and Jessup there, well, you just settle for being blessed double."

By the time the stock market crashed and Black Monday slammed down on us, our valuables were in a tin box locked in a trunk in the bedroom. Business acquaintances in Savannah warned us to get the money out of the bank, and we listened. It was a good decision. We managed to keep the store going through the first two years of the Great Depression, and our folks had regular work.

Toward the end of 1931, though, there was another path that we had to take and find out where it led. What drove the decision was family, the day a letter came from his brother David, and you understand it was the first and last piece of written communication we ever had from the Jacksons.

"We been trying to figure what's got into Ma, and can't nobody offer no more than she's a bit tetched, wore out from life being too hard on her. Since you has been outta baseball Joe, something's different in her mind. Like it is all filled up with the bad things what's been done to her eldest." You could see where he touched the pencil lead to his tongue and pressed it back to the paper to start up writing again, the gray smudges pretty close to coloring over the words.

"What she does is walk the streets from Brandon to uptown, wandering now and then down Pendleton and out around Augusta Road, stopping folks and asking them to sign a paper she keeps in her apron pocket to get her boy back into the major leagues. There ain't no paper, Joe. She's just tired of having her child being tore apart by nasty folks. Come home quick as you can."

My man sat in one of the ladderback kitchen chairs, leaning forward with those big hands hanging between his knees. Didn't bother to wipe the tears that ran down his face and splattered on the tile floor. He made no sound, no sniff nor moan, it was just the tears that wouldn't stop. I went to him, knelt there, cradled his head against my shoulder, lifted it after a bit so I could press my cheek to his, our tears mixing together.

"I'm needed, Katie. It's time to go home." My man spent near his whole life disguised as an illiterate no-nothing linthead, and few would recognize the sensitive person sitting there with me.

That simple. The few words set us on a hectic two weeks of getting things settled, looking for a buyer for the store, present staff guaranteed to be kept on, of course, at present salary. We said a brief goodbye to Lefty and Lyria Williams, much longer ones to Slim and Jessup and their families. Gave notice on the rented house, and closed the bank account, putting our cash carefully in a tin box. And a million other things. It was late December when we pulled out one morning headed to Greenville, our car packed full and our other stuff to follow, shipped on the train.

What was it like? Don't know that Joe and I ever talked about how it felt pulling back into the town where we grew up, where it ceased to be home after the trial in '21, where now we didn't know if we were to be wayfaring outcasts or welcomed homefolk. Coming in, we saw that the Mansion House had been torn down and replaced by the slick Poinsett Hotel.

"We'll head there for supper one night soon, Missy. Take Mama. But you know, that corner of Main and Court just ain't going to be the same without the old Mansion."

A bunch of new stuff was added since we'd been gone. Two new theaters, the Carolina and Rivoli, Belk-Kirkpatrick Department Store, and the Woodside Office Building. Heard they had their first Christmas parade a few years back, with Santa Claus coming in on a special train lit with red torches.

The mule drawn trolleys had given way to their electric-powered cousins, and moved all over downtown. And get this, the townies even included the lintheads in all the go-getting 1920's progressive thinking, with the Belt North and Belt South lines running out into all the mill villages. These good economic times before the Crash seemed a million years gone.

"Don't seem to mind us coming in more than the one day they used to allow. Remember Mill Workers Day, Missy? Give the townies warning not to come in until the trash was gone. Guess they need all the money they can scrape up now." We drove on down and turned onto Academy and moved toward Brandon.

He was called back to take over for his ma, to be the one to make decisions for the family and guide them with a wisdom borne of suffering, like she did all those long years. Joe felt bad because he hadn't been right there all along.

"Damn, Katie," he had said our last night in Savannah, and repeated now, "it was my place! And I let 'em down. Maybe Mama wouldn't be like this now...", and then he was quiet.

Miss Martha would have more good days now that her Joe was back close.

Chapter 7

"Mama?"

They were sitting together on the porch steps, mother and son. The sound of shuttles clacking in new Draper E-models moved through the open windows of the mill and floated out, settling with the darkness over the village.

"You remember when we'd walk through the field there, up to the Wynn's house so's you could talk to Katie's ma, you and her sharing alls sorts of secrets, girl talk and such, while us kids played? You remember, don't you, Mama?"

Miss Martha Ann reached over and patted her eldest son's hand, touched his hair just like back then, and smiled. "'Course, Joe. And you wasn't playing near as much as you was watching out after all them other chaps. You was always good like that."

They sat quietly, a lot longer than I ever could to be sure, 'til one of them got a notion to speak. Wasn't ever much idle chatter in the Jackson household, the legacy left by Joe's pa. It was comforting, I think, to Miss Martha Ann and Joe, when over in the evening she'd lean her head against his shoulder and softly hum "Just As I Am" or "Standing on the Promises" like she did years before. Sometimes she fell asleep there.

"Come on," I whispered from inside the screen door, and held it open while he picked up his frail ma and carried her inside, laying her across her bed, slipping the shoes off and pulling the sheet to her waist. Then we stood there kind of like I pictured us doing for our own children, making sure she was asleep before we tiptoed off to our bedroom.

There were several evenings like that, some with me and Jerry, David, Hortense, and Gertrude all there, but mostly it was just the two of them. Each trying to ease the pain of the other's soul. Trying, I thought, but never quite able to pull it off. Sometimes Joe would be missing her, and find her later on the village streets, or up on Washington or Pendleton with her piece of paper, asking folks to sign up and support her boy.

"Innocent he's always been," she would say in a loud voice to everyone in the general area. "A mama knows that 'bout her boy's own heart. Raised him to be God-fearing and truthful. Can't see he turned out no different."

Joe, he'd put his arms out and gather her to him, and off they'd walk back home. Most folks felt kind of sorry for her and him, but occasionally some real jerk would toss an insult or two, and that hurt Joe. Only saw him go after one of them.

"Bitch who raised a thief!"

My man was out of shape, and the big talker outran him, or the sheriff's boys would have been seeing to a killing, I think.

Three things came about as we got settled back in Greenville, all tied close together. The worsening Depression, union organizing, and textile league baseball. At first we were busy with Miss Martha Ann and getting settled in, so wasn't time to get to a bank and open an account for the money we earned in Savannah. We didn't jump into business right then, not with short time at the mill, cotton prices that were lower than what the farmers paid for seed, and families who couldn't afford food and clothes, much less paying rent. And we saw the foreclosures on stores and homes as bankers called in their markers.

"If we was all in it together, Missy, it would be different." We walked through town one Sunday evening, looking at empty storefronts, or the last sticks of personal belongings thrown out on the sidewalk. "But it ain't that way. All you got to do is look at some of those bankers and other merchants getting fat off other people's misery. Even some of the supers at the mills are acting the same way."

He shook his head, and we walked on in silence, me able to feel his big heart aching at what he saw. With that bunch of nickels and dimes he took to carrying, Joe was an easy mark for apple vendors, dirty faced kids, or mamas with kids holding hands and strung out like a kite tail. We made it back home later, his pockets empty, his heart eased, and a little bit of a smile on his face.

"Lord knows we got more than we need, thanking you for your good sense, too." And I reached up to kiss him tenderly on the lips and hug him, safe and quiet, wrapped in those big arms. Old Joseph Jefferson made a difference to folks, don't let anyone ever tell you different.

Toughest thing I ever saw him go through, more even than being kicked out of baseball, was happening up on an eviction of a family from one of the mill houses on a neighboring village. He had been over there to talk with them about playing some ball. He stepped between the mill representative and the family.

"Union lover," he heard somebody say, and you could see anger starting to well up.

"And what the hell difference does that make when you get a passel of young'uns out here in the rain with nowhere to go." He picked up the littlest girl and held her close, wiping tears and a runny nose, wrapping her dirty, cold feet inside his coat.

"Faded daisies on a soiled old blue dress, reminded me of one you wore when you was just a chap, Missy, and I couldn't leave." Soft hearted and generous to a fault, it was a wonder the loveable old fool didn't catch his death a cold sometimes.

"Don't matter, family goes same as the papa who got fired." The big fellow spoke, hauling out another chair held together by baling wire. "Super says he ain't been doing his job, and got to move on."

"Where?" The daddy said as he and his wife came out, toting the few clothes they could pack and keep dry for them and the girls. They looked at Joe. The other three girls had found their way into his heart too, one each holding to a leg, the oldest one clenching his hand.

"Obliged to you," said the man. "They're good girls, and know when to trust. You got four good votes."

"This union stuff I ain't got no understanding of, but figure its mostly like politics. But if a man supports what gives him a better chance, can't be no crime, nor no harm." Joe always spoke straight.

The big man walked by, made a move to push the oldest girl into the muddy street, but saw my man's jaw stiffen and decided not to test one of those big hands balling into a fist. See, Joe never demanded respect, but he could earn it real quickly the way he handled things.

"Still got to go. Can't live on the village with no job in the mill." Big Boy locked the front door and walked away, giving my man no chance to talk this thing out.

"Hear there's work over in Anderson County, and maybe I can keep my mouth shut," the young man offered a feeble smile. "Wife's got an older sister here in town, maybe my girls can stay 'til I walk over and find a job, maybe in Belton or Honea Path." Shook my man's hand with a strong grip, and the girls hugged him and cried as they walked off.

"You take this," Joe said and shoved seven crumpled dollar bills into the father's hands. "It ain't much for you two and them babies. Some apple trees down behind our house, pretty much the way you going to be walking. We'll get you a sack full, and see what Mama cooked today. It'll give you a good start on that journey you're going to take.

"Besides," and he picked up the littlest one again, his newest special friend, "it'll give me time to talk to the princess here while we walk." She snuggled right into the spot I'd broken in over the years, the little hollow on his right shoulder, and went to sleep as we made it back to Brandon.

"I'll see you and pay you back proper one day, sir, proper and all," and you knew he meant it. Never asked my man's name, but you could tell he knew about Shoeless Joe. Folks never talked to him who did not receive encouragement in return.

"Mills are funny things," my man said to me as that family walked off to a world of insecurity. "Good man runs it, it's a good place even in these bad times. There's food, work spread around equal and short time held down much as it can be, and folks pay the rent when they're able. Ain't no organizer going to find much there to work with.

"Now, greedy man gets up to the super's job, and it's hell to pay for everybody, like I saw today. Union trouble, everybody suspicious of each other, plain bad."

"You already turned down playing over there before you met up with these folks, didn't you? Knew you didn't want any part." I smiled, laid my head on that special shoulder and closed my eyes. "Joe Jackson, did I ever tell you how much I love you?"

He kissed my forehead and then lifted my chin so that our lips met.

"Yes'm." He smiled. We sat awhile longer on the porch, listening to the easy rain splash in the puddles in the yard, two hearts with love enough for the whole world, but the world around us too hateful to listen.

Even with the bad times, folks still came to the ballparks to watch textile league baseball, maybe more to forget life that had grown hard and unforgiving. Good place to catch up on the news, and if you were young and thinking about being in love it was a wonderful courting place. Heck, Joe and me proved that years ago. In '32 the Spinners, semi-pro and outside organized baseball, came calling to ask for Joe's services the last month or so of the season. Almost a quarter of a century since he'd last played for them, so I guess we really were back home now. Getting ready to leave for a game one day, Joe introduced me around.

"Missy, you remember old Sammy Fayonsky, him and me used to go at it in mill ball. And Mr. Wakefield here, he's business manager now—shoot, they got as sophisticated 'bout baseball here in Greenville as up in the American League."

"Nice to see you again, Sammy, and to make your acquaintance, Mr. Wakefield." I filled in after Joe stopped, knowing there wasn't an American League for him any more. We boarded the train, heading to Newberry for an exhibition against their All-Stars. Trains leaving from that old station were always special, ever since I was a little girl and Papa used to bring me to watch them.

Back then they were headed to or from Chicago, New York, Boston or New Orleans, the engines filling the air with cinders that filtered down like so much black sleet that crunched underfoot. The grand entrance tower looked almost like a church steeple, and the waiting room was lined with long polished benches. A slight breeze

126

moved in and out through the open windows, offering folks respite from the heat.

Crowds gathered when vaudeville troupes or baseball teams arrived in town, and everybody who was anybody in Greenville loved to be seen all decked out in their best Sunday go-to-meeting duds. Barefoot kids might hustle a nickel running an errand, carrying a bag, or fetching a bottle of mineral water for a thirsty stranger. What I still miss most are the gas lamps lit in the evenings, the soft glow one of the most comforting things I've ever known.

"This is fun, Papa," I started to say, my mind a good many years distant, but caught myself before anything slipped out, I think. Leastways none of the men gave me any sideways glances.

Somehow before we got there to play ball, my man managed to lose his uniform, glove, and two pairs of shoes. More than one pair meant less chances at blisters, you understand, like way back when in Anderson. Hero for the Spinners that day was Horace Long, who walloped three home runs for the win, while Joe was still learning to time his swing to the lively ball.

He sported the number "five" on his jersey now, first time he ever had one, and he felt pretty special being identified on the field. They had a Homecoming Day for him early in August and the fans gave him a real warm greeting. But if you looked close, you saw that the mayor and most other city folks stayed away from where my man was. Some things are never going to change, no matter what.

"Katie Jackson!" I turned, but before I could get a look the ump grabbed me, picked me clean up and whirled me around, much to the delight of onlookers who laughed and clapped as my blue dress fluttered in the manmade breeze.

"Walter Barbare, I ought to..." but could only hug him more, this old National Leaguer and mill player. He and Joe Jackson went back a long way.

"What in the world are you doing here today?" I managed to get out between the gasping and laughing.

"Chief umpire in the South Atlantic League now that my playing days are over, but I got today off to come up here and be with Joe. Ain't no way I'd miss something as special as this homecoming thing."

"Don't let him sucker you too much with his gab, Missy," my man said, jogging by on his way to batting practice. "Ballplayer's eyes start to go, he becomes an umpire." He laughed as Walt bellowed, "You're outta here, Jackson!" and made out to kick him before he got past. It was all great fun, their antics, the crowd cheering, and the sounds of the game. You couldn't help but notice, though, how quiet it got when

127

Joe stepped into the batter's box. Like God was fixing to add to His creation with a little extra work on the eighth day.

"Always been like that, Katie, from when he was a stringbean at Brandon, all through his years in the majors. I can remember an old pitcher, Ernie Shore when he was with the Red Sox, saying that he could be blindfolded over in the Boston dugout and still tell when it was Joe hitting a baseball.

"'Course," and Walt turned away and launched a stream of tobacco juice in the general direction of the backstop, "his choice of words was bit a more colorful than what I offered you. Pitchers get sensitive when their best stuff gets tattooed against centerfield fences." He smiled and excused himself to go over and meet the managers.

Walt was right. Folks crowded into those splinter-rich bleachers running up both baselines, and others sat behind the thin safety net of a chicken wire backstop twenty feet behind the plate. The cleats dug easy down into the loosened dirt in the batter's box, and old Joe took a solid stance. Low and outside was where the pitch started, and Betsy whipped out after that fastball. What a sound of solid contact, the feel I knew moving up through his hands and into his forearms. It was smooth, like ice cream sliding over your hot lips before surprising your tongue.

One after the other—curves, changes, spitters, emery—and every location in the strike zone. Betsy was a restless rattler, striking out at everything horsehide. Those balls rattled the weathered boards of that outfield fence, starting in right and working all the way back around to left. The guy standing over by the dugout, waiting to hit next, didn't seem in any hurry to move Joe away from the plate. Don't think the folks would have been too happy if he did.

All at once I just gave a belly laugh, because I knew this was as close to heaven as my man could get and not be shaking the hand of St. Peter. No hurt, no people talking down their noses at an old linthead, no wondering what might have been. Here, time just kind of froze like a trickle of water in January. Swish and crack, again and again, a rhythm like a shuttle thrown across a loom making just about a perfect weave.

A few minutes? An hour? I can't begin to know where the time went, but all at once folks just stood and started cheering, like it was one voice starting from inside the heart. And when it came out it was loud and filled with love and caring. Oh, you may think I'm making all this up, but if there was ever magic, it was out there on those ballfields right next to the cotton mills. There wasn't any close cut grass like we saw in New York or St. Louis or Philadelphia, but never was anything more beautiful.

'Look at his smile,' I remember thinking. You could just about hear his laughter. The catcher walked off, leaving his mask there on the ground, and went and leaned up against the backstop. Heck, you get the ball around the plate with Mr. Jackson primed and ready to hit, about the most useless position on the field was catcher. He wasn't going to have a thing to do except sit and figure how far that ball was flying and how hard it was about to hit the fence. Had the best seat in the house, too.

"Ty Cobb would call that the science of hitting," Walt laughed as he walked back to get the game started. "Joe just says it's hitting hell outta the ball. Jeez!" Last one he hit cracked as loud off the fence as it did off the bat. Walt's expletives were lost as the cheering got louder and louder.

"Joe! Joe! Joe!" It was like Gabriel calling home the chosen, the sweetest words ever spoken.

The last six weeks of that season, I think the Spinners played everywhere they could get a game. Union, Anderson, even Gastonia and Forest City up in North Carolina. That last town, Joe hit a long homer and his good friend Fletcher Heath two of them for a 6-5 win in fourteen innings. It was in the papers, and folks came to the park excited to see Shoeless Joe play ball.

He'd give them a show, like at Drayton Mill over in Spartanburg. Made a clean steal of second with a perfect hook slide, so the frisky old fellow took off for third on the next pitch and got nailed by two steps. He and that third baseman got up laughing, everybody clapping and hollering in the stands, and that forty-two year old chubby kid walked to the dugout with the biggest grin on his face and blood dripping down his chin from a busted lip. It was as good as Philadelphia, Cleveland, or Chicago ever had to offer us. Maybe better.

We opened another business just after the season ended, something a little different for us. From the Savannah Valet Service with two shops, J & K Worldwide Enterprises now included the Barbecue Cabin, a modest restaurant where we we'd be providing drive-up service. Even the restaurant had a baseball connection.

See, it was on Augusta Road and kind of between the old Graham Field, where Joe played with the Near Leaguers back before we got married, and the new Graham Field, home to the new edition of the Spinners. I was hoping somebody would give him a chance to ease away from the playing part of ball, and maybe be a coach or batting instructor for one of the mill teams. I was afraid he was getting too old.

Not hardly.

Folks down at Poe Mill came over to talk with him one day when we were working to get the Cabin ready to open for dinner. They huddled over at a corner table over cups of coffee, and came up with a deal for the season. Took about twenty minutes, then they were gone.

"Pretty good money, Missy," my man offered, "and I think I'm going to take it. Give me a chance to manage the club, too, and I think I'd like that, working with the younger players to make 'em better hitters and stuff." His belly was about to pop buttons off his white shirt, and I patted him there, then just looked at him and gave him a hug.

"Money, Joe Jackson, has nothing to do with you and baseball! They could have given you two pieces of bubble gum and a uniform and you'd have been there. I got the oldest chap in Greenville County, and I'll be chasing him to another park this coming season."

Wiped my hands on my apron, grabbed a broom, and swatted him square in the behind when he wasn't looking. "Now get to work! Got to do your chores before you go off to play. That's what I'm supposed to say, isn't it?"

I laughed as he wrapped his arms around me and squeezed tight, cried when he kissed me gentle on the lips, answered his quiet "I love you" with the same words deep from the heart, and thanked God there wasn't ever a man in my life but him.

The tears weren't ones of being lonely or bitter. No, they were of a different sort, knowing that life had changed, and us along with it. We both knew, and probably had for years, that we were not going to be blessed with children. I don't think anybody understood how our hearts ached, and though we loved each other so much, there was an emptiness inside that wasn't ever going to be filled.

"Maybe it's selfish, Missy, but I always thought having a little girl looking like you would be just about perfect." He took a long drag from his Piedmont cigarette, exhaled, and followed with a sip of coffee. It was a rainy Tuesday morning, and the November wind was kicking up, probably a slack day for the eating crowd. "Yeah, that would be an answer to my fondest dream." And he covered my hands with his there on the table top.

"I wanted you to have a ballplaying little boy," I spoke quietly, working hard to control the tears just waiting to bust through. "To be proud of, to teach and watch him become as great as his daddy. And I wondered if wanting you for myself all those years sort of...you know, ruined that for us. I'm so sorry, Joe."

That was it, and the waterworks gushed forth, splashing off the table, keeping up at times with the steady drizzle outside. Joe always said I cried silently, no sobs or dame type stuff, just tears so hot he wondered they didn't scald my cheeks.

"Lord, Missy, couldn't anything better than you ever happen to me. Besides," he pulled me into his lap and cradled me there, "we may not chase each other round the bed anymore, but our moments together seem..."

"Sweeter, more tender. Like we share more." I finished for him.

"Yeah. Wouldn't take growing old with you for nothing, except maybe putting the 'Closed' sign in the window, and spending the rest of the day at home with you." And folks said we'd give up anything to make a buck. Well, what they didn't know...

We stopped by Cunningham's Cafe down on Court Street, taking advantage of our declared day-off celebration to partake of their wonderful blue plate special: three vegetables, a meat, dessert, and coffee for a quarter. Joe savored his meatloaf, turnip greens, colored butter beans and mashed potatoes. My tastes ran to country style steak, mashed potatoes, green beans, and cream corn. We did manage to agree on the apple pie with ice cream for the final course.

Joe took over and managed the Ravens down at Poe, acting the big kid, working with his players and offering them what he learned, packing in the crowds because everybody knew my man was going to swat a few at batting practice. That, according to the placards tacked up to every pole and tree and flat surface all over the mill village the team happened to be visiting that day, was worth "Twice the Price" anybody was having to pay to get in.

To keep things interesting, Joe occasionally showed up as a pinch hitter, like he did over in Anderson one hot July day at Appleton Mill. His single tied the score and the Ravens won in the ninth. There was a little boy that day went down to the well with an oak bucket, brought back water and charged a penny for a big tin ladle of water. "Cold delight," we all praised his drink, the metal tapping against our teeth, and you could even hear yourself breathe as you got every drop of the offering.

Up at Ware Shoals a month or so later we were trying to get the game in before thunderstorms swept over Riegel Field, and Andy Hawthorne got two strikes on Joe so quick he about spun my man's cap around. Wasn't even worrying about the men on first and third. On an inside pitch, Joe leaned in at the last second, his jersey sleeves flapping in the gusty wind. Catcher lost the ball in all that movement and the winning run crossed the plate on the passed ball, because we held them scoreless in the ninth.

"Must be a thousand ways to win a ballgame, Missy." He winked as he walked by carrying the equipment bag slung across his broad shoulders, heading for the flatbed company truck and a bumpy ride back up to Greenville. We had to get back and take the supper shift at the Cabin.

Something real interesting started happening that summer, and you'd have missed it if you weren't a baseball fan. Every now and then on the sports page an old ballplayer who knew Joe up in the majors would be talking about some part of my man's game, like Walt Barbare said Ernie Shore did. Old Scoop Latimer down at the *News* got these items in the paper, and I started collecting them in the scrapbook that I kept under the counter at the restaurant. Folks asked to see it pretty regular, and if they made a comment I'd letter it real neat next to the clipping.

"Wonder what Landis thinks, now that people proved they ain't forgot Joe?" This fellow was right about the Judge being mad as hell, and I had to smile because couldn't anything the commissioner did make folks forget my man.

"Joe Jackson hit the ball harder than any man that ever played in the big leagues, and I don't mean except Babe Ruth." That was Big Ed Walsh, fine pitcher and a teammate for a couple of years, I remember Joe saying. And next to the item was "Pa, does that make Mr. Jackson better than the Babe? How come he still ain't playing?" Never did get to hear what the father's reply was to his boy.

"Made me feel stupid," Jimmy Dykes of the A's confessed. "When he hit the ball to you at second base, it came roaring, the only bouncing line drive I ever saw, and it could eat your hand off."

"Serves him right being on the team that treated Joe so bad" was next to it. Littlest sister Gertrude would, I think, have been happy to see a one-handed Philadelphia infielder.

"It was a pleasure to see him swing, and when he hit the ball there was a ring to it that pleased the ear," was the way Mr. Eddie Collins put it, and I wrote what new friend Horace Long had to say back to him.

"If Eddie cared so much for him, why didn't he take up for Joe at the trial?" I read that to Joe, and there was a lot of pain in his face, acknowledging Horace's glimpse of truth and yet still wanting to believe only the best of Mr. Collins.

It could be Ty Cobb saying that any time he thought he was a good hitter, he'd stop and look at Joe. Or maybe Walter Johnson talking about giving my man the best he had before he ran over to back up third base. Or even Branch Rickey sermonizing that if God ever permitted birth to a natural hitter, it was Joe. It could even be Joe himself, kidding Waite Hoyt about being ordered to walk him, then slamming a pitch way low and inside for a homer in '20.

See, it was all this talking from ballplayers about Joe, coming forward after fifteen years of silence, defying the Commissioner who tried to control their every move. They spoke the truth about one of their own, and no one could stop them.

I pulled out the scrapbook one evening as we were cleaning up, getting ready to go home after a busy day, looked at my man and said,

"It's time for one more letter to the Commissioner's office. With all of what's being said, we can't miss the opportunity, Joe, can't let this show of support slip by. People out there still care about you, about what baseball's done to you."

"One last letter," he said quietly, crushing out his cigarette in the seashell ashtray. "No matter what happens, if he condemns me to hell or don't even answer, there will be no more exchange of pleasantries between Kennesaw Mountain Landis and Joe Jackson. But we'll make it a good one, Missy."

My man was right on the mark, one of his perfect one-hop throws. The letter came back with a two sentence reply, ending with, "Judge Landis will not rule on an issue of reinstatement."

And signed by a secretary. That was all the answer, all the dignity allowed to a man who had just poured out his heart and saw it get stomped on and sent back.

We were sitting around Miss Martha Ann's kitchen table the next day and read the letter together. Everybody had something to say. David and Jerry spoke along the line of tarring and feathering the idiot, Hortense and Gertrude insisted that it was time to get a high-powered lawyer, like the Clarence Darrow fellow who defended the Scopes boy up in Tennessee few years back.

"Can't say as I like the idea of coming from monkeys, but that lawyer won him the right to teach science right along with the Bible, and I bet he could win for Joe and get him back in baseball." Gertie folded her hands on the table, bowed her head and took a big breath. I smiled at this girl who just said more than is normal for her in an entire day, reached over and patted her shoulder.

Joe looked around at all of us.

"I was innocent of any wrongdoing in the Series, and God is my judge, not Landis nor anybody else who's seeing fit to keep me out of baseball. There ain't going to be no more lawyers, no more appeals, no more letters. Because I ain't never begged for nothing and I ain't starting now. The matter is closed." He got up and started for the door, heading back down to the Barbecue Cabin in the bright winter sunshine.

There was scandal after scandal going on in major league baseball that sometimes made the paper, and sometimes we heard it from folks inside the game who continued to remember us. Landis would contradict himself before you could turn around, ignoring nose-on-your-face affronts with the likes of Hal Chase, even Cobb and Speaker, then pound away on my man and Buck Weaver. But Joe never wavered from what he said to the Jackson clan that day, only adding, "If they want me, they can send for me."

Seems like when these things came up and sapped our strength, we'd be off for a change of scenery for a while, and baseball was always providing that convenient outlet. On a couple of warm February days my man was out on the field at Brandon playing some softball, a game just getting started, and Joe kidded that, "Me and my buddies are old, and the bigger ball is a mite easier to see and hit." Then he'd start laughing and catch me in a playful bear hug.

Two gentlemen came down there with a business proposition for him, and Mr. Jackson agreed to an offer by Henry and Roger Huff to manage and occasionally play for the Royal Cords of Winnsboro Mill. And that meant we'd be going topsy-turvy again. We put the Barbecue Cabin up for sale, and because we'd run it right, kept it up, and turned a right nice profit, it was bought pretty quick by Julius "Cap" Capri, nice Italian gentleman who did well by his purchase.

Then Joe was up and gone again, the biggest kid in the world doing what he loved best. I stuck around Greenville, running the dry cleaning store and looking around for other ideas that we might be able to do well by when the season was over, and traveling a couple of times a week to catch the Cords in action, either in Winnsboro or around here.

One game in June up here, Dunean killed them 14-7, and maybe for the first time I wondered if the game had passed him by. Joe put himself in as a pinch hitter in the ninth, giving in to the crowd who wanted to see that perfect swing. None of them got the chance. First ball came whistling, way too far inside, and I watched him unable to move fast enough to even begin getting out of the way. Scared that kid Suddeth so bad, thinking he must have busted every rib on my man's right side, but there was a good deal of padding on that frame now. It was a point not lost on Pete Frye when he tried to get his skipper off the ground and wound up getting pulled on top of him, to the thunderous laughter of Joe, the fans and every ballplayer on the field. Just wasn't anybody like him, who could make any day in the bleachers just like the best Christmas ever.

In '38 Joe got a chance to do something he'd waited for, and that was being on the same team with one of his brothers. Jerry was a pretty good pitcher at Woodside Mill, and my man got hired as manager.

"Fat and fifty," he laughed and told me one day, "and loving the life I've been given." He didn't pencil his name into the line-up much anymore, content now to offer encouragement to the younger guys from the safety of the third base coach's box.

Never said this to him, but for as good a player as he was, I just don't think he was cut out for that managing thing. Lord, he couldn't hurt one of those boys by being nasty to them, never jumped on them or rode them or anything, and his teams kind of did like Mr. Mack's

134

Athletics in later years. They played hard for the old man, but the fire just wasn't lit. Joe, he was as generous, loving and caring to them as he was to the kids who used to tag along and wait for him to buy ice cream for the gang.

One of the things I remember most is how youngsters used to congregate outside the liquor store, because Joe wouldn't allow them inside. But they'd stand out there, little white and black boys, and an occasional girl who I swear after watching her throw a ball was every bit as good as the boys she competed with, and call in, "Miss Katie, could Joe come out and play?"

How much I laugh at that now, knowing that their ideas of Joe were right on target. He was just like Peter Pan, never growing up, so at home down one on the vacant lot near the store, finding a rock or board or piece of paper to serve as a base, with a manhole cover for home plate. Then I just listened as the afternoon hours passed, the shouts of excitement never fading, the mounting score of 50 to 35 and then 72 to 68 accurately kept as sundown crept up on them.

"Just one more inning, Joe!" The squealing voices were all I needed to know what Joe's answer had been, the very same one he gave day after day and years on end. He never wanted to disappoint, feeling I think the specter of 1919 and what the kids might have thought of him even if it wasn't true. Sometimes those marathon quadruple headers ended only by streetlight, coupled with parental threats floating through the evening air, "Get home, young man, or else!"

But no one ever left without a Co'Cola or ice cream readily available next door at Bolt's Drug Store. Ask any of them who worked there over the years and they'll tell you how Joe would buy for everyone, including himself, and then walk the kids home, the group getting smaller and smaller as the streets around West Greenville were traveled.

Then my man would walk back home alone, passing through the patterns laid by shadows curling through the dim light, the magic of Pan unsustainable after nightfall. It was then I'd glimpse the old man he'd become, taking on those ghosts that would never let him go. And I'd cry for him then, but was careful never to let him see my tears.

We heard little official word from inside the game, little enough until there was talk of Greenville getting a minor league team, and of Joe being brought back as manager. Then guess how quick things got into motion?

"Sorry, Mr. Jackson, but we'll be bringing down one of the guys from the big league club. They want to make sure we maintain continuity on the team, develop the kids to fit right in."

135

Break the code and it said, "Landis stands by the guilty verdict, and the sentence of lifetime banishment from organized baseball, and there is nothing we can do about it." To believe in Joe Jackson was to set yourself against the righteous many, the righteous powerful many, and sometimes folks had to back off for their own good. Joe and I understood that. If getting hit by that pitched ball up at Dunean didn't show us the game really had passed us by, let me tell you plain and clear that getting shunned like this sure did. And I lived to see something I never thought I would, and didn't want to. Baseball finally hurt my man so bad he walked away.

We saw a lot of things changing around us in the textile leagues. Appleton's women's baseball team over in Anderson and one at Poe here in Greenville played games, and even night baseball came to the mill hill.

"More folks will come, Katie girl, but it won't ever be the same no more. What's the game without green grass and sunny days and skies so blue it hurts to look up?" It was almost a prayer for the dead he offered.

We were invited over to Greer for opening day of the King Cotton League, '37 or '38, sometime in there, when Pelzer and Greer Mill had at it. What folks came to see was the reunion of that fine Victor team Joe left Brandon for, way back when. Mayor Lanford made the first pitch to Joe and my man missed and laughed, laughed more when his old buddy Bob Patrick made two swings and misses at one easy pitch. Funny that the two of them at home plate were the only ones able to take an active part in the game.

I reached up and brushed back the hair blown across my face, and my fingers ran along my cheek, feeling the start of wrinkles where smooth skin once was. Used to I didn't worry about sweaters on opening day, but the wind seemed to bite extra hard this year, and I was glad I remembered to bring one.

My man went on and did another show in '39, agreeing to bat in the third inning for both the Eastern and Western Carolina Textile League All Stars. They were mill folks, and he wasn't about to let them down, and you should have heard three thousand voices screaming his name when he rifled out doubles both times up. Would have been inside-the-park jobs in the old days, so you can guess how hard he hit the ball to make it all the way to second base in his condition. Got replaced by a pinch runner real quick.

"Somehow this old gut just didn't manage to hurt the swing none," he laughed and reached over the grandstand wall and hugged me. He was breathing heavy. "It was a long way, old girl." I held on tight to those big, loving hands, afraid to let go.

136

Chapter 8

It took another war to finally bring the hard times of the '30's to an end, though Greenville had done okay after about '35 and most of the mills ran a pretty full schedule. The way the lintheads kept playing baseball, you'd of thought there wasn't a thing wrong, but maybe that's how we kept our sanity during those years.

By this time we'd run Joe Jackson's Liquor Store down on Pendleton Street for awhile. Another real original name, don't you think? It was something we enjoyed, meeting the people from all parts of the city, and when you sell liquor and wine in the Bible Belt, there's bound to be some interesting times. Like when we heard one of the local Baptist churches, where we had gone a few times during the years, needed an organ for their sanctuary.

"We'll be happy to buy one for the church, Pastor," Joe said to him one morning after everybody cleared out for Sunday dinner. "It's something me and Katie talked about this past week, and we'd like to do it for the church long as there's no big deal made of it." He chose his words carefully, the character of a quiet man showing through.

All that man could say as he turned away after a limp handshake was "I'll take it up with the deacons." Dear Lord, here was the crucifixion one more time, put-on righteous indignation from proper society saying, "How can we accept a gift so tainted, from people who own a liquor store? From one with suspicion upon him for misdeeds!" And here I am getting madder than I've been in a long time, and that may be saying a lot.

"Come on, Joe," I said, loud enough to be heard half a block away. "We'll not be selling out the back door of our store to half of his flock, including most of the deacons, like we've been doing! Let the damn saints parade through the front door to obtain their holy spirits!"

Thank the Lord my anger was so hot it boiled away all the tears before they could sneak out and run down my face. We walked arm in arm back home. Safer to travel in pairs, we always believed.

The store was a nice enough place, next to Bolt's Drug Store, and safe enough to keep Black Betsy there. Old hickory bat with the beat up barrel and warped handle with "Ferguson" etched down near the knob, and sometimes my man would have her out taking some practice swings right in front of the counter. Fifteen minutes at a time, as if he ever forgot how. It was just holding on for old time's sake, I knew, but just when you think you got it figured out, wrong again.

Early in April of '41 Joe ignored Dr. Clatworthy's orders about playing ball and agreed to do an exhibition game over at Dunean for under-nourished kids. Understand, for Joe Jackson the words "no" and "kids" were never meant to be used together. So here's my slightly overweight husband, who hasn't seen pitching in several years, and has never swung a bat in a night game, batting twice.

Same old sure eye. Same old powerful swing. Same old results. Two terrific line drives to right center slamming way up on that high score board a good 425 feet out. Right with the rest of the crowd, I jumped up and screamed like crazy for both of those monster shots, and listened as the cheers rang down on him.

"Hooray, Joe, ain't lost a thing! Best there ever was," said a fellow about my man's age.

"Go, Mr. Jackson! My daddy told the whole truth 'bout Shoeless Joe, that ain't nobody could crack a ball like you!" one tow-headed little boy screamed, clutching the hand of his father, and everybody clapped and yelled even louder for that one.

I was praying nothing bad would happen, that he would stand on second and soak up all the love and goodness flowing to him right then. That for a moment or two the years would melt away and his pure love for the game would be all that anyone would ever remember. This time, I didn't catch the tears before they started.

"Missy, you love this near as much as me, I do believe," he said as we walked to the car after the game was over, the last ones to leave the field as usual except for the groundskeeper who finally turned the lights off. Joe hugged me close.

"Love it as much as you do," I said, then reached up and kissed him. "Love you more, though." And us there in the moonlight smooching like two teenagers. God said "I love you" to him on many occasions, and I think that night was one of them.

Even times as perfect as this could get ruined, and not long after the *News* retold stories being printed up around New York bashing Joe and running him down. When I read them in the store one morning, he showed little feeling whatever at words like "ignorant cotton mill boy with nothing but lint where his brain ought to be."

"That was alright with me," Joe said to Gene Estes and Wayman Garren, who had stopped by. My man stood up, straightened his tie and went on. "I was able to fool a whole bunch of pitchers and managers that way."

Some stories never made it to the big papers, like when I answered the door one Saturday evening in the summer of '42. About dropped over in a dead faint.

"Mr. Lajoie! How long...how did you find...please excuse my lack of manners and come in." Not exactly the perfect hostess, huh?

"It is so good of you to come. Joe, get in here!" And the two of them hugged and slapped each other on the back.

"Put on some coffee, Missy, while I clean away the supper dishes and I'll call Scoop and get him over. He'll get a big kick out of meeting my friend the Frenchman, best second baseman I ever saw, and a great manager to play for." That pretty much set the tone for the evening, Joe and Larry and Scoop and me drinking coffee and talking about long ago days in the big leagues.

"Show you how special Joe Jackson was in Cleveland," Larry offered, grabbing a second or third cup of coffee. Always liked it strong, I remembered. "They put up a screen ninety feet high above the right field fence to keep this man from knocking so many balls into the street! And still couldn't stop him, not altogether."

One story after another. Addie Joss, Ray Chapman, the Cobb-Lajoie batting title chase, the Cobb-Jackson batting title chase, and poor old Scoop writing fast as he could on his scratch pad, going "Uh huh. Uh huh." And not doing a thing to stop either one of them because the stories might not get rolling again. Not bad for a brainless mill worker to be looked up to by one of the best men ever to play the game. Sometimes Joe's life was like a good book, story after story just drawing you into his very heart.

We didn't keep a radio in the store, except maybe during World Series time, but one of our early morning rituals was going over the newspaper together, finding out things that were happening, war news especially, and all that it was doing to the lives of those around us. We'd hear that Joe Dimaggio, Bob Feller, Hank Greenberg, Ted Williams and other big leaguers were joining up, and of course every day there would be several more stars in the windows close to home as families remembered sons and husbands heading overseas. Doesn't take a lot of people to change the world, just a committed few willing to make the necessary sacrifices.

When people came into the store, and a lot of them hung around to talk about their young men going off to war, we'd listen. Folks said we were a good couple that way, never volunteering much about ourselves, but giving a sympathetic ear whenever we could. We always tried to care about our neighbors and family.

Ned Clay over at Bolt's always said I was friendly and courteous, but a bit too quiet. "You walk in here pretty as any girl in all of Greenville," young Ned would flatter me, "business woman dressed snappy, proud, walking with your shoulders back and never in a hurry, always purposeful. But most of your conversations are made up of 'good morning' and 'thank you'." He brought me my usual BLT and Coke for lunch, while I twirled ever so slightly from side to side on one of the counter stools.

"Miss Katie, how'd that easy going old ballplayer over there ever hold onto a prize peach like you all these years? Reckon there might be a version of you out there not taken yet?" And he could have added 'younger', but Ned was too nice for anything like that.

"Thank you, young man," I said, paying and leaving him a tip. I did pat his hand as he reached for the money, something out of the ordinary for me, but with all the war news...well, Joe and I couldn't bear to think of bad things happening to any of the West Greenville kids.

Something else was going on those early years of the war, and I never understood the timing, but my man started to get a bunch of letters from fans of all ages, from all over the country. It was like when the stories started showing up in the papers about ten years ago, ballplayers remembering Joe and talking about him so favorably after nobody saying anything for years. Then, of a sudden everybody wanted to talk and remember all over again, for no particular reason. Joe, he loved it every time we sat down to read the letters, and pretty soon he'd memorized most of them.

The easy ones to get by were the autograph seeker type, the kind where the first sentence gave it all away. "No collection would ever be complete without the greatest hitter of all time included."

So I'd laugh and call out, "Toss me a ball, man o' mine." And I'd sign it 'With Regards, Joe Jackson'. Got lots of folks out there with collections still incomplete, and Joe always chided me about my mischievous streak.

Some folks never asked for anything, just sent along a special memory that Joe was part of.

"I was lucky enough to see your last game in Chicago and I'll not soon forget what a wonderful player you were."

Some of them came addressed "Joe Jackson, Baseball Player, Greenville SC". Two or three were just "Shoeless Joe, Greenville SC." All of them were delivered.

People must have thought we were sitting around with nothing to do, and Joe could put together a pretty good comedy routine, acting out some of the offers people sent along, about like old Al Schacht would have done.

"Dear Old Joe," he'd croak, "how about keeping racing pigeons as a sport to keep you occupied? I'll furnish you da boids free. Say de woid and youse got 'em." Ned and Gene and the guys from Bolt's would stop over, bring us a malted or Co'Cola, and take in the show.

But when it was a child there was no kidding around, and my man would take in every word like it was the sweetest thing he ever tasted. That was when he was most alive, listening while those young'uns poured their hearts out.

140

"My daddy says you were the greatest hitter ever in baseball, and he seen you break in with Connie Mack, then Cleveland, then the White Sox with that black bat of yours." Eleven year old Peggy from up in Massachusetts was quite a fan.

"I met Mr. Mack at the Brunswick Hotel in Boston once," she went on, "and asked him who the greatest hitter was. He said Mr. Cobb for speed and a quick mind, Mr. Ruth for raw power, and Mr. Jackson as the most natural." Now Joe, he'd smile at that, but when she closed with "Please answer and thank you very much and God bless you Mr. Jackson", well that did him in. He sat there quietly for minutes on end, a tear or two winding down his cheeks, and thoughts so deep I wouldn't dare intrude.

"Missy," he said just above a whisper, "please give me a pen. Got to take a minute or two to draw my name for her on this ball. It'll make her happy, I think." Probably did, but oh child not as much as you made him, and I hope your life was as blessed as you made my man's that day.

Kids. When they were around, the sting of not having any of our own was taken away, and thankfully they stayed around most of the time. Grown-ups, they could do most anything, make fun of us, ignore us, insult us, take advantage of us, poison the world a little bit more with their evil intentions, and usually there was a group around willing to do all of them. Joe, he'd smile and go on about his business. All because the kids loved him like he was big brother and daddy all rolled into one.

Here's one you might enjoy, Landis coming uncorked when J. Taylor Spinks allowed an article on Joe to run in *The Sporting News* sometime around '43. The commissioner tried to declare my man's memory illegal, forbidding one and all from bringing it up again. Old J. Taylor basically told Mountain Man where to stick it, too, when the good judge threatened action against the magazine for printing the truth. The thought of anything positive being said about my man usually sent Landis into fits of apoplexy, especially when players talked about Jackson in the same breath with Ruth and Cobb. Somehow, though, old Kenesaw couldn't keep folks from believing in Joe.

"Ain't never a failure 'til you give up," Daddy used to say. Maybe I should add "or until people give up on you," which, thank the Good Lord, they never did on Joe.

"When them young'uns come calling, Missy, the whole crazy world goes away - the bad memories of the game, this damned war, they chase all the bad away."

And out the door he'd be heading, featured guest at the sandlot or in the street or at the field in one of the mill villages. All kids. Lintheads and Negroes and townies, they all thrilled to the sight of him, and they shut their yaps if one group was putting another one down, knowing he wouldn't stand for it. The black kids that came running from over Queens Avenue or Union School, lintheads from Monaghan or Poe or any mill hill you might have heard of, well off kids from the fancy neighborhoods up on Augusta Street, he taught all of them catching and hitting and running. And respect and caring for each other.

"All right, gentlemen! Let's play some baseball!" He'd let out a big yell, walk to the mound in the white Panama hat, white shirt with sleeves rolled up to the elbow, tie flapping in the breeze, glove in one hand and Black Betsy over his other shoulder 'til he tossed her to the kid blessed to be first up. Back trouser pocket bulged with a bag of penny candies ready for when the game was over, just rewards for his band of merry men.

"He freely gave kindness, encouragement, and though he didn't know it, inspiration to those of us whose daddies were overseas, or those of us who were just scared of growing up in a torn up world," one of them said to me years later. "Wasn't no way to ever forget how great a man he was."

"Mrs. Jackson!" They'd be at the store next day right after school, standing at the front door entrance because Joe wouldn't allow them inside. Made that clear to each one of them and each of their parents.

"Can Joe come out and play?" How may times was it I walked down to where they were playing and had to be the old meanie? Standing with arms folded meant supper was ready and the game, for that day at least, was over. Some people are always getting ready to live, but never get around to doing it. My man, he never missed a beat.

Had real nice neighbors up on East Whitner, the Rogers, and their kids got to be special to us. Joe played catch with the boy in the yard, and the little girl came in the house where we'd play make-up duets on the pump organ. And there was Co'Cola and vanilla ice cream for those occasions, a staple of the Jackson household.

"Why do you get so quiet like this sometimes, Mrs. Jackson, and just look at me funny?" Betsy Ann asked that when I got lost in her laughter and enjoyment of life. Hope she'd never have that empty space in her heart that even the love of a great man was not able to fill.

When he turned fifty-four, I think, all the kids brought gifts up to the house and gave their big buddy a surprise party. Couple of their mamas carted up, you guessed it, cake and ice cream and Co'Cola. Little guys saved up and bought Joe a replica of Black Betsy.

"It ain't the same," both of the Thompson boys yapped out at the same time, "but maybe Mrs. Jackson will let you bring it inside 'cause it's smaller and you could keep it next to your chair." Now I only saw

Joe cry one time up 'til then, I mean really cry, and that was when they buried his ma, but he came awful close as those kids stood around and patted his shoulder and shook his hand.

Haven't spoken much about the war, but we felt it like everyone else, the boys gone, the horror when a uniformed soldier got out of a U.S. Army car and walked slowly to the door with news that a young man wasn't coming back. The blackouts and rationing and all that stuff we endured as well. In '44 something happened to make it real personal. Joe always told it a lot better than I ever could.

"Some things what gets on an old ballplayer's mind, and stay there, ain't what you'd be expecting. No, most times it ain't about games or hard hits or long throws from the outfield, but about somebody who was feeling worse off than you.

"Got a letter from a fellow that year, the war was still going strong though things had turned in favor of the Allies. This soldier, think his name was Jack, had a buddy in an army hospital up in Michigan. Charlie had lost both legs in the Battle of the Bulge. After fighting for his country, he was now fighting for his life. In a conversation between these two guys, Charlie remembered how his pa had taken him to see the White Sox play a lifetime ago, and told Jack that old Joe had been his idol. And wasn't no changing that, didn't matter about 1919 or nothing else.

"Jack thought a letter from me might do Charlie some good. So after Katie finished reading, I kind of told her what I'd like to say in return, nothing all that special, just that we was all proud of what he'd done, and how it would be more honest to say that folks like him was the real heroes to folks like me. Then I said I'd pray for him to get better.

"When she finished jotting all that down, I asked the old girl to pass me the letter, took out a folded paper from my shirt pocket, and pressed it flat on the counter so's I could draw my name at the bottom of the page. Did the same thing with a baseball that was laying in the drawer. Packaged them up and got them off in the mail that cold afternoon.

"The kid was kind of like me in a way. In the wrong place at the wrong time, even when you thought you were doing the right thing. Him getting nearly blown up, me going to the shipyards back in World War I 'cause my pa had died and I had to support my ma, brothers and sisters. Him at death's door and me being chased by ghosts. Folks made it out I was a coward and run from service on the battlefield when there wasn't no other choice for me. And folks probably thinking Charlie was a hero when all he'd like to be doing was hauling in some fly balls somewhere on a field up in Michigan in springtime.

"Later, me and Katie got two Christmas cards from up in Michigan, and she read to me what they said. The first was from Jack, and he said I'd brought a lot of happiness to an unlucky kid, that he watched that boy with no legs laugh over the gift of the baseball and the card from his idol, Shoeless Joe. Said he couldn't keep back the tears. Then he said, 'May God go with you, Joe Jackson, as he does with the great.'

"The second one was from Charlie's brother, who let us know that the boy was much improved, and said my letter had raised his spirits. He closed with, 'To Charles and all of us you will always remain the immortal Shoeless Joe Jackson. God bless you, Joe. We have never lost faith in you.' Now couldn't no man be worthy of what them two said about me, especially when all I did was write to a kid who was hurt and talk some baseball with him. Shoot, I enjoyed that as much as Charlie did. That kid was the hero, and the real gentlemen were Jack and Charlie's brother, who stuck by him during them hard times. Seems they had a little of the cotton mill people in them—sticking by those they love and believe in.

"Think I cried a little when Katie finished reading them cards to me. I do remember walking round to the cash register, giving her a big hug, wishing her a Merry Christmas, and planting a big old kiss smack on the lips. Did that even though the mistletoe was across the room, hanging from the ceiling just inside the front door."

Joe, he just never could realize how much he was loved.

Just before the war ended, Commissioner Landis died. Scoop, Jimmy Thompson, Red Canup over in Anderson, them and several other sports writers came by to talk about it, speculate really that maybe it was time to slap baseball back, make them say Shoeless Joe Jackson got a raw deal, and Buck Weaver, and others along the way, too. Got to admit I wasn't all that opposed to such a course of action. I squeezed Joe's hand as I sat there beside him that Sunday afternoon and looked into his eyes for some flicker of fire that would let me know the battle was on.

"Ain't nothing more needs to be said, because nothing's changed since Judge Landis passed away. I'd a done gone out of my mind if there had been, brooding all these years, living in regret." He ran his right hand over his bald head, stood up and took a couple of steps to the window. Our Chihuahua Skippy hopped to the floor as Joe got up and sat there patiently beside the couch until his master's lap was ready to occupy again.

"I gave the game all I had, and no man or woman can truthfully judge me otherwise. My conscience is clear. Bitterness, it can eat you alive, and I ain't never allowed that to happen. Let it rest." He stared over at the vacant lot where those kids would be gathering soon, running up the steps to get the Big Kid so the game could start.

"Joe..." I looked toward Jimmy, who was speaking as he got up to leave, but only that one sound came out. The man was fighting back a lot of emotion.

"Don't think God made any better than you, not for what you've been through and how you held your head high." Scoop and Red filed on out after offering pleasant good evenings. They all shook hands with Joe there on the little front porch.

"He knows I'm innocent," Joe said real quiet, and he put his arm around my waist. "That's all that matters with me."

We went down to the railway station a few months later to pay our last respects to President Roosevelt, standing quiet as the funeral train passed through on its way from Warm Springs to D.C. I expected tears from the young'uns and the women, but I never saw so many grown men cry. Must have been half of Greenville there, lintheads and townies, black and white, kings and thieves, but all of us united, at least for a little while, in our grief.

Probably just a notion in an old woman's head, but after what we went through as a family when Joe's nephew McDavid died, I remembered things we did almost like taking pictures with a camera. I'd watch what was going on with my man, noticing more without really trying to, holding on to all the little details that made moments so special. Always figured it was too bad we learn how to do that only after we get old, but the Good Lord probably blesses us that way to make up for slower steps and creaking bones and such.

On a slow day he'd sit in the store and play a game or two of checkers with friends who stopped by, and those intense eyes of his didn't miss a thing. It was just like when he'd step up to the plate and maybe get fooled one time by a pitcher, but know for certain it would never happen again. I'd be at the register doing the counting so the books would stay straight, and Joe, he'd look up and say to anyone in the store, "I've been blessed with having a good banker—Miss Katie Wynn. 'Cause handing money to her was just like putting it in the bank." But when it came to numbers and how much people owed, Joe Jackson was sharp as a tack. Maybe reading and writing were things he couldn't do, but keeping figures in his head, he was a regular mathematician.

My man had a reputation for being tight with a dollar, and you'll get a kick out of this. Workers had taken up the flooring in the store. We were having it replaced because it just couldn't be patched any more. Gene Estes happened to step in from over at Bolt's, saw Joe standing there in the middle of old tile and sub flooring, and couldn't resist.

"Hey, Mr. Jackson, you drop a quarter?"

Joe, he didn't miss a beat. Lit up a Piedmont cigarette, strongest thing I ever smelled, and shot back, "Uh, uh. Nickel."

Young Estes, he was in the drugstore the day Joe needed witnesses to the signing of his will.

"Can you spare a few minutes for an old man to get his affairs square so Miss Pretty there behind you will get all the riches I done stashed away?" He laughed and put a big hand on the young man's shoulder.

"Yes, sir, I will, but you ain't so old if you can hold onto a good looking woman like Miss Katie all these years. Look at how you still run around that new Packard ya'll bought from Mr. Bridges and open the door for your bride. Give her a nice diamond ring and all, too. Shoot, figure ya'll going to be lovebirds another twenty years at least." Estes matched his laugh.

Joe "drew" his name, a word he used when he meant copying. He'd look real hard at how I wrote it out, then would move his hand very slow to fashion each letter. Looks shaky, doesn't it? And no wonder, it took him almost five minutes to complete the signature. Folks sometimes said we never had any close friends, and maybe that's right, but everybody Joe helped, or who helped him, like Estes being witness along with Scoop Latimer and Jimmy Thompson, they were all friends to us. Don't think anybody who knew him didn't fit into his circle.

And he could get about anybody on his side, let me tell you. We were sitting at a Brandon game in early May, one of the perfect days your mind conjures up when you think of spring, bit of a cool breeze and a high sky. Not unusual for us to be there, since we were given season passes to the Western Carolina Textile League, the Greenville Spinners, and the Asheville Tourists. That last one, Joe loved to go to the mountains and take in a late season tussle now and again.

I noticed Joe Anders, young boy from around Easley Joe took under his wing and worked with on his hitting. Tall, good looking, and had a girl named Katie, too. They reminded me a lot of me and my man years upon years ago. He walked over to the Woodside dugout to chat with Floyd Giebell, once a pitcher for Detroit and now managing the Wolves. Both of them looked in my man's direction, Giebell shook his head, and then Anders started walking over. I couldn't believe what I was hearing when he got to where we was sitting.

"Joe, I'd like you to pinch hit for me. Back's kind of tender just now, and Mr. Giebell said he ain't got no problem. 'Sides," and his quiet, courteous voice might just move the heart of an angel to do his bidding, "good crowd, and the folks going to remember this moment for a long time." He signaled over to Wayman Garren in the announcer's booth.

146

"Ladies and gents, you have got the treat of a lifetime, because pinch hitting for Anders tonight is Jackson. As in Joe, Shoeless Joe!" The words took a minute to float down over the bleachers, but when they did, goodness what yelling and whooping, nigh on to a World Series game.

"Set up and pay attention, all of you!" Mr. Garren said, and I sat there smiling, taking in the joy that had descended upon that ballpark, then I glanced over at my man.

"Joe?" He hadn't moved, hadn't said a word. Just staring. And when he finally did speak, his voice seemed like it was coming from a thousand miles away.

"Always knew there would be a last time, but didn't figure on my insides coming apart." He took my hand, raised it gently and kissed it, like the first time when I was just a little girl there at that same ballpark, and I knew we had begun courting.

"We'll give 'em something to remember the Jacksons by."

He climbed down and made his way to the Brandon dugout, emptied his pockets, rolled up the shirtsleeves and proceeded to swing three bats like they were toothpicks. Then he looked up and smiled at me as he walked to the on deck circle. Hadn't even taken off his Panama.

"Whatever God starts in a life, He finds a way to finish it in fine fashion," I remember thinking.

The kid on the mound may have heard of Jackson, but he still came inside with a good fastball, to back my man off the plate and show him who owned it. A mistake, but you can't fault the kid because Walter Johnson and Chief Bender and Hod Eller and a bunch of others tried it over the years in the majors. The bat resting so easy on Joe's shoulder moved quick as lightning and met the ball with a sound echoing all through that park. The ball didn't even think about stopping 'til it smashed into the top of the centerfield fence, some 420 feet away. The only thing stopped was my heart.

Sounds. I was aware of the cheering before I finally remembered to breathe again, and if the very angels at heaven's gate sing any sweeter, well I can't imagine it. Young Anders had arranged to run for Joe, and he had no trouble circling the bases, coming home and putting one arm around his old buddy, pumping the other fist in the air as the crowd shouted.

"Jackson! Jackson! Jackson!" until they were just about hoarse. Told you we never had dull moments at the ball fields.

We made some visits, and had some visitors now and then. Being more particular about his health, Joe had pretty regular appointments with Dr. Clatworthy, and I can't believe what he brought back one evening. A prescription allowing "one piece of fatback per

147

week", written out on one of those prescription forms you see hanging up at the counter over at Bolt's. Truth be known, he'd been giving me a fit about this, so Joe's old pal was going to let him get just a taste. Good for remembering, but not too much to hurt him.

Spring of '47, two gentlemen pulled up in a black Buick sedan and came in the store. It didn't take folks too long to gather around one of them, because it was Ty Cobb, and there wasn't anything shy about the Peach playing to a crowd. I met him and his buddy at the front door.

"Miss Katie, good to see you again, and your beauty's outlasted the years." Nice to hear, though I didn't believe much of it at all. Well, maybe a little, or at least wanted to. Crowd kept getting bigger, as more folks from Bolt's and from all up and down the street came running in to see the Hall of Famer.

"This gentleman..." and a voice from the back finished, "Is Grantland Rice, one of the finest sportswriters it was my pleasure to meet." Joe made his way out to where we stood. That way he knew the kids he wouldn't allow in the store would get to see the immortal Cobb and the smooth talking Granny.

"Rice told me he was stationed up at Paris Mountain, Camp Sevier I think it was, during World War I," Cobb said, and reached for Joe's hand.

"A wonder I survived the flu in '17. I remember lots of boys who didn't." Rice turned toward my man. "A long time, Joe," and stuck out his hand in greeting as well. My man took it and smiled warmly, though Rice had never been particularly kind in the things he chose to write about Shoeless. Not real nasty, just not very supportive, I guess is what I'm trying to say.

"We've been down to Augusta to watch the golf tournament Mr. Jones puts on, and nothing would do but that Ty drive to Greenville to speak with Joe Jackson and," he jerked his thumb toward the door, "to purchase a fifth or two of your finest bourbon." Rice's voice was swallowed up by Cobb's.

"Greatest natural hitter," we heard as Ty was warming up the crowd. "Your man here put us all to shame. Me, Ruth, Hornsby, day-in and day-out none of us could sustain the pure rhythm of his swing, the flow of power, the sheer beauty of it all."

He sounded about like one of those revival preachers, always coming through and putting the spirit into a Saturday night tent meeting. And when he paused, I couldn't help but jump in and say what I was thinking.

"And all that beauty and power and rhythm moved from his swing into the way he lives his life." Said it sweet and smiled. Didn't

148

want to offend Ty, though I would have if he tried to take my man to task. He and Rice both smiled, and it was Granny who spoke.

"That much, Mrs. Jackson, is obvious by the youngsters gathered around here just now. Oh, they may be here to ogle at Mr. Cobb, but my guess is they aren't strangers at all to this location, or to you and your husband."

"Joe plays ball with us near ever day, sir, over there in the vacant lot, or sometimes down at Brandon. Don't you, Joe? Don't he Miss Katie?" That young Burgess boy spoke for all the kids there.

"Now why doesn't that surprise me?" Cobb laughed and slapped Joe's shoulders with his hands. "Loved the game more than all the rest of us put together, Granny," and I swear I heard Peach's voice crack. "Cherished it deeper than any of us ever knew how to do." Sunset came on and the baseball talk quieted as boys went home to supper, and men back to work that stayed unfinished these last couple of hours.

The travelers purchased their bourbon, the best brand we had, and headed back down the road toward Royston, Georgia, for some hunting before Granny got back on the beat. It was odd watching the three men there in the fading light, glimpsing how much more empty the world would be when my man, Peach, and Granny were gone. Whether you liked them or not, giving credit to their greatness was not an option.

"Phone, Joe." It was a few days later just before lunch.

"Yeah, remember you when we was both in the majors. Ottaray, yeah, know where you are. Be nice to see you. We'll talk.

"Old ballplayer passing through, wanted me to join him for dinner down at the hotel. I'll be back around one or so." He gave me one of his sweet kisses right on the lips, and oh that man could still make my heart flutter.

I was, however, surprised the way he came back home. A squad car pulled up, and my man got out with the sheriff. When they got inside, Homer Bearden told how my man busted up a con game, though Joe held up his hand when the man's name was about to be called.

"Wouldn't do any good, Sheriff. You go ahead and hunt and catch him, but don't butcher his honor 'til you know the whole story and who else might be involved." Man would have walked across the street to keep from sneezing on a caterpillar, afraid he'd give it a cold.

"This gentleman, then," he smiled at Joe and kind of shook his head like he couldn't believe it either, "was going to stage a poker game to bilk money out of...". He let the name of the wealthy man go unsaid. "He was going to get Joe to introduce the two of them. After listening awhile, Mr. J. here remembered he should call you regarding a bank transaction ya'll needed to take care of, and excused himself to go to the phone in the lobby."

"Had 'em call the sheriff while I went back to talk with the fellow, keep him there, but..."

"Wasn't no keeping him, since he was done gone, back through the kitchen, one of the waiters said," the sheriff interrupted. "Turned and trotted off toward the train station at a pretty fast clip. Two trains he could of jumped, since I don't think he would of stopped to buy a ticket, so we'll get 'em checked."

My man, heart attack and all, honorary deputy and undercover man. Elliott Ness would have been proud. Me, I was amazed one more time at how he couldn't stand to see anybody get hurt. Not the uppity townie who was about get taken, and not even the con man, at least not until he had a chance to do some explaining.

"Thank you, Mr. Jackson," the lawman said on his way out. "Always a pleasure to do business with an honest man." Old linthead never knew any other way to be. His own heart formed his true honor, not what others thought.

Still got occasional letters, too. Not from fans and autograph hounds this time, but from friends way back. There were even a couple from Hercules Television Productions asking about doing a movie on my man's life. They requested rights and all, but nothing ever came from it. A shame, too, because it would have made a great story.

Two of the letters were from Bill Steen, a teammate when we were up in Cleveland, a so-so pitcher, but a good man. Then there was a wonderful one from Hod Eller, three pages handwritten, talking about the '19 Series and the Scandal. You know Hod won two of the Reds' five games, and oh he went on and on about plays he remembered and funny things that happened. Started right in with John Philip Sousa leading the band in "The Star Spangled Banner" during the opening festivities at Redland Field.

"Think it was Weaver who lined a ball just in the corner of our dugout that first game in Cincinnati, and rattled pretty hot down where Mo Rath was sitting. Said he and Joe played together down in New Orleans when they were in the minors, but you wouldn't of known him after he swallowed a big wad of tobacco while dodging Weaver's rope. Green as a frog in a minute or two, he hightailed it back to the dressing room to throw up. Can't imagine these fellows today being as rough and tumble as us." Joe was laughing by the time I finished reading.

"There's more," I said.

"Joe, I watched every move you made in those eight games, and know you played your heart out, all on the level. Ballplayers know that lots better than sportswriters ever could. Maybe now people will start

150

talking about it with Landis dead and all. Time's long past for this thing to get set right."

"Good to hear from the old guys," was all he said as he answered the call of another customer at the counter. He was polite and carried on idle chatter for a few minutes, but his gaze was thirty years distant.

I remember a special evening over at Brandon, a time like I've never seen before or since. Drizzly night in mid-July, cool for that time of year, and here came nearly three thousand folks to attend ceremonies honoring a man, my man, older now and no longer in the best of health.

Wayman Garren, PA announcer for the Braves all through the '40's, introduced him in that smooth talking way as "Shoeless Joe, Pride of Brandon." Folks got up and cheered and stomped and clapped. Minute after minute the sound just got louder and louder, swirling around the outfield wall from right to left, then rushing down one foul line to home plate and darting back out along the other. Repeated again and again. Five, ten minutes, maybe fifteen, and what can you do but sit and cry?

Which is what I did, and very well, thank you. Just before Miss Martha Ann died, she said she was watching her whole life dance across a movie screen, all the good and all the bad mixed in. What I was seeing now was our life together, me and Joe, from being young'uns, to marrying, us running half undressed one night on that Delaware beach because we couldn't wait to get to our bungalow and enjoy one another's love. New Orleans and Savannah, Cleveland and Chicago. Dear heaven, what a journey we had, him and me. He read my thoughts.

"Wouldn't change a thing, Missy," he said, leaning over to kiss me, and the clapping and cheering just got louder and louder. He never let go of my hand, just kept it cradled in that big meathook of his. Apart from one another, I don't believe we ever really amounted to all that much, but together I think we had everything.

"Kind of a big birthday party, ain't it?" Sixty-one and looking older to all these folks who moved around us, I'm sure, but he was always my handsome young man. Oh yes, my passion still stirred for him, fine hunk of ballplayer that he was.

Lots of gifts they brought along, too.

Suits of clothes. "Ain't no linthead going to wear that except to church or get buried in."

Rocking chair. "Look here how comfortable, Missy." He sat there behind home plate as townies and lintheads alike made their feelings known about Shoeless Joe Jackson. We moved back up in the grandstand as the rain and wind picked up a little bit.

151

What surprised us most, as always, were letters from people we didn't know, talking about a man they'd never met, telling him how much his ballplaying meant to them. No, more than baseball. They were granting him the full measure of a distinguished gentleman.

The boys from Hobby's Garage up in Kentucky, saying they remembered driving to Cooperstown and telling folks there wasn't a reason to have a Hall of Fame if Joe Jackson wasn't there.

One from folks in a retirement home in Florida, encouraging my man to always swing for the fences.

A Brooklyn mother talked about her son, whose dream was to hit a baseball as hard as Shoeless Joe and send screaming blue darters down the streets of Flatbush.

A court clerk up in Pennsylvania who said there wasn't a finer man alive than Joe, and all you had to do was look at how he handled the bad times with dignity.

A farmer in Alabama wondered if they were kin, having the same last name and all.

Man in Connecticut asked what he could do to help clear the good name of Shoeless Joe.

"Glad it's Wayman having to read these," I whispered to my man, tears still falling just like the rain coming down. He patted my hand, put his arm around me and drew me close to him, like he always knew when I needed him most.

"Me, too, Missy. Dear Lord, folks we ain't never met offering that kind of praise, and to a old broken down ballplayer." He chuckled and wiped a tear or two away himself.

"Don't make much of a difference 'bout being in baseball's good graces long as people take your side, 'cause they somehow know your heart. Ain't no man could have been luckier." He understood better than most that the true measure of a man's character is how he responds to the trials and temptations that come his way. Folks notice that kind of stuff.

I reached up and kissed that wonderful man square on the mouth, and folks around us hooted and cheered again and again. A photographer who came over with Scoop took a lot of shots that night, my favorite always being Joe out at home plate with some of the Brandon players.

After the heart attack, his face was thin, drawn, his huge arms giving way to little more than scarecrow broomsticks, thirty pounds at least under his playing weight when we broke in with Cleveland. Wore his favorite Panama with the black band, long sleeved white shirt - even let me starch and press it, thank goodness, - which he then ruined by rolling the sleeves up a turn or two. I had taken up the gray suit pants at the waist, but it still took tightening that black belt to the last hole, and I think it was a new one he made with his knife, to hold them up.

Ralph Harbin, Harry Foster, and Joe Anders, young Braves and all very good players, stood around my man, who looked strangely out of place until Anders handed him a replica of Betsy. Joe took his grip and gently laid her on his bony shoulder, and wasn't out of place any more.

No, he was the center. Every eye was on him, the players, fans, umpires, every man on both benches. Things got real quiet. It was like all of us knew it was one of the perfect moments we're graced with two, maybe three times in our whole lives.

There wasn't any hitting exhibition this time, not even any loud urging from the stands. He shook hands all around after talking a minute or two, then turned to walk back to where we were sitting in the grandstand, midway up the third base line. You could hear, or it sure seemed that way, every footstep in the wet dirt. Then it started, soft at first.

"Joe! Joe! Joe!" and before he reached where I was waiting you could have heard the echo clean to Christ Church, down Main Street, around the Woodside and Poe and Southern Bleachery mill villages, running on to Paris Mountain and mingling with ghost soldiers at Camp Sevier, and then I swear moving straight on up to heaven.

"Joe! Joe! Joe!" and it died out only after the game started, us sitting there for the full nine innings though the stands were emptying pretty quick now that the mist was getting blown around by a steady north wind. I stared out at those footprints dissolving slowly back into the infield as the rain fell. The game was called in the bottom of the sixth, Brandon up on Woodside 3-1.

Some folks say that picture of Joe and the Brandon kids summed up all of textile league baseball. Joe started out right here way back forty-five years ago, and now it was playing out as more and more mills dropped their teams. Nobody wanted a part of what had brought the villages and the people through labor trouble, the Depression, and two World Wars. No matter how good Harbin, Foster, Anders and all those other young players were, didn't matter any more. It turned out we were the last ones to get up and leave, sloshing out to the Packard where, as always, Joe opened the door for me.

Chapter 9

Joe and I still went to the store every morning together, wouldn't either of us have wanted it any other way. Once a week we'd leave home a little earlier, park the Packard and walk down to Tucker's, a new restaurant not far from the store, so Joe could order his favorite breakfast, fatback and milk gravy, with coffee and biscuits. Thin as he was, I was happy to see him eat. Me, I'd stick with the coffee and toast, trying and largely failing to hold off the midriff bulge.

One of the pictures that showed up in the papers a few years ago showed him on the sidewalk outside, half toothless grin, fat, with a tie barely coming halfway down to where it was supposed to be. The caption described him as sitting there, only able to dream about the roar of the crowd. I could almost hear people talking again about the dumb southern linthead who cheated his way right out of baseball, and look what he's become. But there's another image of him I kept, a more accurate description of how he was in business.

"Morning, Zeb Eaton," he said to the man stepping through the door, "and if you'll get in here quick and close off that draft we'll all be staying a mite warmer."

"And all the years you spent in Cleveland and Chicago hasn't prepared you for a January cold snap in Greenville? Would of expected better, Joe!" The two of them exchanged pleasantries.

Nothing special about the sale, other than the day was real cold. No deep friendship shared; Zeb was a customer, like Joe an old ballplayer, an acquaintance. I just watched my man, graceful doing his work as he ever was running down would-be triples and letting them die in his glove, explaining the difference between brands of blended whiskey, and the best quality for the price. Three-piece gray suit, black striped tie, a silver watch chain running from button to pocket on his vest. The man once reviled by New York sportswriters as a "cowardly, ignorant country bumpkin" was quite a successful businessman, and looked the part.

"Distinguished," I whispered, "quiet and loving and caring as any man could be." He turned and smiled as Zeb was leaving, and I counted again in my mind all the reasons I loved Joe Jackson, now more than ever.

We had gotten on well in life together, accepted the bad things like not having children and how people could still throw the Scandal in our face. Sometimes I'd get fiery, ready to go to war for me and my man, but Joe, he faced it all with great dignity, never showing bitterness toward the game he loved so much. You can't imagine the pain we lived with. Yes, more tears every time I think about it. But I can promise you

154

nobody saw the pain, or my tears, or how we always wanted to be accepted but never were. Not really.

That Joe Jackson night, it sure stirred up people all around to talking about him, from Atlanta to New York and all points in between. Maybe, just maybe, I hoped, this would be the time he was welcomed back in.

"I'm not what you call a real strong Christian," he said to Furman Bisher one Saturday morning, the two of them sitting under a tree in the front yard. "But I believe in the Good Book, that what you sow you shall reap. I have always asked the Lord for guidance, and I'm sure he gave it to me." I helped him slip on his black sweater as the interview lasted a bit longer than we figured. Furman drove up from Atlanta, and Joe wasn't about to disappoint him.

I got a copy of an article run on Joe in one of the New York papers, of all places, where the sportswriter got on his soapbox and said "no evidence produced made Jackson a guilty man, and he is innocent of the crimes of which he is accused."

On down a bit, he pops them harder. "In the United States, innocence is presumed when there is uncertainty, and there was enough reasonable doubt concerning his role." That man's going to make me have to re-evaluate my opinion of Gotham writers, his was such an honest look at the situation.

Seems *The Sporting News* thought highly of my man, too, including him in a baseball history book they were publishing, *Daguerreotypes*. Got the material in the mail, and Joe and I sat at home one rainy evening and I read it to him. He caught me off guard a bit with his actions, though. Oh, he was pleased enough with the stuff Taylor Spink was going to use, but it sparked a lot of things in Joe's mind that made him restless.

Biggest thing to come out about this time, of course, was the formal resolution adopted by the South Carolina Legislature calling for the reinstatement of Shoeless Joe Jackson to good standing in organized baseball. John Snow of Williamsburg and Frank Eppes of Greenville brought it up and, like that New York writer, wanted this wrong set right.

Joe happened up on Mr. Pete Hollis one day, I think maybe the two were watching a baseball game at Parker High School. Hollis, remember, was pretty much accepted as the man who brought basketball to the south and started the Southern Textile Basketball Tournament here in Greenville. Though my man didn't understand all that much about the game, he thought Mr. Hollis a real nice man. That feeling was returned in kind.

"I can tell you, Mrs. Jackson, he never uttered a word, as far as I know, about the Scandal and what happened after it. Not in the hundreds of conversations that have passed between us over the years. But yesterday he seemed to want to."

The dear man had dropped by Bolt's, saw me at lunch with my usual glass of milk and BLT, and stopped to talk. I never saw him decked out in anything but suits, white shirts and ties. He was elegant as usual, but make no mistake, he was a real champion of mill folks. He may have dressed differently from them, but in his heart the lintheads were the salt of the earth. He pushed a piece of white hair off his forehead and continued.

"'You know, Mr. Hollis, I don't deserve this thing that has happened to me. But I have paid many times over for the company I kept.' That was it.

"I've been around a lot of people in my life, and think I can judge character pretty well. Never has there been a doubt of your husband's innocence in my mind, and if the world could have heard the tone of his words, seen the resolute look on his face as we talked, there would be no doubt. Folks speak of the Gettysburg Address saying a lot in few words, but your Joe topped Mr. Lincoln in the succinct telling of the truth."

He got up to leave. I extended my hand, and he took it in his.

"You are both to be greatly admired," he said, then walked slowly away. Lots of good folks in this world, I can tell you, to offset the bad ones we ran into time and again.

We had a lot of great things happen to us, and this move to get him reinstated was certainly close to the top of the list. But I swear if sometimes we didn't have the most rotten timing of anyone in the whole world. Here we are with the first real effort to clear Joe's name going on, and the biggest story on the sports page is the college basketball scandal. It almost made you hate Mr. Hollis' game a little bit. So instead of seeing Shoeless Joe Jackson's name there in the papers, you saw Al Roth, Ed Warner, and Sherman White.

"I don't believe this!" as loud as I could yell there in the house. Joe sat, holding a cup of coffee, and watching the sun set back over behind Judson Mill.

"Aren't you the least bit mad?" I could have choked him, I do believe.

"Missy," he took my hand in his big warm mitt. Light grew dim that November evening. "I'm at peace with myself. Lots of folks can't say that and mean it. You and me know all about 1919, and I feel I'm innocent of everything except hanging around the wrong people on the team. Maybe all of them except Weaver, I don't know." He was thinner

156

now, way less than even a few months ago, and he made hardly a sound crossing to the kitchen window.

"Got most everything I ever wanted. Wonderful wife." Here came the tears again, me giving Niagara Falls a run for the money. "Nice house to live in, children coming by to see me all the time and talk baseball. Ain't that about enough for one lifetime?"

I circled my arms around him, rested my head on his back. He turned and hugged me, just held me until it was pitch-black dark outside.

All the attention given to clearing his name began to stir interest in areas we never thought of. A phone call came in to the store one day, and Joe answered, but for the longest time he didn't say anything, just stood there. After a while he spoke real soft, "Yes, thank you, and we will be there December 15th. Yes, we look forward to it."

"Joe?" He stood staring out the window. "Joe?" I said again, went over and touched his arm. "Anything wrong? Not bad news, is it?"

"Missy, they want me to come be on *Talk of the Town*, with Ed Sullivan, to tell our part of the story on the Series and all that's gone on since then. That fellow on the phone was Mr. Sullivan's schedule manager, and said they were looking forward to having us. Matter of fact, he said a good deal of the city up there was already buzzing about it." He laid his hand on mine and gave me the sweet smile that melted my heart for the million and first time.

"We're going to close the store this afternoon, go shopping for you a nice new gray suit. The color looks awfully good on you, you handsome cuss.

"Joe," I looked into those deep-set eyes and brushed his cheek with my lips. "Folks are going to listen now. They'll know the truth."

"Yes," he said. "Folks, they might listen."

This go round, it was God's timing that was lousy.

December 5th was a Wednesday, getting on toward Christmas with the streets decorated and the weather turning colder. My man didn't feel well, and stayed home while I went on to the store by myself. Like most merchants, we couldn't afford to miss being open even a day around the holiday rush. Folks asked about Joe, wanting to be remembered to him, telling me to wish him a Merry Christmas. I called him early in the afternoon to make sure he was okay.

"Kind of cold, didn't crave much to eat." Suspected he might have a touch of the flu.

"Just going to lay here and rest, Missy. See you when you get home." I was pressing the phone hard to my ear, his voice so much softer than usual.

I closed up early and headed home. He managed to get some soup down about seven o'clock, and we ate and talked, me sitting on the edge of the bed holding his hand. I was more than a little bit worried.

Called his brother David to come over about nine, just to sit with us. I hadn't seen my man so weak, but maybe it was just that flu going around, or a cold, or something not too bad. Pretty soon they were talking baseball and old times, the old blue-tick hound dog and their pa, my mama and Miss Martha Ann, so I eased out into the kitchen and put on a pot of coffee.

"I smell that," Joe said. "Going to be good to sip some, Missy."

Awhile later, after they stopped chatting and I was finishing my first cup, I heard him gasp and call "Katie" real hoarse. It was a three-step sprint to the side of that bed for me, and David reached to touch his brother's shoulder as Joe closed his eyes and tried to breathe deep. Somehow I got to the phone and called Dr. Crossland and Dr. Clatworthy, asking them both to hurry.

"The preacher, Katie," the younger Jackson whispered before I could hardly turn around, "and quick." Don't even remember dialing and asking Reverend Turner to get over to house fast as he could, but he and David both said I did. Wouldn't leave the bedside, wouldn't let go of those big hands. The clock struck some hour, I couldn't tell which. He looked up and smiled at me.

"Missy, I'm going to meet the greatest umpire of all, and He'll be calling me safe at home. Don't never you doubt how much I loved you every second of our life together." He squeezed my hand and closed his eyes.

Gone. I didn't, couldn't move. Couldn't let go. Couldn't talk. David and the Reverend finally took his hands from mine and folded them on his chest. They eased me into the rocking chair not far from the foot of the bed.

"Joe?" I gasped now. The men stood by, quiet, not really able to offer anything in the way of comfort.

"You're not going to leave me alone for Christmas, now are you?" Hot tears opened up, some splashing on the rocker arms, some disappearing into the throw rug. Never wailed or did much crying out loud, they told me later. My man wouldn't want me to do that, you know.

"Joe?" Waited a bit.

"Joe?" I didn't try to speak any more.

I remember something Mama told me when they buried my granddaddy. 'The big things, they just sort of wait until you're ready to pick them up and think about them later. But the oddest details get burned into your memory that you'll remember all your life. And I made

158

myself remember everything, over and over and over, not wanting to forget even the smallest things.

The day after Joe died it was cold and windy with dark clouds running through the sky. I went from place to place with David and my sister Mattie, trying to make arrangements for the funeral. Mr. McAfee and his folks were a big help, and we chose a copper coffin and their white hearse with a leather top to carry Joe. We went to Woodlawn Memorial Park and picked out graves one and two, lot 333, section five, for him and me. I asked Reverend Turner and Reverend John Wrenn to conduct services at Brandon Baptist Church, and they said it would be an honor to talk about Shoeless Joe Jackson. Nobody ever had a name like that.

'That long heavy coffin up all those steps,' I remember thinking.

"It ain't going to fit—can't turn quick enough." I think it was young Anders talking to the McAfee folks, all of them struggling to move the casket into the living room. Finally they had to decide on opening a window and sliding it in that way.

"Miss Katie, I'll stay if you want," Anders offered as the other people were getting in the hearse for the ride back to the funeral home. Guess they'd all had a pretty long day, too.

"You run on home and rest up, and I'll see you and your lovely Katie later this evening. Thank you for being here," and I hugged him and sent him out into the twilight. Much as I had dreaded it, there was a need, a deep ache to spend an hour alone with my man, just him and me like it was so many times during our lives. It took a bit of doing, but I managed to raise the top of the casket until the hinges caught.

The lines on his face were softer, resting now, no more hurt to keep from the world, no more set jaw to keep from saying what you knew wouldn't matter anyway.

"You look good in that suit, Joseph Jefferson, did the day you tried it on when we were getting ready to head for New York." I reached down and kissed his cheek. Hard. Cold. A tear fell there, ran down to the collar of his shirt, stopped and glistened in the light a brief instant until the fabric soaked it in. Picked out his gray suit for him, the matching tie, silver watch chain from vest button to pocket.

I pulled a dining room chair over and sat there, once in a while running my hand along the copper, once in a while standing up just to look at him, touch his arm, smooth his hair along the temples. Sat back down, and I guess for the first time, and the only time, all the grief and hurt and bitterness and new-found loneliness came pouring out, gushes of tears. And deep sobs, coming from so deep down it was hurting even to breathe. That, and the sound of the clock ticking in the hallway, was all I could remember for thirty minutes. Me against the whole blackness of forever, without him to lean on for strength.

Called me the strong one, they did, but oh my dear God if they only saw me now, just begging for five minutes to talk with him, ask him what I ought to do, how to act when all these people started coming around. Which of them I could tell to go to hell and not feel bad about it. Which I could hug and know that they cared.

"Bound to be some gawkers, Joe, and you know I've never liked buzzards. Them and snakes, never could stomach them." I heard myself say it, and got tickled. Think he probably would have, too.

There was a little tiny room that branched off the front hall, only about four foot by ten foot, and ever since we moved here Joe always kept scrapbooks and trophies and pictures and such littering it up. So here I am carrying on a right lively conversation with my dead husband, laying out some mementos so people could have something to do besides look in the coffin and say, "Oh but he looks so natural." Don't you just hate that?

"Remember, Joe? Up in Delaware with the Harland team? Me and you skinny dipping in the ocean on those summer nights, and even when we got cooled off in the water we could go and heat that night right back up, couldn't we?"

I walked over and touched his face. Before too long, I'd arranged a pretty nice display of all the stuff that marked the married life of Joseph Jefferson and Katie Wynn Jackson.

Took a bath, probably soaking up all the water I lost bawling my eyes out, and felt the wrinkles and a little too much fat in too many places. When I ran my hands over my body lathering up, I just closed my eyes and one more time pictured it was that sweet man's touch. It was a comfort to think like that.

I won't try and tell about all the folks who came by during the evening, but a couple of the mothers of those kids talked to me in a special, sweet way.

"My boy, he ran off to his secret place right after he knew Joe died." Both Mrs. Thompson and Mrs. Burgess said of Joe and John. "Finally came on back home when they realized the tears weren't going to stop, and it was pretty close to dark."

Old friends, ball players, kids, acquaintances, it was a line that kept on moving through the house until a bit after ten o'clock. Lots of hugs, lots of tears, lots of kind words. Must admit, I didn't really have to chase away the buzzards.

Men, women, children from every walk of life came to Brandon Baptist Church the next day, paying respects to my man. Old major leaguers like Champ Osteen, Walt Barbare, and Sid Smith sat together

160

up front, behind the row of honorary pallbearers - Mr. Bolt, Doc Crossland Doc Clatworthy, Scoop Latimer, Leo Hill, and Frank Eppes were part of the two dozen I chose for that honor.

Reverend Wrenn spoke to the younger generation sitting there, who were removed from my man in age, yet touched by him just the same.

"If these kids, who used to drop by the store to ask for his help on baseball's finer points, dare to dream as big as Joe did, whether they make it in baseball or medicine or nuclear physics or as a worker in a cotton mill, it doesn't matter. If the seeds of excellence are planted because of the memory of Shoeless Joe Jackson, then his life mattered to the fullest degree." He kept his voice just above a whisper, but I don't think a word was missed by anyone. You could tell because there wasn't a dry eye to be found.

And Reverend Turner closed with words that cut to the quick. "As long as we remember his name, those who tried to hurt him will have failed in their attempts to ruin a great man."

It reminded me of what folks said the night before at the visitation, telling Jerry and David and me what Hubert Holloway had broadcast from a radio station up north.

"And here's my final word on Jackson. Now that God has put His hands on Shoeless Joe, we can take ours off." Amen, and again, amen.

"Cold rain and whispering wind," his brother Jerry said as we came out of the church. Bringing the casket down the steps was a hard job for eight men, even the young and muscular ones like Joe Anders. About three steps down, Mr. McAfee touched Wade Ridgeway's shoulder and got him to hustle and help get the heavy load down that steep passage.

"Old Wade, he'll be telling folks about this years from now, Katie. For twenty years he served up egg sandwiches and coffee and such over at the mill canteen, but to him it was a small price to pay for getting to know Joe Jackson," David whispered to me. He was right. All you had to see was the man's face, the pride of being able to help lay his friend to rest.

I was grateful to be kept busy the days after the funeral, writing to thank folks who sent flowers and telegrams. It was so much like when the players of a sudden started talking about him several years ago, after not saying anything for so long. Now he was standing much taller in death than he ever did in life. To everybody but me, that is.

Senator Burnet Maybank offered "my deepest sympathy in the death of your husband and my friend." Lefty and Lyria Williams sent along condolences, as did Charles A. Comiskey, the Old Roman's grandson, and Ed Sullivan. Even got a cablegram from Joe's friend Colonel Alan Hale, stationed way over in Oslo, Norway with the Navy.

And Lord how many printed notes from those boys, and yes a few girls, too, who called the biggest kid of all their friend. Some of the papers were grimy, stuck under the door, or maybe just dropped on the porch before anyone saw who left them there.

"Mama says I done cried myself to sleep three nights in a row, and I'm wondering when I'll stop." Me and you both, little James, me and you both.

"I ain't welcomed up in the white section, but when Joe was there it was okay for me to walk with him. Me and all the others here around Queen's Avenue and Doe Street loved him 'cause he loved us and you could tell." Wouldn't anybody dare give my man grief about walking along with the Negro children, not with him carrying Betsy around on his shoulder. To Joe, see, all kids were good.

"He let me bat and play third base if I ran home and changed out of my pink dress. Wouldn't let none of the boys laugh at me either, said as long as I tried my best I was every bit as good as them." There wasn't a soul alive that old linthead couldn't uplift.

A little bit later some of baseball's big names offered their thoughts, too, though none as eloquent as the kids. Mr. Mack said baseball sinned against Joe more than he sinned against baseball. And Commissioner Happy Chandler, he was nothing if not right to the point.

"I have joined in defending your husband because he received bad treatment, and this is an injustice that ought to be corrected. This is a mission of mercy that we now join in together."

A package came one day early in January, I think, from the Cleveland Baseball Club, and I thought about how many years passed since Joe and I walked from home to League Park, how long since the Sumners and Lajoies and Josses touched our lives.

"Open it, sister," Mattie said. Think she was about as curious as I was, and pretty quick we'd unwrapped a small gold mantle clock.

"Dear Mr. Jackson," it said right there on crisp white official Indians letterhead, "our fans have recently voted on inductees into the Cleveland Baseball Hall of Fame. Your name had not been included on our formal listing, but such a write-in campaign ensued, demanding your inclusion, that you were selected on the first ballot. Congratulations to a most deserving gentleman and baseball player." Cleveland, it seems, never lost its love for Shoeless Joe.

"Oh, Mattie Wynn," I broke down in sobs. "I only wish he could have lived to see it." Why does it take death to be appreciated, to be seen for what you were all the years you were alive? Maybe we just learn a lot more because we have reason to pay attention now.

Found that out first hand when I opened the bottom dresser drawer a week later and saw the small mahogany box he'd been given on Joe Jackson Night three years ago. Thought a lot about us, where we'd been, how we'd lived, how I'd been blessed.

Joe always said these blue eyes were so bright that they burned with a love of life most uncommon in the world he and I knew. When we were young and in love and starting out on our own, that was most likely true.

But I wonder if he knew deep down that I changed after all the ridicule and accusations came our way? If he knew that sometimes these eyes were flashing anger at the injustice hitting him square in the face?

My man, I don't know that he ever held a deep down anger at anyone, not even Judge Landis. There was that gentleness about him, and it could only have been a gift from the Good Lord because I certainly was not blessed with it. Maybe that was the source of the strength he imparted to me. I've come to believe it grew out of the grace that was at the very core of his being.

That strength I needed the week after he died, when I went through and found bits and pieces of his life. The pocket watch was probably the only thing his pa left him, scratched on the outside from rough handling around mill machinery and the tools used in his butcher's business. Funny how the edges of the stem were worn about smooth, like a man obsessed with time wanted to make note of the exact hour when he glanced at it.

A child's crayon drawing, I think it came from McDavid, Joe's favorite nephew. You might remember him dying just before Christmas in '47. He couldn't have been more than four or five when he did this; pink trees, brown clouds, dark blue water. And how Joe loved that boy. We wanted to adopt him, but things just never seemed to work out, so we stayed Uncle Joe and Aunt Katie instead of Mommy and Dad.

Couple of train tickets to New York, October of '17. The World Series and us beating the Giants four games to two, Joe hitting .307 and being part of a championship club. It was so exciting, the hugging and yelling and sipping champagne and going out to eat at fancy restaurants.

"No, sis, it's okay, you just sit quiet and listen to the radio. I'm just straightening up some things of Joe's that I ran across."

Funny, isn't it, how all these little things spoke volumes about his life and what he valued, but they are only a soft whisper to the good memories he left me.

"Just talking to myself, sister, like I always heard widows were apt to do."

163

Now and then there was someone in the newspaper who would write about him, somebody on the radio say something, or maybe a letter or postcard would come asking what he was like. And then there might be someone from out of town who would show up on our doorstep wanting to talk. It happened that spring after Joe died, when Scoop brought a young man by, tall and skinny like my man was when we first got married.

"Katie, this is Ted Williams," the old sportswriter offered. The Kid everybody was calling the greatest hitter alive, was compared every now and then to Joe. He was too late to talk hitting with my man.

"Long way from Boston," I smiled and held the door open for the two of them to come in. "And take that hat off, Scoop. Be a gentleman."

"Never changes. Bossed Mr. Jackson around the same way." Scoop laughed, and young Williams smiled kind of shy, so much like Joe. But his voice, his passion for baseball showing through, just froze me right where I was standing. A carbon copy he was.

"Mrs. Jackson," he said, "I made one damn big fool mistake a few years ago, not stopping by to talk with Joe about hitting." Once he mentioned that word, forget saying anything because you weren't going to break into the conversation. But couldn't anyone mind, he drew you right into that passion.

"My biggest regret, and it was something so easy to do." He took a sip of ice water, leaned a little bit forward on the couch, and revved up again.

"The Red Sox were through here for an exhibition, and I knew that you folks were here, but didn't take an hour to come by and talk. He's the only one of the great hitters I've missed. Talked to Ruth, Cobb, Hornsby, Paul Waner, Lefty O'Doul, but not having Joe in that line-up is a sin I've committed and can't undo."

He paused then, raising his eyes a bit to meet mine. Couldn't help but like him, not me anyway, and I bet he did talk with those fellows, picked their brains for everything he was worth.

"George Herman and Tyrus are rare birds, and God could have only had enough gumption laying around to fashion one of each." I couldn't help but laugh, remembering...Joe... his smiles when he talked about men he battled in the field, men he had so much in common with.

"Come in here, and at least I can show you some of what Joe Jackson was about." We looked through the scrapbooks and the baseball photographs. Williams was like a detective as he studied each piece of evidence, sometimes letting out a low whistle, sometimes stopping to brush back that wavy black hair of his.

164

"Both of you are about legendary when it comes to eyesight, though Joe and I took in a movie every once in a while. I understand you don't." Young Ted thought picture shows were bad for his eyes, I remember Scoop telling me once.

"Wife of a ballplayer," Scoop chimed in. He had been watching the Kid go through all this stuff like it was Christmas morning. "You're not going to put much over on her, and I'd advise against trying, because she knows the game real well."

"Wouldn't think of it," he said with a warm smile that melted your heart just like my man's could do. "Always had too much respect for Mr. *and* Mrs. Jackson, you know that, Scoop." He looked my way again.

"You husband swung at a lot of bad balls, and still blew them out of the park or knocked some poor sap's glove off with a line drive. Me, outside or inside, I don't swing, so that's a difference. And..."

"Both of you hit well against all kinds of pitching, and even being left handed, handled portsiders pretty well, I recollect." I interrupted him, but Ted didn't seem to mind. "Something else you both shared, evident since you stepped in here, and that's the passion you have for the game, especially the hitting."

When he picked up Black Betsy, and other bats like Dixie and Old Genril, he stepped out in the back yard and swung each one of them, full stride and everything. There was a reverence, a purity about him then. I closed my eyes, and the lumber whistling through the air, why it could have been my man, the sound so close to what I remembered.

"Got to get you back and ready to catch the train," Scoop interrupted him. "Sorry to break up a great afternoon tea."

"Not half as sorry as me. Mrs. Jackson, thank you." He shook my hand a lot like when Joe used to take it, covering mine with both of his.

"It doesn't hurt so much now, not having talked to Joe, I mean. You helped me understand a lot," he said. The two of them turned to go.

"You tell Mr. Eddie Collins hello for me. Joe thought the world of him." I called after them as they reached the end of the sidewalk.

"Up in the Boston papers, Mrs. Jackson, he compared me with Shoeless Joe, and I consider that a great compliment."

"A good man, Mr. Williams, you'd do well to listen to." I enjoyed the banter, and liked Ted a whole lot.

"I'm here most any time. Know that you're welcomed." He waved, and then he and Scoop were around the corner and gone. It was a good day.

Time passed, slowly to be sure, without my best friend near where I could talk to him. And I got lonelier, first with Scoop's death, and then Mattie's a year or so later. They were the only people I ever talked to a whole lot, especially about Joe and the life we had in baseball. Pretty soon I just went to work, went to Bolt's for lunch, came home and read a little until bedtime. Made it to church most Sundays.

Did you ever have somebody sneak up on you and take a picture, at just the wrong time and capture everything bad about you? About how you felt, and looked, and really didn't care about remembering any of it? It happened to me, and I guess what made me mad was that it painted my life without Joe, and there was not a thing there to see.

I ran the store on a year or two after his death, and it helped pass the time, keep me in touch with folks. Most of the day was spent sitting on a stool behind the counter, all the different bottles lined up in neat rows on the five shelves. Customers were always nice, taking a few minutes to tell me a story about my man, little things he did to touch their lives in a special way. Meant well enough, but when they left, it was like the loneliness was multiplied, and I'd feel the hot tears running down my face again. There was no mascara or make-up to streak then, just water splashing from old tired eyes and getting channeled one way or another by wrinkles on a right worn out face. Probably can't explain it well, but if you've been there, you'll know what I'm talking about.

Only time I'd leave would be to scoot next door to Bolt's Drug Store, eat a bite and sip a glass of milk or an icy soft drink. Young fellow in there, Rex Carter, jerked sodas and he made a darn good bacon-lettuce-tomato sandwich with just a bit too much mayonnaise. Always nice and polite, so I never worried about correcting this little indiscretion.

Late afternoon was the hardest time to get through. The kids didn't come by any more to stop and get the biggest kid in West Greenville to go play ball with them. No laughter or a dozen voices yelling, "Hurry up, Joe, 'cause it's already going to get dark too quick," or bare feet slapping the sidewalk in a mad sprint to Ebbets Field or Yankee Stadium or whatever it was they called the vacant lot that day.

No, they were all dealing with their grief privately, like I do. Mrs. Burgess, my paper boy's ma, said her son John sat by himself and cried the day after Joe passed away, and I think a lot of them did the same. He meant a lot to them.

You can't make that up to the kids. They know better. Me offering them a Coke or ice cream wasn't the same as when my man did it. Like so many times before, I rubbed the counter with a damp cleaning rag laid close by to shine up the wood one more time with a splatter of tears.

At the end of the day I'd total up, making sure everything balanced, sweep the place and put it in order, cut the lights out and head on home. Sometimes before opening the door of the Packard I'd freeze, for some reason waiting for that big hand to reach around and open the door for me. The sound of a passing car, or someone calling my name, would call me back to the reality of an old woman standing in near darkness, wondering which way to turn.

It's not right, Joe. It should have been me that died first, couldn't we get that one thing right? It should have been me... should have been me. If not for me, you should have lived on for all those little kids who needed you. Damn...Joe...oh God.

Always knew of folks called 'crazy old man' or 'crazy old woman' because of funny ways they had, and I wonder if maybe now that group doesn't include me. If somebody was walking up our street at that gosh awful hour, they might have been calling for the Bull Street Special down in Columbia to come and cart me off to the psychiatric hospital. A restless night wasn't all that uncommon for me since Joe's death, but the loneliness was worse, like I couldn't get my breath it was so oppressive.

Shivered when I got out of bed and dressed quickly in the dark, and before I could think I walked into the closet and pulled out his heavy brown overcoat. A mile too big, but bundled it up and I was out the door. Winter night, cold and cloudy, streetlights had haloes around them, like a remembrance of Christmas when the decorations were still up.

By the time I reached the field, the wind was blowing hard out toward center, me standing in the swirling mist and clouds hanging low enough I could touch them. Walked to first base, planted my foot on the bag and kept a quick stride out to where the road formed the field boundary. Turned then and headed toward center and the deepest part of the park, and if I squinted real hard I could make out the oak tree behind the plate. Bare and dying.

"Can't anybody remember what those warm Saturday afternoons were about, how we didn't ever give them the honor they deserved. We went and swapped them for another life we were better off maybe never seeing." Didn't know if the words were only echoes in my head, or if I really spoke them out loud and they were taken by the wind to every corner of the sacred ground.

Rain splattered on his coat about the time I touched third and completed the walk around the old mill village baseball field. It was home, his, mine, for a lot of years, and maybe our happiest times were spent right here with people we knew and cared about. Two kids in love with each other and the whole world, until things moved us too far from home.

I hurried away, the darkness and silence of a sudden becoming burdensome, stuff I didn't want any part of. Shivering, I started off for home, walking fast, conscious of the crunch of frozen earth under my feet, of the rain and the wind. It was like being on a hell-bound train, all your sins and your supposed sins and every bad dream leering at you. Ghosts coming out of a foggy lamplight glow at every stop along the way. Dear Lord, the longer the ride goes on the more you abandon any of the hope that maybe was left. Until it's just easier to accept the abandonment, the loneliness, the separation, the cold. That last one's worst of all, the cold. Because it's inside and outside, tearing at your heart and numbing your hands until you just can't hold on any more.

I wanted to get home and not be cold, not be wet. Wanting just to sit, watch first light ease into the kitchen, to be warm. When I reached the steps, one of the clocks downtown chimed four a.m. I stood there shaking, cold rain running off the coat. Maybe I was the last person in the world. The saints already taken to heaven, the sinners damned to hell, and me the lost soul forever between the two.

"Crazy old woman," I think I muttered as I opened the door and stepped inside.

When Dr. Williams finally diagnosed cancer, after I wouldn't go to him for months on end even though I knew something was wrong, don't know what I really thought. Maybe I didn't think at all, just kept working at the store, going home and eating a little bit of supper, not much appetite, you know. Sleep an hour or so at a time, then walk the floors, or the streets, near as long.

"The disease is pretty far along." He was a dear soul, struggling hard right then to keep his voice from breaking.

"I don't think surgery would benefit you much, but there have been great strides in radiation treatments." Like watching the burns on your skin multiply at every session until you resembled fresh hamburger, and you hurt a lot. I asked some questions on my own, and knew pretty much that was a road I didn't want to walk down.

"Loneliness since Joe passed away, that's been the pain I've lived with, not what's happening right now in this worn out old body," I said, a little surprised at the steady voice, the even sound. "The death I was afraid of happened a few years back, Doctor, so facing my own is a little easier."

I reached over and patted his hand, smiled at him, and got up to leave. "If you could be there maybe when I needed a little something for the times it does get the best of me..." and moved toward the door of the examination room.

"Look at this," the young man smiled, "I'm the care giver supposedly comforting a..."

168

"Dying woman," I finished for him. "It's really not so bad to say, Ernest."

"And you're the one lifting my spirits, Miss Katie. You talk about how wonderful it was sharing your life with Joe. Well, I can tell you he was a pretty lucky man to have you for a wife. You remember that, Mrs. Jackson."

Guess we were even on the spirit-lifting thing.

Watched items come up on Joe now and again. Branch Rickey, as he was rebuilding the Pirates' organization, picked my man as part of his all-time outfield, along with Tyrus and George Herman, and was bold enough to defend what he did.

"He was blacklisted for cooperative knowledge of a fix," he said, "but there must be a kindness in God's justice that permits his redemption. He suffered a lifetime. I know about it and make no apologies to anyone by including Jackson." Didn't ever get to meet the man, but I'm right positive we would have gotten along.

Of all people, Chick Gandil gave his story to *Sports Illustrated*, and when Joe Anders and Leo Hill, two of the Bolt Store Regulars, ran over with the magazine, I was prepared to read the worst about my man. But Chick was kind to Joe, telling folks, "Fame never spoiled him. He had no education, but a good head, despite reports to the contrary." Maybe Mr. Rickey was right about there being a wideness in God's mercy, especially if Gandil broke and said something nice about Joe after offering nothing all those years, not even acknowledging his death five years ago.

Leo Hill, another of the youngsters Joe befriended and encouraged, went on to become a lawyer, and I called him over one day to set up an appointment to do my Last Will and Testament. We sat there in the store late one Friday evening, after I closed up, and planned everything out. Didn't take very long, and when it was through the estate of Joseph Jefferson Wofford and Katie Wynn Jackson was split square down the middle. Joe's half to the American Heart Association, my half to the American Cancer Society.

Same reasoning for that like it was for dispensing with the $5000 we tried to give Comiskey back.

"Put it where it'll do some good," my man had said, and I was following through with that one more time.

"Quite a thing you did, Miss Katie, providing for others with this will," Leo said, finishing up the last sentence of all that legal stuff. "But you and Mr. Joe, you were always like that. How many times he'd offer a handout to folks he just happened up on in the streets. You're the same way, not wanting anyone to know, and I've always admired that about you."

"And as always, you're too kind, young Mr. Hill." I smiled at him, reached over and patted his hand, old wrinkled skin over his youthful glow. "Get on home, I've kept you too long."

"No, Ma'am, you didn't. I'll finish these papers tomorrow and drop by to see you. We can go over to Bolt's and get some of the guys to witness the documents. Then I'll treat you to a vanilla shake. Let them all get jealous."

He headed for the door, turned to me as he opened it. "Can I wait and walk you to your car?" Suppose he was saying 'should I', since I was a little lighter, and maybe weaker, too.

"Lord no, child. I'll finish tallying up here, then head home. You get on."

"Yes, ma'am. Goodnight."

"'Night, Counselor," I called after him, cheerily as I could. It had gotten to be a long walk from the counter to the door, a longer one still from the front door to where I parked the Packard along the street. Funny how my shadow looked, kind of bent and leaning to one side, moving through the streetlight glare.

It's hard for people to know what to say when you have a lingering illness like mine. "Hope you feel better" sure doesn't cut it. And "Boy, it'll be Christmas before you know it" isn't all that bright and cheerful, either. Didn't dwell too much on anything except trying to get affairs in order, and what I did with Leo was just the beginning. Took care of the big things, but still had all of the personal items Joe and I collected in our lifetime together.

Most of the clothes and shoes, that was easy enough, bundle them up and send them on to the Salvation Army. Lots of folks not as fortunate as I'd been needed stuff like that all the time. For furniture and jewelry, I'd be making a list of family and friends. Then there wouldn't be any disagreement on splitting up the goods.

One day that autumn, felt like I just needed to walk, though it was hard on me now. Closed up a little earlier than usual, drove over to the mill village, and began to wander around.

It was more than just wanting to go—,it was stronger, like I had to be there and wasn't given a choice in the matter. The leaves had started turning, and I remember it was a chilly Thursday afternoon moving toward sunset.

Joe and I used to love this time of year, no matter where we were, but especially here at home. We'd always be listening to World Series games on the radio, and I'm still doing it. Isn't it refreshing to see the Milwaukee Braves scaring the heck out of the Yankees and threatening to take the Series two years in a row? Usually we're putting up with the Yankees all the time against whoever gets lucky in the

National League, but maybe things are going to be changing. We'd get out of the store and before heading home would walk up Pendleton Street and the bakery, and wander back along Augusta Road for a spell. Sniffing the air, holding tight to each other, sharing thoughts and not ever having to break the silence to let it be known how deeply we loved and were loved.

But now I'm here by myself, going down past the house on Mason Street we once shared with Joe's folks right after we got married. No matter which road I took it seemed to wind back toward the center of the village, and the mill, and the ball park. Some of the windows were tilted open, allowing for air and humidity to condition the weave and spinning rooms especially, and the sound of the looms sneaked out and mingled with the autumn afternoon. Probably first frost by morning.

I stood there for a minute or two, and looked, and listened to where my Joe spent hard years as a little boy. Thank God that child labor is over now, because it was something I never could abide. Made kids grow up and take on adult ways too fast, getting married young since they didn't figure to see many birthdays past forty, working overtime because what they made in regular hours was hardly enough for rent and food, raising kids when they ought to be going out on a first date. And being denied the pleasure of an education because there just wasn't enough time to fit it in. No, I hated it all when it was going on, and nothing has happened to make the memories any sweeter.

I've only been back over to the ballfield a few times since they had that Joe Jackson Night back in '48. And after my man died, I just didn't have the urge to go over and watch the mill league games. The leagues were pretty much heading downhill then, too. One or two good years after the war, but then poof, and what we thought would last a lifetime dried up and blew away with the infield dust.

The field isn't used much, weeds and such crowding the infield out, about like what life is doing to us old folks now. Watch these slick youngsters in the majors, and I believe they could run circles around most of the players in Joe's day, though none of us would ever admit it.

Ever thought about the end of time? Wondered maybe if what I saw today, the setting sun and the silence and a favorite place now dead, if that was going to be what it looks like? And being scared to turn around, because those you've loved for so long might not be there, and you couldn't begin to stand the pain? The walk back to the Packard was a long one.

I remember one night, heavy misting rain in early April, the kind where the cold eats right through your bones. Sat down in the floor and pulled out boxes of stuff. Scrapbooks, photographs, letters, rings and necklaces and such, gloves and bats, trophies, one or two old uniforms

171

my man kept, spikes, a White Sox blanket with a likeness of him weaved in. I took that old scratchy thing and wrapped up tight in it, not unlike dozens of cold early season games in Chicago, laid there and felt like I was close to him again.

I'd be holding a glove, or maybe reading a letter, and then I'd drift off to sleep. Don't know if it was sleep exactly, maybe more like in between, when you see and hear things so much clearer, voices and places long gone but for some reason still alive, never willing to die and leave you empty.

Mama and Daddy, Miss Martha Ann, Joe's pa, Hyder, Mr. Joss, Mr. and Mrs. Lajoie, George Herman, Mr. Williams, Tyrus. My man, too, reaching out his hand to take mine.

"Missy, you're as beautiful as ever. Let's walk down to the ballpark. Big game, you know, and we can't let the likes of Woodside beat the very best that Brandon done put on the field in years. Got an hour or more before the game starts, so we can walk real slow and talk. Ain't got to do that much lately, you being so busy and all." Touch of that man's hand could still make me melt.

"Miss...Mrs. Jackson," it was Dr. Williams, leaning close and smiling down at me. "Had the sweetest look on your face, Miss Katie, like a kid eating an ice cream cone on a summer day." I looked past him to the rain splattering on the window panes, and ran my hands over the crocheted blanket one of the kid's mamas had given to me a couple of months back. Some of the letters and baseball stuff was lying on the bed.

I noticed something else, too. The tears in that gentle doctor's eyes. Guess he figured I was lonely, with visits from family and friends kind of few and far between. He was only half right. Lots of times I was pretty happy with the choice of company coming by.

I did have one order of business to take care of with the family, one I'd thought about a long time, trying to get the words just right so there would be no room for mistaking what I was going to say. I remembered how corny I always thought that was, family gathering around the deathbed to get final instructions on living, like the one dying had any better idea than those standing around her. And here I was doing the same thing.

Crazy old woman.

"It's time to put an end to letting people use us," I looked closely at all of them there. Jerry and David, Gertrude and Hortense, nephews and nieces. I asked Dr. Williams and Leo to step into that circle, because both of them were just like family to me. Smoothed the bed cover, my favorite habit I guess, in this bed Joe and I shared.

"So many lies have been told about Joe's life, and we haven't been able to set very many of them right. In his best interest, and mine,

172

too, for that matter, I ask the family to stop talking about it. Let Joe Jackson rest in peace."

Gave a big sigh and sat up straighter in bed, Leo pulling the pillows up so I could lean against them. Surprised myself with what followed, and smiled when I figured it was my man whispering in my ear.

"Folks who can't forgive carry a heavy burden down the path they're walking, and every man has need to be forgiven. And this woman, too. Don't judge harshly those who wronged Joe. I figured that's what he'd say to you."

Settled down to rest a bit after they all left. But my thinking was speeding up even as my body was just begging for quiet for an hour or two. I closed my eyes.

The fragrance of roses, the plum tree, and the wisteria slipped through the open windows in the bedroom, past the blue and white curtains, and filled the room. Some of the boys kept the yard up, stopping by when it needed cleaning, keeping it tidy like Joe always did. Cut grass smelled good, fresh like early morning should be.

The breeze eased in one window and billowed the curtains, sneaked out the other one and sucked the fabric behind it. The cool air felt good against my face and bare arms.

Then he whispered from somewhere far off and called me back.

"Missy, don't be feeling bad, because nothing's ever been that the two of us ain't licked, can't lick, together."

My man. In the end all we had was each other, and that was more than enough. It was everything.

ABOUT THE AUTHOR

Thomas K. Perry earned both a BA (1974) and MA (1977) from Wake Forest University. He is the author of *Shoeless Joe*, a play about Joe Jackson (1995), *Textile League Baseball* (1993), and co-author of *The Southern Textile Basketball Tournament* (1997). Perry has researched the life of Shoeless Joe Jackson for more than twenty years. This is his first novel.

www.ingramcontent.com/pod-product-compliance
Lightning Source LLC
Chambersburg PA
CBHW050658290626
47170CB00015B/1644